MISSING PIECES

By Jamie Zakian

MISSING PIECES

Limitless Publishing, LLC
Kailua, HI 96734
www.limitlesspublishing.com

Formatting: Limitless Publishing

ISBN-13: 978-1-64034-108-1
ISBN-10: 1-64034-108-0

Dedication

For my mother.
The day she died, the brightest star in my sky
burned out.

Chapter One

Sasha stepped off the elevator, onto the checkered carpet of a Manhattan high-rise, and tripped over her own two feet. Her hip crashed against a shiny table in the dimly lit, ghostly hallway. Its metal edge thumping the wall was but a whisper compared to the loud "Fuck!" that slipped from her mouth and the giggle that followed from the woman clutching onto her arm. Although Roxy's snicker traveled farther down the hall than Sasha's stumble, crash, and outburst, Sasha couldn't say shit. For the entire elevator ride up fifteen floors, she'd lectured Roxy about being quiet. Then, like a goddamn spaz, she wrecked the place the second her feet touched plush carpet. She blamed the shimmer of the silver trim on the walls. This hallway, the floor-length window at its end showing off the twinkle of city lights, and the penthouse she and Roxy were walking toward were too fancy. She couldn't concentrate with all the fucking glimmer, the constant distractions.

"I'm gonna wait outside," Roxy said, glancing at the elevator.

Sasha pulled Roxy closer to her side. The streets of New York City were vicious, even in Manhattan, and she wasn't letting their claws dig any deeper into her girl.

"No." Sasha glided her thumb along the puffy scars on Roxy's wrist. Of all the strippers, in all the boroughs, Sasha had managed to find the one more damaged than her own fucked-up self. It should've been an easy feat, except most the strippers that rode her lap were hard-working, well-adjusted gals. It seemed hardly anybody was beaten, locked in a tiny room, and tortured these days.

"Everyone should be crashed out," Sasha whispered, leaning close enough to Roxy to get a whiff of cigarette smoke and Seven and Seven. "Just raid the fridge. I'll hit the safe."

Sasha stopped in front of the penthouse door, staring at its golden knob. The people beyond that door were hardcore motherfuckers, mean bastards, and they didn't like to be messed with. They definitely weren't going to enjoy being robbed. Now *she* wanted to scurry back into the elevator and wait outside.

The door in front of Sasha flew open, and she jumped back. Her gaze drifted along ripples of muscles hidden beneath a tight black t-shirt, ending at Dez's glare. He looked exactly the same as the first time she'd laid eyes on him over a decade ago, sexy as hell and pissed the fuck off. If only she could be the same Sasha that he'd first laid eyes on. The scars that ripped across her cheeks, arms, entire body, coupled with the emptiness in her stare, had to be ugly as shit to look at. Nobody could ever say that about Dez, though. The man was still everything Sasha admired and always wanted to be. His dirty blond hair might be a little longer now, graying at the roots. The disappointment behind his intense leer burned brighter, for sure, but the confidence that radiated around him still lit the air in electric sparks.

The corners of Dez's eyes wrinkled as he glowered, and Sasha couldn't help but smile. Dez was fucking irresistible, especially when he was fuming. She hadn't realized it until now, but she missed the feel of his lips, the roughness of his hands. When he stopped touching her, or why, she couldn't remember. He seemed so far from grasp now, even though he was standing right in front of her.

"I'm sorry," Sasha said, lowering her stare from Dez's face. "Did I wake you?"

"It's seven pm," Dez damn near growled. "Where the fuck have you been?"

The rigid tone in Dez's voice, along with the way he curled his fingers, reminded Sasha why she stopped getting near that asshole. Dez was a great father, but she didn't need any more of those.

"I told you." Sasha pushed Dez's big ass from the doorway, grabbed Roxy by the hand, and barged inside the penthouse. "I had some business to handle."

Dez snatched Sasha by the collar of her flannel. He yanked her to his side, and her clutch on Roxy broke free. "That was three goddamn days ago," he said through clenched teeth.

"Mommy!" Tyler yelled, running down the stairs.

Sasha elbowed Dez in the gut, ripping herself from his grasp just in time to bend down and catch Tyler's strong hug.

"There's my man," Sasha said, squeezing Tyler tight. His little shoulders wiggled, and he squirmed from her embrace.

Tyler took a step back. His stare hardened, and he propped his hands on his hips. "Where the heck have you been?"

A mix between a snort and a snicker erupted from Sasha's mouth as she rose to her feet. Staring down at Tyler was like gazing at a tiny Dez. Although cuter than a June bug, Sasha didn't even have time for one Dez, let alone two. Especially if that many days had really passed.

"I'm sorry, buddy," Sasha said, stepping around Tyler. "Mommy's been crazy busy."

"I'm gonna wait outside," Roxy said, scrunching down as she backed past Dez and toward the open door.

Dez pulled the door open wider. "Good idea."

"No!" Sasha rushed forward, taking Roxy by the arm. She pulled the woman close. Roxy had become somewhat of a blanket to Sasha. The first two months of her return to the real world had been hell. She'd escaped a tiny stone room only to be placed in a bright, spacious tower that was crammed with sympathetic leers and promises of brighter days. The last month, after Roxy slinked into her life, had been a complete blur, which was exactly what

Sasha wanted.

Her grip on Roxy tightened, and she headed for the stairs. "I just gotta grab something from the bedroom. Then…" She stopped on the bottom step, steered her glare to Dez "…we'll be out of your fucking palace."

Tyler hurried after Sasha, stopping short when Dez slammed the penthouse door shut. The boy's little legs rocked in place, his tiny fingers twisted into the ends of his shirt. "You're leaving again?"

Tears welled inside Tyler's eyes, and Sasha turned away. She couldn't soothe the child. The only way she knew how to dull pain was by pumping heroin into her body, and she wasn't about to try that method on a five year old.

"Don't worry, little dude." Sasha took the steps in a sprint, practically dragging Roxy behind her. A clank of charms and dangly pins rang out from Roxy's jean jacket, the frilly pink lace of her skirt rustling as she hurried to keep up with Sasha's pace. "I'll be back before you head off to school."

"Tomorrow's Saturday," Tyler yelled just as Sasha opened her bedroom door.

"I know…right," Sasha called out, which was always an appropriate answer to shit she wasn't listening to.

Roxy squealed as Sasha shoved her into the bedroom, flinched when Sasha kicked the door shut behind them.

"Your son is awesome," Roxy said, taking her signature scared kitten stance. The woman's bottom lip quivered, her shoulders trembling as she inched toward a corner. It would be annoying, if Sasha didn't completely understand. The three months Sasha had spent in a rat-infested cell, dosed on LSD and brainwashed to become her dead mother, was nothing compared to what Roxy had endured. Roxy spent ten years of her life in a closet, an actual living room closet. The woman's own father had locked her in there when she turned five, kept her in the dark. Roxy had no light beneath her door, no voice to tell her stories. Just a drunken father to beat and rape her on a whim. If Roxy wanted to cower in a corner every single place they went, then that's what Sasha would let Roxy do.

"And your old man." Roxy's back hit the wall. A sigh of relief skated past her lips as she flattened herself against the bright, white wallpaper. "Dez? He's fucking hot!"

"You wanna bone him, don't you?" Sasha asked, dropping to her knees in front of the nightstand.

"Yeah." Roxy nodded, slow, a wicked smile lighting her dark eyes. "Don't you?"

"I do," Sasha said through a groan, opening the nightstand's drawer. "But that guy wouldn't be down."

"Not down?" That drew Roxy away from the wall, a half-inch. "For a double-team?" She ripped open the flaps of her jacket, flaunting a long stretch of brown skin between her sparkly halter-top and low hanging skirt. "With us?"

Splinters dug into the tips of Sasha's fingers as she groped the underside of the open drawer. "Probably not. Any minute now, he's gonna come tearing ass in here, demanding I do some dumb shit. Then—" A small paper baggie, taped under the drawer, stopped both Sasha's jaw from wagging and the frantic search of her hand. "Found it!"

Sasha held up a half-empty dime bag of sweet china, then flipped open its top. Before she could snort a nail-full of powder up her nose, Roxy sat on the floor beside her. There was only two things Roxy loved in this world, would sacrifice everything for—fucking and sticking needles in her arm. They didn't have time to boot, not with Dez lurking around, so tokes would have to suffice.

"Here." Sasha shoved the little bag into Roxy's palm, wiping her nose as she wobbled to her feet. "Take a few hits." A warm tingle crept beneath Sasha's skin, slowing her steps toward the closet. "I gotta...the money."

A stumble and a stagger later, Sasha made it to the closet. This fucking room was bullshit. The way it grew longer when she walked, how it tilted to the right when she leaned left. A fucking asshole, that's what everything was for ganging up against her. She needed another toke, since her retarded brain had decided to kick on and ruin her high.

"Don't do it all," Sasha yelled, louder than she intended.

Roxy jumped but didn't drop one bit of heroin on the white carpet. "I got you, baby. You want me to bring it to you?" Roxy climbed to her feet, faster than Sasha could wave a hand.

"Nah. Just save me a hit or two."

"Or three," Roxy snickered as Sasha dug through shoe boxes.

"I don't even know what I'm looking for." Sasha ran her hand along a row of Dez's shirts, neatly

7

hung on silver hangers. The long leather trench coat, which she'd never seen draped on his shoulders, looked so worn, weathered. She pulled it close, buried her face inside the collar, and took a deep breath. The scent of Dez filled her lungs, bringing with it a piercing sadness. How she longed to roll in that scent, let it wrap her body in its warmth, instead of relying on a sniff of heroin to spread heat beneath her skin.

"Bring it now," Sasha said, pushing Dez's jacket away.

Roxy hurried across the room, stopping just outside the closet door. Slowly, she raised her hand. The little bag between her fingers quaked, and the trinkets pinned along her sleeve jingled as her arm trembled. "I can't go in there, Sasha. I…"

"Oh fuck." Sasha tripped over a pair of boots as she rushed out of the closet. "I'm sorry. Fuck! I wasn't thinking." Roxy clutched the bag of heroin to her chest, and Sasha almost snatched it from the woman's grasp.

"I trust you." Roxy clung to Sasha's flannel shirt with the hand that wasn't bogarting the drugs. "You know that, right? I just can't go in there with you."

"No, I know." Sasha wrapped her arm around Roxy, and the woman's tight body loosened. A few kisses, some soft Spanish words, and that bag would be free for the taking. "Sorry, doll. I fucked—"

The bedroom door flew open. Its shiny handle crashed against the wall and Roxy yelped, then scurried into the farthest corner.

"What the fuck, Sasha?" Dez walked into the room, getting right in Sasha's face.

"Jesus, asshole." She pushed Dez, but he didn't budge, so she strolled away. "You scared my friend."

"Fuck your friend!"

"Hey!" Sasha stopped in the middle of the room, turning to hurl glares at Dez. "You better be nice to her." The words came out venomous, with more spite than she ever thought possible. "*My friend* is gonna be around for a while."

A long, slow huff streamed from Dez's mouth. Pain, Sasha saw pain in his stare as he ran his hands through his tangled hair.

"I'm trying really hard to understand what you're going through right now," he said in a near whisper.

The laugh that burst from Sasha's mouth wasn't a funny one, or a mocking snicker. It was a bit of a crazed-person chuckle. "Oh wow. You're actually waiting for me to magically poof back, aren't you?" She took a step toward Dez, ducking to meet his gaze. "My ugly, ripped-up face isn't going away. Neither is my disgusting body, or shitty attitude." The sight of anguish on Dez's face nearly broke Sasha's hard stare, but this was what she'd become. Hard, revolting, broken. That's what she was now.

"Get used to it," she said, mostly to herself. It felt wrong. The words that spewed from her mouth, the thoughts that flashed through her head, didn't fit with the Sasha she'd built. She'd forgotten. The Sasha she'd built had been torn to shreds, all its little pieces stolen. It was a damn shame. The only piece of herself she'd been able to salvage was the part that harbored hate.

Before she could drop to her knees in front of

Dez and beg to be forgiven or saved, she turned her back to him. "Come on, Roxy. We're out of here."

"Sasha," Dez said as Roxy hurried to Sasha's side.

The tremble in Dez's voice, the finality in that one word, should've stopped Sasha's feet from shuffling onward. Except it didn't, and she had no idea why. Almost against her will, she walked from the bedroom and headed down the stairs.

"I'll be back," Sasha called out to Dez without bothering to turn around. She didn't want to push her luck. It was already pretty damn amazing she'd made it through the five-minute interaction with that man, considering the near microscopic amount of drugs in her system at the moment.

Sasha removed her arm from Roxy long enough to blow Tyler a kiss, then headed for the front door.

"We won't be here when you come back," Dez said from the top of the stairs.

The speed of Sasha's feet slowed but only a tad. She pulled the penthouse door open and pushed Roxy into the hallway. "Yeah, whatever."

Sasha followed Roxy into the hallway, closing the door behind her. This could be one of *those* moments, when destinies changed depending on the direction a person walked. In the movies it would be *that* moment. Sasha was stuck in reality, where misery rained down in every direction. It didn't matter if she turned back or walked forward. All roads led to the same destination–despair.

Her shoulders fell into a slump as she followed Roxy to the elevator. Dez was full of shit. The guy couldn't leave. He had nowhere to go, just like her, just like everybody who ended up in New York fucking City.

"You got my bump, right?" Sasha asked, yanking Roxy to a stop in front of the elevator. She wrapped her fingers around the front of Roxy's jacket, squeezing. Any second, she'd start pillaging through the woman's thieving pockets. Goddamn, that woman had a fuck-load of pockets too.

A smile lifted Roxy's cool brown cheeks and she held the bag, with its pathetic minuscule of dust in one corner, up in front of Sasha's eyes.

"Fuck!" Sasha grabbed the bag, looking back at the penthouse. "I fucking forgot we came here to steal a briefcase full of money."

Chapter Two

Not only was Sasha two days late for a meeting with her dealer, Reid, but she didn't have the five grand to cover her order of six pounds of pure heroin.

"I'm gonna get fucking shot tonight," she said, weaving between the assholes littering *her* sidewalk.

"No," Roxy said, almost a scold. "Reid will understand. I can blow him if you want me to."

"He's probably gonna make us both blow him."

Some guy stared Sasha down as he walked by. The bastard probably heard the words "blow him" and was looking for the line.

"You'd do that?" Roxy asked, shock taking her pitch into a screech. "Blow Reid?"

"Fuck no!" She wasn't getting on her knees for no man. Well, except Dez. And maybe Vinny.

"That's what I'm talking about," Sasha said, waving her arms in the air like a natural-born city folk. "I'm gonna get fucking shot."

"We don't have to go," Roxy said, stopping in front of a ratty apartment building on the fringe of Harlem. The same busted windows, crumbling brick apartment building they were supposed to meet Reid in.

Sasha stared at Roxy as if the woman were dense. "Not go" equated to "no drugs." No drugs meant memories of dead eyes staring at her through the slit of a steel door and the unending shakes that accompanied no heroin. She'd never survive that, and neither would Roxy.

"Don't go?" Sasha said in somewhat of a snarl. "Then what? We're out of shit, fucking idiot."

Roxy lowered her gaze, taking the abuse Sasha constantly seemed to dish out. It was too easy to treat Roxy like shit. One of the many reasons Sasha kept the woman close. Agony clung to every inch of Sasha's body, and to let it out on a weaker person relieved a sliver of the ache. How she hated herself for that, even more for not caring enough to stop hurting a woman who'd already suffered a million torments.

"I'm sorry, doll." Sasha slid her hands around Roxy's waist, backed her against the apartment's cracked brick wall. Roxy's soft skin floated beneath Sasha's fingertips, but she couldn't feel it. There were red-hot prickles running through her veins, and they blocked out everything but their burn. It wouldn't stop. The curvy ass she just gripped, the breasts pressing against her chest, wouldn't stop the spikes grating the insides of her flesh. She needed a fresh bag of powder and five minutes alone with Roxy's needle. Then she could enjoy the sexy body of the crazy woman in her grasp.

People slowed to watch Sasha grind against Roxy against the front of a building. Fucking people were goddamn perverts. The city was going to shit. Two girls couldn't even get it on against the front of a building anymore without drawing a goddamn crowd.

"It's okay, baby." Roxy slipped her hands beneath Sasha's tank top. "You have so much stress."

A finger circled Sasha's nipple, and warm breath flowed over her neck, but they were just distractions.

"I can help you relax," Roxy whispered. "Let's sneak into that alley."

Sasha pushed Roxy's hands from her body, taking a step back. Nothing that Roxy could do in an alley would relax her, not right now. "No. We need to get some shit. There's still someone I can call." She held her hand out, palm up. "Quarters."

Sasha fidgeted, then started tapping her foot as Roxy dug through a large purse. That woman had everything in her bag a homeless person would need to clean themselves in a public restroom, and then some. It had to be the reason she was taking so fucking long to find some damn quarters.

Shiny coins jingled as they fell into Sasha's palm. She picked out the pennies, tossing them over her shoulder, while staggering backward down the sidewalk. Her legs wouldn't stop trembling, her head on a non-stop race to insanity. God, she needed a hit.

"Just…go in there," Sasha said, pointing at the

apartment building's busted front door. "Stall Reid. I need like forty-five minutes."

"Me?" Roxy's wide eyes bounced between the door and Sasha. "You're sending me in there? Alone."

"You'll be fine." Sasha eyed a payphone on the corner, silently praying the fucker wasn't busted. "Reid's *your* buddy."

"He's not my buddy, Sasha!"

Sasha waved her hand, which seemed to tune out Roxy pretty damn well. "Do the blowjob thing. Forty-five minutes."

***

Vinny

Vinny leaned against the wall in Dez's bedroom, watching his brother stuff handfuls of clothes into a duffle bag.

"I'm done," Dez said as he kicked the bottom drawer of his dresser shut. "I tried, really fucking tried, to be patient with her." He pulled open the top drawer a bit too hard, and it crashed to the floor. Its wooden side fell apart when it striked plush carpet, spilling t-shirts on Dez's boots. "Fuck," he muttered, kneeling down to gather the last of his clothes.

Only twenty minutes had passed since Dez called Fat Tonys and screamed at Enzo about heading for the hills. Vinny ran five red lights to get home, but Tyler's suitcase had already been packed. Now that the last of Dez's shit was loaded into duffle bags,

Vinny realized how serious the man was.

"Dez. Fuck! She spent three months in a dark cell. We went to that house, saw that shit." Vinny cringed. He could live to be one-hundred and never glimpse anything as horrible as what he saw in that place. The rotted bodies that greeted him when stepping inside that farmhouse, Ellen's childhood home, wasn't shit compared to the basement. Damp stone walls, tiny cells with steel doors. One of which had Sasha's blood painted on the walls, along with bits of her flesh dangling from a rusty metal cot.

"You can't leave her," Vinny said, trying to sound like the Capo of Manhattan and not a whiny little brother. "Sasha needs you."

"She don't need me. Sasha got herself some Mexi-cunt to play with." Dez zipped his bag, slung it over his shoulder. "That bitch hasn't been home in three days, except for the five minutes she breezed through here and broke Tyler's heart. Again."

"What about me?" Vinny called out, slowing Dez's sprint from the bedroom. "You just gonna ditch me?"

"Do you even live here anymore?" Dez stopped in the doorway. "You never come home. She never comes home. This place doesn't feel like a home anymore. It feels like a fancy jail cell."

Dez looked over his shoulder, his sad, tired eyes settling on Vinny. "If I stay here, I'll wring Sasha's fucking neck."

And with that, Dez walked from the room. Vinny should be relieved. With Dez out of the way, he could finally get some alone time with Sasha. It was Dez and his pussy attitude that had warded Sasha away these last few weeks. It had to be.

"No, Daddy," Tyler yelled. The boy's cry echoed through the penthouse, grating Vinny's ears. "I don't wanna go. Uncle Vinny, help!"

Vinny ran out of Dez's bedroom. His feet locked up as he stared over the banister at Dez pulling Tyler across the living room below.

"Don't let him take me," Tyler screamed, tears flowing down his red cheeks. "Please, I don't want to go."

Fire seared through Vinny's chest. He was gripping the solid banister so hard he was shocked it didn't break to pieces.

"It's all right," Vinny said, hurrying down the stairs. There was no way he'd let that kid leave without at least getting a hug and kiss from one of his *real* parents.

Tyler broke free from Dez's clutch, ran into Vinny's arms. Little hands clung to Vinny so tight they brought the sting of tears.

"I can't go. Everybody's here," Tyler sobbed, burying his face into Vinny's chest.

"You have to listen to your pa." A tremble cracked Vinny's voice, and his fingers quaked against Tyler's back. No matter how hard he hugged the boy, he couldn't quell the ache in his chest. "Your pa wouldn't steer you wrong. He knows what's best for you."

"But—"

Dez ripped Tyler away, and the kicking and screaming started up again.

"Stop!" The boom of Vinny's shout flinched his own body and put a halt to Tyler's struggle. "It's not forever." Vinny reached for Tyler then drew back. He couldn't. If another one of Tyler's tears grazed his skin, he'd beat Dez's ass for doing this.

"We'll all come visit," Vinny said, forcing a smile. "Soon, but Kentucky needs you now."

Tyler nodded, sniffling.

"Good luck," Dez said, hurling Vinny a regretful leer. With a suitcase in one hand and Tyler in the other, Dez walked out of the penthouse.

The door closed away Tyler's pout, leaving Vinny alone to stew in his own agony. There was no sound but the pound of his aching heart, and the echo of its wild throb hammered inside his head. Rage circled his body, clashing with the anguish that already dwelled within. Any second, he'd fall to the floor and weep like a fucking baby. That would be unacceptable. He ran Manhattan now, sat at the side of Othello Lazzari, had the biggest boss of the largest crime syndicate in his pocket. Crying like a little bitch wasn't an option.

A roar burst from Vinny's mouth, and he slammed his fist into the wall beside him. Skin peeled from his knuckles, plaster crumbled as his hand drove through the wall. It helped. The pain ricocheting from his fist, the hole now blemishing this once pristine and somewhat clinical foyer, actually helped soothe Vinny's jagged soul.

Mobsters waited a borough away, serious men who wouldn't appreciate being stalled, but Vinny didn't give a shit. He walked into the living room and plopped his ass down on the sofa. Sasha would be back, eventually. That girl was like bad luck; she struck in threes. There were still two more rounds of pain she had to dish out, and the word patience wasn't in Sasha's vocabulary. It wouldn't be long now until she stumbled through that door. Then he could lay into her for fucking shit up with Dez and Tyler.

***

Sasha

Sasha crouched down in a narrow alley between two buildings. Not only had standing become iffy with the shake of her legs, but the bright shade of her skin in this neighborhood could only bring trouble. Normally, she'd welcome trouble. But fuck, all she could think about was getting another hit. Her every muscle scraped like hot glass, and exhaustion weighed her eyelids down, but she couldn't focus on that. She was so close to getting enough smack to last her a month, two weeks at the least.

A black sedan parked down the road, and Sasha poked her head out of the alleyway. The passenger door opened, Kev climbed out of the car, and a grin crept across Sasha's lips. The guy bumbled his cracker-white ass down the sidewalk of Harlem, briefcase in hand, which warped her grin into a glower.

"Kev," Sasha called out in a whisper, keeping to the shadows of the alley.

Kev's free hand flew to his holster as he inched

closer to the alleyway. The second he saw Sasha, peeking out between two buildings, he rushed to her side.

"Sasha! Jesus fucking—"

Sasha wacked Kev in the gut with the back of her hand. "What the fuck, asshole? I told you to come alone. Who's in that car?"

"Fuck." Kev rubbed his stomach, glancing back at the car down the street. "Mickey drove me. I don't know where 127th and Malcolm X is."

"Yeah, well, I don't know who the fuck Mickey is."

"Neither do I." Kev pushed Sasha deeper into the alley, backed her against a dumpster. "Where the fuck have you been? You look like shit."

"You look like a douchebag."

Kev chuckled, wrapping Sasha in a tight hug. "God, I miss you. I'm stuck with all these stuffy Italian bastards. They're so fucking boring."

"Get off!" Sasha shrugged away from Kev's embrace. Her skin felt like a combination of broken razorblades and bits of barbed-wire rolled beneath it. "Did you bring the money?"

"Yeah, but…" Kev handed Sasha the briefcase, stepped back, and cringed as if awaiting a slap. "There's only two g's in there."

"Shit, man. I need five."

"I know, sorry. It was all I had, and you said I couldn't tell Otis and Vinny." Kev peered back out onto the sidewalk. A group of young men strolled by, oblivious to them, and Kev placed his palm on the butt of his holstered gun.

"You ain't never seen black folk before, have

you?" Sasha said, snickering as Kev slid against the slimy wall and back to her side.

"No. I mean, one or two here and there, but...what the fuck are you doing in this neighborhood?"

"My friend's in the building over there." Sasha gestured to the apartment complex across the street, the one her eye had been on this entire time. Some very unpleasant things could be happening to Roxy inside that place. Everyone would eat bullets if one drop of blood had been shed from her beautiful girl's body.

"I gotta go," Sasha said, pushing Kev toward the sidewalk. "Get Otis's little narc motherfucker out of here so I can split."

"Sasha." Kev grabbed onto Sasha's hand, squeezing tight. "Will you come back to Fat Tonys tomorrow, please? Vinny's never around, and Otis is...different now. It's weird there. I'm all by myself."

"What about Cory?"

"He went back home. His mama wasn't taking Cash's death well." A strange look crossed Kev's face, like he might run away, then he pulled Sasha's hand to his chest. "I know what it's like to put flowers on your grave. I don't want to do that ever again."

Sasha yanked her hand from Kev's grasp. That didn't sate her anger, so she shoved him. She hadn't asked for no one to put any flowers on some grave. Hell, she hadn't even asked for anybody to dig her a fucking grave.

"Stop being a freak," Sasha said, shoving Kev

again. "Now get, and don't tell nobody you saw me."

"Yeah, all right." A long sigh flowed from Kev's mouth as he turned toward the sidewalk, walking away.

Sasha crept to the edge of the alleyway, watched Kev climb into the passenger seat of the awaiting sedan. She should be at his side, in that car, on her way to Fat Tonys. She would be, if she were Sasha Lazzari. Sasha Lazzari had died.

"Poor girl got herself shot in the face," she muttered.

The car busted a U-turn, sped toward the glimmer of tall buildings, and Sasha hurried across the street.

Chapter Three

As far as drug deals go, to walk away from a buy instead of being carried out from one in a body bag constituted success. It didn't matter that Sasha had to watch her girl suck some guy off while she tossed out excuses to her dealer for coming up short. The fact she handed over all the money and only got a tiny, near non-existent fraction of her promised amount wasn't much of a factor either. She'd just walked away from a place where every wall had holes between the smears of shit, where people convulsed in the hallways from overdosing on hot-shots, with her girl and a quarter of china. All and all, a good score.

"We need to find someplace," Sasha said as they hurried along the sidewalk, back toward Upper Manhattan. Sasha eyed every alley they passed, every dark corner, but they were all occupied by junkies, hookers, and homeless people.

"That place." Roxy pointed at the building lit in a red glow across the boulevard. "Sharkies, they have hourly rates for rooms."

"I don't have any cash. Fucking Reid ripped me off big time. After we load up, I wanna go back there and drag my knife across his throat."

"No," Roxy said through a snicker. "We still need him." She took Sasha by the hand and strolled into the street without bothering to look. Tires screeched as cars swerved around them. A pinto nearly sideswiped a van beside them, yet Roxy didn't spare a glance as she pulled Sasha across the road. Not even when a car's front bumper squealed to a stop inches from her knee did she flinch.

"Fuck, woman!" Sasha hurried out of the street and away from the people shouting cusses. "You wanna fucking die?"

"Cowards die many times before their deaths; the valiant never taste of death but once."

"What?" Sasha pulled Roxy to a stop in front of Sharkies Motel. The woman may be delirious, having never gone this long without booting up before. "You're talking gibberish."

"It's Shakespeare." Roxy tugged Sasha's arm. "Come on, I wanna get inside."

"I still don't have any money," Sasha said, keeping one hand in her pocket to clutch the bag of powder within.

"I have money." Roxy stopped in front of the motel's glass door and pulled a wad of twenties from the waistband of her skirt. "I made those guys pay for their blowies." A smile spread across her lips, her jaw smacking the gum that rolled around inside her mouth.

"Nice." Sasha glided her hand along Roxy's

side, and she latched onto the woman's curvy hip. She drew Roxy close, dropped a kiss on her soft neck. "Let's go, doll," she whispered, licking Roxy's ear.

***

A steady thump echoed around the narrow motel room as Sasha drummed her fingers against her leg. The two big lines she'd snorted had barely taken the edge off. It seemed like she'd spent an eternity sitting on a thin mattress in this dumpy little room, staring at a brown stain on the wall while Roxy drifted in and out of a heroin haze. Finally, a light snore flowed from the woman's mouth.

Roxy was too deep into her nod to notice Sasha swipe the small leather pouch from her lap. Sasha's heart raced as she staggered toward the bathroom. She stopped in its doorway to glance back at Roxy. Her girl was still conked out atop the ripped bedspread, so she crept into the bathroom and closed the door. This had to be quick, quiet. Every day, Roxy forbid Sasha from booting up while slamming a needle into her own arm. It was an unreasonable demand. Sasha could snort a twenty bag in one sitting and only walk away with a nose bleed. All her time, for what felt like weeks straight, had been devoted to finding *that* high—the one she'd experienced the first time she snorted a nail-full of powder in the backroom of a strip club. The sensation of an endless orgasm existed. She had grazed it, once, when the horrors of the world had faded from her mind for a few blissful hours.

Sasha slid down the bathroom wall, sitting on the floor. Her fingers shook as she unzipped the small leather pouch. She could find that high again. A little more juice this time, not as much as Roxy's shots, but more than halfway up the syringe. Then, maybe, she could grasp the fringe of release.

After the smack had been cooked and the needle loaded, Sasha kicked off her boot. A red stain blotted the tip of her sock, turned cold once hitting the air. She pulled off her sock, wincing as the fabric tore off a scab between her toes. Her right foot couldn't take many more pinpricks. She'd have to start shooting in the other soon.

It took a few minutes for Sasha to find a spot between her toes that didn't ooze puss or blood. The outside of the little toe was all she came up with. It was going to hurt, later. Right now, she was finding it a little hard to give a fuck about later.

The tip of the needle quaked as Sasha jammed it into her skin, pulling back to slip into the sweet spot. She pressed down the plunger and warmth flooded her body. The heat rushing through her veins scorched away the pain of her flesh, clouded every dark memory ravaging her mind. Tingles led to a powerful slump. Her back slid down the wall, hiking up her flannel as she fell to her side.

A cockroach scurried in front of Sasha's eyes, and patches of black mold surrounded her. It was all good. The filth would fade, as soon as a haze crept up to claim her vision.

"Sasha," Roxy called out from behind the closed bathroom door. The locked knob jiggled, and the door rattled under a barrage of knocks. "Sasha!"

"Be out in a minute," she slurred. A spin had gripped the world, but Sasha was numb to the sway brought on by drugs. Her palm slapped the cool tile of the floor. She pushed herself to her knees and glanced around the bathroom. Shit was fucking everywhere. Her boot sat in one corner, a bloody sock in the other, and the tools of her forbidden deed were scattered around her.

As Sasha reached for her sock, the needle rolled across the dirty floor. She dove for it, brought the syringe close to her chest.

"Fuck," she said, searching the floor for Roxy's favorite spoon. She had to get this shit back in its leather pouch just the way Roxy liked it, or the jig would be up. After making certain the pouch was back in perfect order, she pulled on her bloody sock and shoved her sore foot into her tight boot.

Sasha smoothed back tangles of her dreadlocked hair, stashed Roxy's pouch down the back of her pants, and left the bathroom. The tiny motel room didn't seem so bad now. Earlier, Sasha considered setting the ripped curtains on fire. The chipped paint on the walls had grated her mind, and the stains on the floor disgusted her. But now, the place felt pretty cozy. It had everything Sasha needed. A bed with a beautiful woman sprawled atop it, and a fresh bag of china on the nightstand. If only she had a joint. Then this moment would be complete.

"Sorry, doll." Sasha snuck the pouch from her waistband, slipped it into Roxy's purse as she dropped onto the bed. "I was washing up."

Roxy climbed on top of Sasha, straddling her lap. "Really?"

Sasha clutched onto the hips riding her. She got about two seconds of groping in before her arms were yanked away. Roxy pushed the sleeve up on Sasha's right arm, then her left.

"What are you doing?" Sasha asked, leaning back against the headboard as the woman manhandled her.

"Looking for track marks."

"I told you." Sasha grabbed Roxy by the wrists, squeezing. Tingles still flowed through her blood. It was hard to glower when she yearned to giggle, but she managed to push out the next set of words between gritted teeth. "I don't shoot."

"I'd never forgive myself if you fell down this hole with me." Roxy's legs clung to Sasha like a vice, the woman's entire body trembling. "It's not too late for you, but if you boot you'll never be able to stop. I want you to stop, baby."

Sasha pulled Roxy to her chest. "Nobody's booting shit." Her hands glided up Roxy's arms, slowing their quake. The shudder of Roxy's bones stopped when Sasha slid her palms over the woman's shoulders. "Relax, doll. It's all good."

Roxy's mouth drew near, and Sasha lunged for it. Their lips connected, silencing the shouts from the room next door. Roxy's eyes rolled around in her head, her body barely able to hold itself up, but the woman's kiss remained hard.

A loud knock shook the motel's door, and Roxy's body grew stiff.

"Time's up," a man hollered through the door. "You whores need to pay for another hour or get the fuck out."

"We're leaving, dickwad," Sasha yelled as Roxy climbed off the bed.

Sasha took one last second to enjoy the buzz circulating throughout her body, then stumbled to her feet. "Now what? It's, like, two in the morning."

"Let's go back to your penthouse. Maybe if we crawl in bed with your old man, he'll give in and fuck us."

The thought brought a smile to Sasha's lips. Dez hadn't fucked her since she'd escaped her cell. They did have sex a month ago, but it wasn't fucking. It was awkward. Dez flinched every time his hand touched a scar, and he kept asking if she was all right. She wasn't all right. It was the only time she ever cried during sex, and Dez hadn't touched her since.

Things could go different with Roxy at Sasha's side. Two broken girls had to equal one whole woman. Together, they could distract Dez from their deformed flesh and actually get loved like real people.

"Yeah." Sasha draped her arm around Roxy and headed for the door. "Let's go molest my husband."

***

The penthouse door creaked, and Roxy chuckled.

"Dammit, woman," Sasha whispered. "You're so fucking loud."

"Me?" Roxy said in a hushed squeal. "You're the one fucking with the door. It sounds like a bullhorn."

A light clicked on in the living room. Roxy

yelped, jumping behind Sasha as Vinny glared from the loveseat.

"That's because it's so quiet in here," Vinny said, leaning forward in his chair.

"You scared the fuck out of me." Sasha ignored Vinny's hard stare and headed for the long couch beside the loveseat. "I'm glad you're up." She dropped onto the couch, stretching out. "You got a joint? I'm fucking dying to smoke a joint right now."

"Dez is gone," Vinny said, turning his glare from Sasha to Roxy. "Who the fuck is that?"

Roxy backed into the corner of the foyer, between a hole in the wall and the open front door.

"Shut that door, doll," Sasha said. She dug through an ashtray of cigarette butts in search of a stray joint as the penthouse door clicked shut. "Where'd Dez go?"

"He split, for good."

Sasha snickered, moving her search for weed to the end table. "Fuck Dez. If that pussy wants to roll, good riddance."

"What about Tyler?" Vinny yelled, jumping to his feet. "You gonna say fuck Tyler too?"

"Tyler?" Sasha rose from the couch. She looked across the penthouse to find three wide open bedroom doors on the landing of the second floor. "That motherfucker can't take my kid."

Vinny grabbed Sasha by the arm, damn near crushing her bone with his tight grip. "What? Did you think Dez would leave a child here, alone, just hoping you'd come back?"

With a shove, Vinny released Sasha. She

stumbled over her wobbly feet, crashed to her hands and knees on the gray carpet. "He can't take my boy," she said to the floor below. "I'll track him down. Put a goddamn bullet in his head."

"What the fuck is wrong with you?" Vinny shouted, balling his fists as he stared down at Sasha.

"Stop," Roxy muttered, shrinking down in the corner. "Please."

Sasha stayed on her knees, her glare caught on the fury that burned within Vinny's eyes. "What's wrong with me?" Rage surged within Sasha, so strong she could taste its bitter flavor. "I spent three months in the dark, in a room that sparkled and bled, with my mother's eyes chasing me."

Slowly, to avoid toppling, Sasha stood. Her chin lifted, gaze narrowing as she stared Vinny in the face. "You wanna know what's wrong with me? I'm scared! Every second, of every day, I'm scared someone's gonna take me. I close my eyes, and I'm scared they'll open to a locked door."

"I'm scared too." Vinny latched onto the sides of Sasha's arms. "I'm scared I'll lose you again."

Sasha fell against Vinny's chest, hugged him tight. His strong arms wrapped around her, and the tears she'd been holding in broke free. Vinny should've hugged her before now. It would've been nice to have his embrace when she didn't need it, instead of having to throw herself into his arms.

"So..." Sasha wiped her tears on Vinny's shirt before she drew back from the refuge of his touch. "You got a joint, or what?"

***

Vinny

Smoke rose from the joint in Vinny's mouth. He sat at the edge of the loveseat, watching Sasha roll doobie after doobie from his bag of weed. There was something off with Sasha. She wasn't drunk, yet she could barely sit up straight. The girl definitely hadn't smoked herself stupid. That wasn't possible for a stoner of Sasha's caliber. Still, something wasn't right.

"Come here, babe," Sasha said, glancing at her friend, who was still cowering in the corner.

This shit was too weird for Vinny. "What's up with her?" he asked, nodding at the woman who crept toward Sasha's side.

"What's wrong with you?" Sasha snatched the joint from Vinny's hand. "You freaked her the fuck out when we walked in."

Vinny stared at the Spanish version of a Cyndi Lauper wannabe. The woman's poufy skirt rustled as she hurried across the living room, showing off her long legs. Sasha sure did have great taste. The hips to waist to tits ratio was amazing. He couldn't help but imagine that woman's ass bouncing in his lap as he buried his face between her silky brown breasts.

"You like what you see?" Sasha asked through a snicker.

Vinny forced his stare to the floor, which made taking the joint from Sasha's hand nearly impossible.

"Maybe," Sasha said, slanting forward to catch Vinny's gaze, "if you apologize for being a freak earlier, she'll let you slide between those smooth legs of hers."

A giggle flowed from the woman's mouth, squeaky, sexy. The flaps of her jean jacket slipped open as she leaned back against the couch cushions.

"Oh damn," Sasha said, taking the joint that Vinny completely forgot to hit. "I think Roxy likes you, Vinny."

"Who is this guy?" Roxy asked, reaching for the joint in Sasha's grasp.

"That's my brother."

"Gross," Vinny said, lighting a fresh doobie from the pile Sasha left him. "Don't call me that. It makes us sound…"

"Nasty," Sasha said, flashing a wicked smile. "You feel all dirty cause you fucked your sister?"

"You're not my sister!" Vinny took a deep breath. He was furious with his own body right now, especially his cock for getting hard at the crap rolling from Sasha's lips. Sasha's full, pouty lips.

"I'm married to your brother. That makes me your sister."

"In law." Vinny pointed his joint-filled fingers at Sasha's smug face. "We ain't blood kin."

"Yeah, all right. I'll give you that much." Sasha crushed her stub of a roach out in the ashtray, grabbed a new joint from the pile, and rose from the couch in a bit of a wobble. "I gotta use the bathroom." She looked at Roxy. "Gimme your purse."

Roxy drew the large leather purse to her chest, hugged it like a baby. "Why?"

"Just give it." Sasha yanked the bag from Roxy's

33

grasp and headed for the staircase.

"I'll go with you," Roxy said, jumping to her feet.

"No." Sasha didn't look back as she climbed the stairs but did wave her arm in Roxy's direction. "You can go next."

Vinny settled back on the loveseat, staring at Roxy frozen mid-step in front of the couch. The top of Roxy's jean jacket hung low on her back, showing the tips of long, skinny scars. It looked like the woman had been whipped at some point in her life, a lot. And it all started to make sense. Sasha had found someone more frightened by the world than she was. It must give Sasha strength to be around Roxy, which was something Vinny could never strip away.

"Roxy, right?" Vinny asked, chuckling when the woman jumped. "It's cool." He gestured to the couch, then held out the joint. "I won't bite."

With her gaze locked on the banister of the stairs, Roxy walked past the couch and sat beside Vinny on the small sofa. Instead of reaching for the joint, she went straight for his belt.

"Whoa." Vinny shooed Roxy's hands from his pants, scooted away from her. "That's…not how this works."

"You don't want a blowjob?" Roxy asked, her face a giant ball of confusion.

"Fuck yeah I want a blowjob." Vinny handed the barely lit joint to Roxy, clicking his zippo to life for her. "But I want a blowjob from someone who *wants* to give me one, not someone who feels like they have to."

Vinny didn't think it possible, but the confusion in Roxy's stare grew thicker. The woman really was gorgeous, in a mysterious wounded bird sort of way. A hint of cleavage spilled over the top of Roxy's shirt as she hit the joint, and Vinny shifted in his seat. Sasha sure was taking her good-ole time in the bathroom. If that girl didn't hurry, shit might start happening in this living room.

Chapter Four

Sasha

Sasha stepped out of the shower in her bathroom, wrapped herself in a towel. It had been so long since she'd washed. She forgot how great it felt, how light to be clean. Shampoo had done wonders for her hair, but that mop of a mess was too tangled to fuck with now.

She twisted her hair into a bun, glimpsing the new marks on her scarred foot. The rats had done a fine job of turning her toes to shreds, but the damages she'd inflicted with one thin needle was far worse. That last jab, five minutes ago, tore the skin open on the side of her right foot. She hadn't been able to bring herself to start in on the left foot yet. Especially for such a small dose. She'd only taken half the amount she usually booted because of fucking Vinny. While that guy was around, she had to appear at least somewhat lucid.

The fog had begun to fade on the mirror, and

Sasha turned away at the first hint of her reflection. She did *not* want to see that horror show. She'd never understand how anybody could stare at her, see the swollen red marks running along her cheeks and not vomit. It made her puke every time see saw her own face. That's why she didn't blame Dez for splitting. He was smart, knew how to dodge a bullet.

Smears of blood stained the white tile every place Sasha stepped. "This isn't gonna work," she mumbled, digging through the medicine cabinet. A smile lifted her cheeks when she spotted a tube of superglue, Dez's favorite tool for sealing busted knuckles.

Sasha brought the tube of glue to her chest. She really fucking missed Dez. Not the strange dude who'd been smothering her the last few months. She missed the real Dez, the guy who put his fist through everything, the man who fucked her hard against a wall, gave her the strength to fight. That's who she'd been longing for. The disappearance of that man was the reason she'd been slamming poison into her veins. She had to erase Dez from her mind, since the Dez she knew wouldn't be coming back.

After dabbing a few globs of superglue atop the open wounds between her toes, Sasha left the bathroom. Her heart skipped at the sight of clean socks in her dresser drawer. Once she slipped those suckers on her feet, she tossed the blood-crusted ones in the trash, tightened the towel around her body, and opened the bedroom door.

Beyond the banister of glass and silver, in the

living room below, Vinny lounged on the sofa beside Roxy. They looked so perfect together, cute. Roxy hid her scars well behind her layers of sparkly clothes, and Vinny wore his marks on the inside. The two of them made a good-looking couple. It was too bad for them, because her ugly, monster ass was about to burst into their love scene.

"Hey," Sasha called out, and Roxy jumped to her feet. "Why don't you guys grab a few joints and come up here? It's more comfy."

Roxy was halfway up the stairs before the first syllable left Sasha's mouth. The woman scanned the bedroom the instant she walked inside, looking for her purse no doubt.

"It's in the bathroom," Sasha said, which sent Roxy into a skip toward the open bathroom door. "You can shower if you want."

With a wink, Roxy shed her jacket and walked inside the bathroom. The woman didn't bother to close the door. Sasha laid on the bed, watching Roxy strip off her tight halter top. The skirt dropped next. Roxy was a vision of beauty as she swayed her hips to music only she could hear, and they were such luscious hips.

Vinny walked across the bedroom, his stare caught on the thin scars that decorated Roxy's back. "What happened to her?"

"Close the door, Roxy," Sasha called out. The bathroom door clicked shut, leaving only the shimmer of city lights from the wide windows to illuminate the room. Sasha didn't care if Vinny ogled her girl, wasn't offended when he asked about Roxy's scars. Roxy had started digging into her purse. That woman would boot up in the middle of a church unless someone told her otherwise, and Vinny wasn't ready to see something like that.

"Her father kept her tied up in a closet for ten years, raping her," Sasha said, nonchalant, as if it were an everyday type of occurrence. In her life, her new life, that sort of shit actually was normal.

Vinny sat on the bed beside Sasha, lighting a joint. The towel slipped off Sasha's leg as she propped onto her elbow, scooting closer to Vinny.

"Then," Sasha said, taking the joint before Vinny could get a full hit. "Roxy ran away from foster care, ended up a whore. Her pimp liked to put cigarettes out on her body."

"That's all kinds of fucked up." Vinny's gaze stayed on the closed bathroom door. He looked pale, naïve, like a farm-boy plucked straight from the hills of Kentucky. "She tried to give me a blowjob," he said, snatching the joint from Sasha's grasp.

"Yeah." Sasha rolled onto her back, caressed the one smooth spot on her stomach untouched by jagged marks. "Roxy likes doing that."

"I don't think she does." Vinny took a long hit of the doobie, then looked at Sasha. "Did you tell her she had to?"

"No! I'd never do that." Sasha didn't know if she should be pissed at the jab or impressed by Vinny's compassion toward a near stranger.

"Do you want me to fetch ya some clothes?" Vinny asked, darting his stare between Sasha's bare skin and his feet.

Sasha pulled off the towel, threw it in front of

Vinny's face and onto the floor. "Nope. Does seeing my body bother you?"

Vinny tossed the joint onto the nightstand and ran his now free hand along Sasha's side. His fingers thumped with each ridge of scabs they glided over. She felt like a reptile, hard-shelled and scaly. A cool chill slithered beneath her skin, clashing with the fire pumping through her veins. She was definitely turning into a beast.

"Seeing your body turns me the fuck on," Vinny said, brushing his lips against her mouth. His fingers glided along her cheek, but she could barely feel it. Scar tissue blocked the gentlest of touches.

Sasha sat up on the bed and pulled off Vinny's shirt. His chest was solid, hard. That, she would feel pressed up against her reptile flesh. "Gore turns you on?" she whispered, biting Vinny's ear.

"I don't see no gore." Vinny slid his hand into Sasha's hair, knocked her tangled waves loose from its bun. "I only see you."

He kissed Sasha, hard, clutched her waist, pulled her hair. His rough hand ran up her chest, and he pushed her back onto the mattress. He didn't ask if she was *all right*; there was no tremble in Vinny's fingertips. His electric eyes scanned Sasha's naked body as he unfastened his belt, and a slight tingle ignited deep inside her chest.

A loud clunk rang out as Vinny's jeans hit the floor. The sound sent shivers down Sasha's spine. It was one she knew well, the thump of a gun hitting the ground. Vinny grabbed Sasha by the hips, yanked her to the edge of the bed.

"Oh, hell yeah," she said with a moan as she

grinded against the hard-on that crept between her legs.

The bathroom door creaked open, spilling bright light over the ink that covered Vinny's shoulders and arms. Roxy froze in the doorway, clutching a towel to her still damp body.

"Come here." Sasha stretched her hand toward Roxy, wiggling her fingers. "Slide your sexy ass between us."

A giggle flowed from Roxy's mouth. The towel dropped to the floor, and Roxy hurried toward the bed.

***

Sasha lay atop silky sheets, under a tangle of arms and legs. Vinny snored beside her, his arm dead across her chest, and Roxy's leg clutched her waist. To crawl out from beneath this jumble of flesh, silently, would be damn near impossible. It was a chance Sasha had to take. The two bastards snuggling against her got to sleep. She should be afforded that luxury too, except sleep would never come while thoughts of a shiny needle floated around inside her mind.

A tiny lift of her head, and Sasha spied Roxy's purse. The big leather bag sat on the bathroom sink's long marble counter, its patches of brown, red, and orange suede reflecting off every shimmering surface.

It wasn't the actual purse that called to Sasha. The dwindling bag of smack and small pouch with every accessory she needed to get truly high was what sang to her soul. She would never rest. Not as long as that grating melody, which only played for her, echoed around the room.

Shivers nipped at Sasha's spine. Her fingers twitched. Fuck everyone in this bed. She could use the bathroom. There was nothing wrong with that.

Vinny snorted, rolled onto his side when Sasha pushed his hand off her chest. That was one naked lover she'd unraveled from. Roxy's sexy brown leg barely moved when Sasha crawled out from under it. The bed squeaked, but Sasha didn't slow her somewhat clumsy departure from the mattress. Her stare had become fused with Roxy's purse.

The shine of the bathroom's overhead lights stung Sasha's eyes, brought a layer of tears to the surface, but she didn't blink. She saw the only object of her desire, and nothing would stop her from grasping it.

Sasha didn't have time to shut the bathroom door, not with Roxy's purse gleaming on the countertop. She grabbed the cool leather strap, pulled the bag close. In seconds flat, she had the powder in the spoon and a lighter lit.

While Sasha loaded the syringe, she eyed her right foot. Her little piggies were fucked. Instead of the market, it looked like her toes had visited the slaughterhouse. The virgin skin on her left foot would be getting sacrificed today. It was a thought that excited Sasha, which also brought a wave of disgust that drowned her.

Just as Sasha brought the needle's tip to the fresh skin between her toes, the bathroom door thumped against the wall. She pulled the needle back, tried to hide it under her leg as Roxy stomped into the bathroom.

A deep stare of betrayal filled Roxy's eyes as she clutched a satin sheet to her body, staring down at Sasha. "What are you doing?" she practically screamed.

"Shh." Sasha looked past Roxy to the bed, and Vinny stirring on it. "What the fuck—"

Roxy dropped to her knees beside Sasha, the sheet fluttering. "Look at your foot." She grabbed Sasha's ankle, her fingers trembling. "What did you do?"

Sasha crawled across the bathroom floor, shut and locked the door. "Damn, girl. Vinny's not cool like that."

"You promised." Tears ran down Roxy's cheeks, the needle quaking in her grasp. "You lied."

Roxy dropped the syringe as she rose to her feet. Sasha stared at the still loaded needle rolling across the white tile, then looked at Roxy hurrying toward the bathroom door.

"Fuck," Sasha muttered, glancing back at the needle. Roxy flung the sheet off her body and yanked open the bathroom door while Sasha dove for the needle. She jammed the tip between her toes, shot half a tube in one quick plunge. There was just enough time to stuff the needle and spoon back in its pouch before a fiery rush tore through her body.

Vinny peeked into the bathroom as Sasha wobbled to her feet. "What's going on?" he asked, gesturing to the room behind him. Beyond the ripples of Vinny's distracting abs, she glimpsed Roxy pull on her clothes. Sasha took a step toward the bathroom door, and Roxy burst past Vinny, stomped up to Sasha, and latched onto the purse.

"This is mine." Roxy snatched the purse and the little leather pouch from Sasha's weak grip, then tore ass out the bathroom.

"Hey," Sasha yelled as Roxy ripped open the bedroom door. "That shit inside your bag is mine."

Roxy stopped in the doorway, looking back at Sasha. "Not anymore, *doll*." Hints of sorrow filled Roxy's lost stare, and then she walked away.

Vinny turned his wide eyes from the now empty bedroom to Sasha. "What the fuck?"

"Just…" Sasha waved Vinny off, staggered over her jelly feet to chase Roxy. "Go back to bed. It's all good." She picked her clothes off the floor, dressing as she headed for the bedroom door.

"Sasha," Vinny called out.

There was no time to think up bullshit excuses, so Sasha grabbed her boots and picked up the pace. She was not going to spend another night trying to score more smack or a new woman, for that matter.

Sasha might've fell down the top half of the stairs a little bit, but she mastered the art of running down swaying steps pretty quickly after that. "Roxy," she shouted, just as Roxy stormed out the front door.

"This fucking bitch," Sasha muttered, almost jogging out the penthouse. Her shoulder crashed against the smooth wall in the hallway, sending a jolt into her bones that slowed her steps. The dim hall stretched out in front of Sasha, longer the more she stared down it. Roxy was at the elevator now, pounding her finger against the button. Sasha had to

44

catch that woman before Roxy slipped into the city like a shadow.

"Wait, please," Sasha said, though the words may have streamed out in a mumble. Somehow, she managed to reach Roxy's side. All the world's weight seemed to fall on her shoulders. The air was so heavy, it dragged Sasha down. She grabbed onto the side of Roxy's arm to keep from tumbling to the floor.

"Here." Roxy shoved the bag of heroin into Sasha's hand. "Just take it and go."

Sasha dropped her boots to the floor, shoved her bloody feet inside, and tucked the bag into her pocket. The drugs were hers. She could walk away and be perfectly fine without Roxy, for maybe three hours.

The elevator door slid open, and Sasha backed Roxy inside. Her girl was no push-over. Roxy slapped Sasha's face, screamed about broken promises, but Sasha didn't let go. She pushed Roxy against the elevator's wall. The second her chest fell against Roxy, the struggle ended.

Although Sasha would love to dive into ignorance, she had to see Roxy's face. She looked up from the silky neck in front of her blurry eyes, only to find a hurt gaze.

"I lost you," Roxy said in a quaver.

"I'm sorry I lied." The strength had faded from Sasha's legs, and she couldn't help but lean against Roxy. "But you don't know me. I can handle my shit."

A short, sarcastic snicker erupted from Roxy's mouth. "You sound like a fucking idiot."

The elevator door opened with a *ding*, and Roxy slid away from Sasha.

"Really?" Sasha said, bouncing from wall to wall as she followed Roxy into the way too bright, far too sparkly lobby. "That's how it's gonna be? You're a fucking hypocrite."

Roxy stopped short, her long messy hair tapping the back of her bedazzled jacket. She spun to face Sasha, jabbed her finger at Sasha's chest. "I didn't pick this life. It was dumped on me. You think I like slamming shit into my veins just to deal? I hate it. I hate myself."

A fuck-load of people had gathered around to watch Sasha and Roxy shout at each other in the middle of the garish lobby. Every one of those assholes in suits, lugging thousand-dollar briefcases could suck it. The dumb fuckers whose bullshit lives Sasha had interrupted didn't much matter to her. Roxy's gentle spirit, the kindness behind her deep brown eyes, the feel of her silky skin was what mattered to Sasha.

She took Roxy by the hand, locked their fingers together. "If you leave now, without me, we'll never see each other again. Is that what you want?"

A lone tear carved its way down Roxy's cheek. "Let's go." Roxy kept a firm hold on Sasha's hand and barged past whispering men and narrow-eyed women. "I fucking hate Manhattan."

Chapter Five

Vinny

Vinny strolled down the sidewalk, ignorant to the sun's rays. It had been a strange fucking night, even stranger morning. For all Vinny knew, the mind-blowing sex with two incredibly scarred women was a dirty figment of his twisted imagination. Except he could still feel Sasha's lips on his neck, his chest, his—

"Where the fuck you been?" Otis called out.

The short tone of the Don's voice snapped Vinny out of his own nasty thoughts. Jesus, he'd walked right though Fat Tonys, up the small steps to the private dining area, and sat in his seat next to Otis. Without even noticing. Fucking Sasha would end up getting him killed.

"I, um…"

Otis shifted in his seat at the head of the table, which made Enzo and Kev fidget in their wooden chairs. "You been chasing Sasha, or Dez?"

"Both," Vinny said, fishing out his pack of smokes. "I couldn't stop Dez."

"I know." Otis waved over a waitress, and a mug of steaming coffee was placed beside Vinny. "Dez called me from Kentucky at five o'clock this fucking morning."

Goddamn did Vinny miss Dez, which was stupid considering he wanted Sasha all to himself. Although, with Sasha, it didn't matter if Dez was around or not. Vinny would never get that girl all to himself.

"I caught up with Sasha," he muttered into his coffee, not caring to elaborate on how *that* meeting went.

Otis leaned on the table, staring at Vinny. "Dez had some things to say about Sasha."

Vinny wasn't surprised Dez had a bunch of trash to talk. His brother liked to blame everyone else for every little thing that happened, but it was that bastard's fault Sasha was acting so weird. Sasha wasn't used to being babied. Plus, Dez was a piss-poor coddler. His dumb-ass oaf of a brother had chased Sasha right into the arms of a sexy, exotic, broken angel, and Vinny wasn't the least bit surprised.

"What the fuck did Dez have to say?" Vinny slammed his mug onto the table, spilling a drop of coffee over its brim. "And you should've seen how he dragged Tyler out of the penthouse. That shit was fucked up."

A low growl streamed from Otis's mouth. Judging by the anger that brewed in Otis's glare, it was probably a good thing the man hadn't witnessed that scene. Tyler may be Dez's "son," but that kid meant something special to every person at this table. Even Enzo looked crushed that Tyler was gone, and he'd just met the little guy a few months ago.

"Dez told me," Otis said, forcing his rage-filled glare into a semi-aggravated glower, "Sasha's been disappearing for days at a time, hanging with some strange Mexican woman."

"Not Mexican," Vinny said, lighting a cigarette. "Puerto Rican."

Otis sat up straight, as if an invisible hand stuck him. "You've met her?"

"Yeah. Roxy."

"Roxy, what?" Otis asked, pulling a pen from Enzo's front pocket and grabbing a napkin.

"I don't know," Vinny said with a snort. It didn't seem like an appropriate question to ask the woman while he was fucking her, or when she threw a hissy-fit and stormed from the penthouse. "I just met her last night. Sasha brought her home."

"So, this Roxy woman was in the penthouse? Did she touch anything?"

Vinny looked down at his lap. There was one thing he could think of that Roxy had her hands all over, but he wasn't about to whip his dick out. "Um…She had a beer. It's still sitting in the living room. Why?"

Otis nodded at Enzo, and Enzo rose from his seat, grabbed Kev by the arm, and headed toward the lobby with Kev in tow.

"What's up?" Vinny asked, his voice echoing around the empty restaurant.

"Enzo and Kev are gonna run that bottle over to our friends in blue. They can pull some prints, tell us who this woman really is."

"You think Sasha's in danger." Vinny's heart jumped into his throat at the thought of some fucker trying to hurt Sasha again. A sudden burst of dread, fury, anguish washed over him. He balled his hands into fists, but the prickles in his fingertips wouldn't fade. Sasha would never end up in a dark hole, alone and scared. Never again. "Do you know something? Are there more Mancinis out there?"

"No." Otis laid his hand over top Vinny's fist. "I just want to play it safe. Sasha has a…"

"Target on her back for predators," Vinny said through clenched teeth.

"A trusting heart," Otis said, sitting back in his chair. "And it gets her in trouble, a lot."

Otis had changed since coming to New York. It wasn't the power to command hundreds of men to kill on demand that had turned Otis ruthless. Vinny's friend grew cold the day they dropped a coffin, thought to hold Sasha's body, into the ground. That's when Vinny's friend became his boss. Not the road captain kind of boss either. In only two months, Otis had become the bloodiest Don in Lazzari history. The killings didn't end when Sasha returned to them, her body shredded almost beyond recognition. Now, Otis was determined to wipe out any threat to every member of his now much larger family, and Vinny couldn't be happier.

"What'd you want me to do?" Vinny asked, wishing "lock Sasha in a tower" would be the answer.

Otis rose from his seat. He stared out at the busboys hurrying to prep the many tables below their private dining area. Each ghostly table got a coat of shimmer for the assholes that would pile into this place, hoping to graze the feel of a wicked life.

"Do your fucking job," Otis said. He grabbed his belt and nodded at the waitress beside the bar. The girl giggled, slinked off to the backroom, and Otis steered his hard stare to Vinny. "You were supposed to shut down an underground poker house last night. Do you think you can run a crew and keep an eye on Sasha? Or should I have Kev do it?"

Vinny sneered. He could take Otis's sarcasm, usually, but Sasha withdrawal was kicking in and he was feeling a bit ornery.

"Motherfucking Kev," Vinny yelled. His chair scraped the floor as he jumped to his feet. Vinny stomped past Otis. His hip bumped the table, launching a mug to the floor. The shatter of glass boomed throughout the quiet room, but he didn't slow his trot down the small steps.

"I was just fucking with ya, brother," Otis called out.

Vinny didn't look back. He lifted his middle finger high in the air as he headed for the front door.

***

Sasha

The squeak of bed springs sent spikes into

Sasha's spine. She dropped her half-eaten hamburger onto its grease-soaked wrapper and looked at the bed. A rusty cot wasn't waiting to rip her flesh to dangling pieces of dead meat; it never was. That didn't mean shit. She still expected to find her jagged cot whenever she heard the squeal of metal springs. Instead, like always, she found Roxy sitting cross-legged on a filthy mattress that centered a closet some asshole dared to call a motel room.

Her girl seemed to light the drab walls in a shimmer of gold. Roxy always shined. Even hunched over, holding a rubber strap tight around her arm with her teeth, she shined.

Sasha inched toward the bed as Roxy pulled the drained needle from her arm. Roxy opened her mouth, a soft moan escaping. The rubber strap slipped from Roxy's lips, unraveled onto the mattress, and Sasha pushed that crap aside to crawl in bed with Roxy. She laid on the dusty pillow, gazing into Roxy's glassy eyes. If there were ever a time to convince Roxy to share the needle, it would be now.

"How'd you get the money for all this?" Roxy asked, gesturing to the hole-filled walls around them that barely blocked out a screaming child's wail.

"I took all the cash from Vinny's wallet."

"That's fucked up." Roxy slapped Sasha, light, playful, keeping her hand firmly planted on Sasha's chest.

Sasha glided her palm along Roxy's hand, clasped their fingers together. "You like Vinny."

"I like you."

"He'd treat you right, Vinny."

Roxy shook free from Sasha's grasp, sat up in bed. "You trying to push me off on your friend?"

"No, I—"

"Oh, I know. You're just trying to distract me so I don't notice you sneaking off with this." Roxy picked the needle off the mattress, waved it in Sasha's face. "You want this shit?" She gathered the blackened spoon and rubber strap, shoved them along with the needle into its leather pouch. "Take it."

Sasha stared at the little brown pouch which Roxy was practically thrusting in her face. It had to be a test. She'd know by the look in Roxy's eyes, except her gaze couldn't part from the pouch.

"Go on, take it."

Before Roxy could finish her sentence, Sasha snatched the leather pouch. Once it was safe in her grip, she looked at Roxy. The woman just sat there, holding a blank stare.

"Do your thing," Roxy said, crossing her arms.

The metal zipper dug into Sasha's thumb as she squeezed the pouch. "You think I won't 'cause you're watching?"

Roxy shrugged, and Sasha pulled open the zipper. She dumped the pouch onto the bed. Everything tumbled out in a neat little pile, except the bag of drugs.

Sasha threw the empty pouch at Roxy. "Where's the stuff?"

"What stuff?"

A deep breath, a tight jaw clenching. Sasha tried

everything to stop the uninvited rage within her chest from building. It was useless. Her fingers trembled, a red haze crept over her vision, and the throb of her temples pounded in her ears.

"Girl," Sasha yelled, her shout flinching Roxy's shoulders. "Now is not the time to fuck with me."

"Sasha—"

"Where's the shit?" A rush of fury surged inside Sasha, blazing hot enough to singe her skin. She had to let it out, before the fires within scorched her insides to dust.

Sasha gripped onto the edge of the nightstand. Her nails scraped wood as she flipped the table over. A lamp shattered on the dirty floor, and Roxy cried out. The sound of Roxy's whimper spiked Sasha's temper. To hear her girl scream in terror infuriated Sasha beyond the point of control. Before she could stop herself, she was on the bed straddling Roxy. Without permission, her arm raised and she rocked the back of her hand across Roxy's cheek.

"No, Sasha. Don't!"

Roxy's shriek, the tears, didn't register with Sasha. All she could see, think about was that bag of heroin. She could almost taste its sticky sweetness on her tongue.

"Where is it?" Sasha ripped open Roxy's jacket, catching sight of a plastic baggie's edge between Roxy's breasts. She yanked the bag from Roxy's bra and jumped off the bed.

The needle and spoon had fallen to the floor, and Sasha dropped beside them. Her hands went right to work, despite their violent quake.

"You said you wouldn't change," Roxy choked

out between sobs, curling into a ball on the bed.

Sasha wrapped the rubber strap around her arm, pulled it tight with her teeth. Virgin veins popped up on her arm, and she jammed the needle into the biggest one. Once a warmth flowed through her body, quelling the fiery chill that circulated beneath her flesh, she could finally breathe.

"You made me do that," Sasha slurred, blinking back a fuzzy haze. "You shouldn't fuck around with shit like that." She kept her stare low, away from the soft cries that erupted from the bed.

"No." Roxy wept. "You're gone."

Sasha tried to stand, but her legs were too heavy. Instead, she crawled toward the bed, pulled herself onto the mattress, and curled beside Roxy. "I'm sorry, doll." She draped her arm over Roxy's heaving shoulder, and its shudder intensified. "I'll never hit you again, I swear. You just...can't fuck around. All right, girl."

Roxy buried her face in Sasha's chest, held Sasha tight. "I won't do this again. I can't. I ruined you."

"You didn't ruin shit." Sasha kissed the top of Roxy's head. If it weren't for the tingles nipping at her flesh, and the slow drag of her vicious thoughts, she'd feel like shit. How she loved heroin for taking away her ability to feel. "Just...no more fucking around."

"I won't do this." Roxy kissed Sasha. Her soft lips trembled as they pressed against Sasha's mouth, but Sasha couldn't move. Her entire body was numb.

"Goodbye," Roxy whispered, her breath tingling

Sasha's skin.

Sasha pulled Roxy closer, held as tight as her weak arms would allow. "You're not going anywhere."

A dark fuzz had stolen the blur that was Roxy's face, and Sasha closed her eyes. Between the nods of dreamless sleep, she heard Roxy's voice echo, "See you on the other side."

Chapter Six

Sasha rolled onto her side. The mattress beneath her squealed, and her eyes shot open. "No more shitty motels," she muttered, sitting up. Roxy's arm slid off her back, thumped to the mattress. Not a sound flowed from the woman behind Sasha, nor did a rustle erupt from the scratchy sheets.

"Roxy?" Sasha looked over her shoulder, and the first thing she saw was a needle sticking out of a badly scabbed arm. "Roxy!"

Sasha grabbed onto Roxy's hand, gasping at the feel of ice-cold skin. "No." She pulled the needle from Roxy's arm, tossed it to the floor. Roxy's head rolled to the side, and empty eyes stared at Sasha.

"No." She fell atop Roxy's chest, hugging the stiff body tight.

Two fresh puncture wounds sat side by side on the still arm in front of Sasha, an empty baggie propped up just beyond. Roxy was a pro, knew exactly how much to boot and when. This overdose had been intentional. Roxy fucking killed herself.

"Why did you do this?" Sasha rose to her knees, latched onto Roxy's shirt, and shook. "Why?"

A rattle of air burst from Roxy's mouth, and Sasha yelped. She jumped off the bed, tripping over the phone. Her eyes were stuck on Roxy's blank stare, but her fingers dialed the operator.

"I need help," Sasha said the moment the line connected. "This is Sasha Lazzari." She fumbled with the crap strewn across the floor, from the nightstand she had toppled earlier, in search of something that would tell her where the fuck she was. Under a food wrapper, beside a broken alarm clock, she found the room key.

"The Roosevelt, room eighteen." She hung up the phone, even though a slew of frantic words rambled through its receiver.

Sasha climbed back onto the bed and pulled Roxy onto her lap. "I did this. I did this to you. I…" She kissed Roxy, breathed in the woman's sweet scent. "Please come back. I'm sorry I hit you. Just, please. Come back."

***

Darkness had swallowed the light outside the window, leaving Sasha in shadows. Women screamed, babies cried somewhere outside this motel room, but Sasha didn't move from the bed. She couldn't let go of Roxy. The woman's body had grown so stiff it cracked with every slight movement, so Sasha stopped moving.

It wasn't until a thin beam of bright light cut across the floor, blocking the city's glow from the window, that Sasha looked up from Roxy's pale skin. A cop walked into the room, making the faded wood beneath his heavy boots creak.

"My girl's not supposed to have such pale skin," Sasha said, caressing Roxy's icy cheek. "Her skin is the coolest brown, like the cliffs of the iron mountains."

The cop stepped beside the bed, placed his hand on Sasha's shoulder. "We have to get you out of here, Ms. Lazzari. Back to Fat Tonys, where you've been all night."

Sasha looked up at the man, his badge shimmering in the hallway's harsh light. "Nice try, asshole. But I've heard that one before."

"I know about what happened to you," the cop said, kneeling down to stare into Sasha's eyes. "About the traitors who turned you over to the Mancini family. Your friends in the blue circle took care of those two rats, permanently. You can trust us." He gestured to his partner in the doorway, a young man practically swimming in his ridiculous uniform.

"What about Roxy?" Sasha looked down at her girl. She was lying stiff like a gruesome mannequin in her arms.

"We'll take good care of her." The cop took Sasha by the hand, guided her off the bed. Her fingers glided through Roxy's thick curls before her girl fell to the mattress, sinking into shadows.

On her way to the door, the needle bumped the tip of Sasha's boot. "My shit." She dropped to her knees, pawed the dark floor for the small leather pouch.

"Is this what you're looking for?" asked the younger cop beside the door as he kicked the pouch with its rubber strap peeking out the top into the light.

Sasha grabbed the needle, then crawled toward the pouch. She shoved the syringe inside, a clink of metal ringing out when the glass tube hit the spoon.

"Thanks," she said, keeping her eyes low as she rose to her feet.

This time, before Sasha allowed two men to usher her toward a possible torturous fate, she looked her dead friend in the face. A gray film had covered Roxy's deep brown eyes. It was horrible, a mistake. She shouldn't have looked back. Now she'd remember, for the next beautiful person she killed, to never look back.

***

Leather crinkled as Sasha squirmed in the back of a police car. The steel cage in front of her, the backs of clean-cut heads on the other side, brought her right back to that night. Her stomach twisted, chest clenched. She had to get just one hit, then these men could slice the rest of her body to pieces.

"Take me to 127th and Malcolm X," she said, clutching the pouch tight.

"That's Harlem," the younger cop said from the passenger seat.

"Why don't I just take you to Fat Tonys first?" the driver said, shifting in his seat. "Then—"

"No." Sasha banged on the cage. "Just let me out here."

"It's cool." The cop behind the wheel hit the brakes, turned the car around. "I'll take you to 127th."

Tall, bright buildings gave way to dark lines of tightly packed rowhomes, and Sasha's foot tapped the metal floor. It felt like ants made of sharp metal had crawled beneath her skin. Every inch of her body burned, even though a chill clung to her bones. Why was this car ride so long? Why did the city have to be so fucking big?

"Here," Sasha said, the second they passed Roxy's favorite diner. "This is good. I can walk from here."

Brakes squealed as the cop steered the cruiser to the side of the road. "What should I tell Mr. Lazzari?"

"Don't tell him shit." Sasha pulled the handle, thanking God the door opened. "You never saw me." She climbed out of the car, shut the door, and knelt beside the passenger window. "Thanks, for not being treacherous douchebags."

***

Dez

Dez stared at the phone on the kitchen wall. Seven o'clock on a Friday night. Vinny would probably be at Fat Tonys, and Sasha...Dez took a step back to peek through the kitchen door, into the living room. Sasha should be in that room, cuddled up with Tyler on the sofa. Not his wife, though. His wife was most likely trolling dirty streets with some skank. He should've bashed Sasha upside the head and dragged that bitch home, caveman style. Instead, he took his kid and ran for the hills to hide with his tail between his legs.

Back to the phone Dez's gaze went, his fingers drumming his side. "Fuck it," he said, walking out of the kitchen. He shouldn't give a shit what Sasha was doing, what she was thinking, how she felt at this very moment. He wouldn't care. His heart, all his thoughts, belonged to Tyler. If he told himself that enough times, it would become true…eventually.

***

Sasha

The walk three blocks to the only buy house Sasha knew seemed to take an eternity, especially without Roxy at her side chattering about soap operas. It was sad. Sasha was more familiar with some fictional Ewing family than the woman she'd been fucking for the last month. That had to make her disgusting, or pathetic. Definitely self-centered. One thing it made her, for certain, was walk faster down the fucking sidewalk.

Her boot landed on the first step of Reid's apartment building, and a scrawny dude crept from the alley beside the stairs.

"What you want?" he asked, his hoodie cloaking his dark skin.

"I'm looking for Reid," Sasha said, groaning as her neck twitched without permission.

The guy eyed her over then stepped back into the alley. "Whatcha looking for?"

Sasha followed the man in the shadows. "Twenty." She patted her back pockets, finding only a crushed pack of smokes. "Fuck!" She'd put her money in Roxy's purse, for safe keeping. It was real fucking safe now, fucking safe and goddamn useless in an evidence bag.

Sasha pushed strands of tangled hair from her face, her fingers shaking. The burn in her stomach whirled faster, taking her into a hunch. "Look." She stared at the bag dangling between the dude's fingers, a tiny black ball glimmering in the streetlight. "I'm good for it."

Itchy, God she was so itchy. Something was crawling all over her, slithering beneath her skin. She scratched her arm, neck, head, but the prickles kept spreading. "Reid knows me," she damn near shouted, shrinking down from her own loud voice.

The guy scooped the bag into his palm, closed his fist tight, and Sasha took a deep breath. She had to get that bag. Every dumb motherfucker within a one-mile radius would be sorry if she didn't get that fucking bag.

"Okay," she said through gritted teeth, staring at the blank eyes in front of her. "I just watched my girl die, and I lost my fucking money. I can go get you twenty bucks, bring it right back, but I need a fucking hit first." Her finger trembled as she pointed it in the guy's stone-cold face. "Reid knows me. If he gets back before me, just tell him it was the crazy white bitch. He'll know who you're talking about."

"All right." The guy backed deeper into the alleyway, waved Sasha toward him. Sasha glanced over her shoulder, as if expecting a twenty-dollar bill to float past her face. It didn't. So she followed the shady man into the dark crevasse between two run-down brick buildings.

"I'll give you this bag, but you gotta do something for me," he said over the sound of a zipper.

Sasha looked down to see a big, veiny cock in the man's hand. A bit of vomit crept up the back of her throat, her muscles almost too stiff to move. "Fuck," she yelled, rocking in place. She really needed that bag.

"You know what to do, girl," he said, one hand stroking his wide dick and the other balled into a fist.

"Yeah. Okay." Sasha dropped to her knees on the dirty, cracked concrete. Icy water soaked through her jeans, but she could barely feel it. She was desperate. Her hand slid down her leg, into her boot. All she could think about was that tiny ball of tar, locked inside that disgusting man's fist. The metal handle of a switchblade grazed her fingertips, just as the man's giant cock neared her lips. She pulled the knife from her boot. Its double-edged blade flipped out with the press of a button, and she jumped to her feet.

Yeah, she was desperate for that hit. Not enough to suck strange dick, though. But she definitely wasn't above gutting this motherfucker to get what she wanted.

The man stumbled to the side. His back hit the

damp wall as he fumbled with his pants, and Sasha jabbed her blade into his side six times. Kidney shots, quick with slight twists. It was an effective method, one she learned about while eavesdropping during her short stay in a prison infirmary. The guy gagged on the spurts of blood erupting from his mouth, swayed on his feet, but the hand holding the heroin remained clenched.

"Why won't you die?" Sasha plunged her blade into the side of the guy's neck, bringing him to the ground. Finally, his hand broke free, and Sasha snatched the baggie from it. She should run across the street, to an alley without a man she murdered in it, but her shaky legs wouldn't budge.

"Real quick," she said, kneeling beside the puddle of blood that oozed from the body right next to her. "Just one little hit, then I'll roll."

Although her hands quaked beyond control, Sasha held the spoon steady. A little bit of non-bloody water from the alley, a pinch of black tar in a spoon, and a lighter flick later, the frost that threatened to solidify her body melted. Black smoke wafted up as the tar cooked. Its thick syrupy scent stuck in Sasha's nose and she retched, dry-heaving whatever bile was in her stomach onto the ground.

"Fucking fuck," she muttered, wrapping the rubber strap around her arm. She'd never felt so bad, so raw. Not even when her metal cot tore her skin did it hurt this bad. Her vision blurred as she brought the needle to the spoon. Its tip clanked metal, and the haze of an amber pool in the spoon disappeared. The tube of the syringe was now so heavy and warm in her hand. It forced her heart to pound the wall of her chest.

The syringe looked a little full, felt too heavy, but there was no time. A blue vein shined in the dim light of the alleyway, and Sasha slid the needle into it. Somehow, she missed the mark—the giant, bulging, almost glowing blue mark. "Stupid idiot," she said, her teeth clamped down on the rubber strap. After two more pricks, the tug of a needle's sharp tip snagged her vein and she pressed the plunger.

A warm rush stole Sasha's breath. She slumped against the wall, closed her eyes in attempts to slow the world's sudden spin. The waves of heated tingles didn't stop flowing, and the weight dragging her down only got heavier.

"Too much," she said, hurrying to gather the tools of her survival. She managed to shove everything back in its pouch and tuck it into her waistband before the last of her strength fled her body. She dropped face down on the trash-covered ground. A giggle slipped past her lips, pushed out by a surge of white-hot ecstasy. She'd found it. Her eyes drifted to a close, shut away the tiny red dots that swirled in the darkness. She'd finally found that high, just like the first one Roxy showed her.

Chapter Seven

Soft hands held Sasha tight, caressed her cheek, tangled into her hair. She couldn't see any faces, hear any voices. It didn't matter whose hands they were; the feeling was what mattered. Those smooth palms gliding along her body brought warmth, love. As long as they touched her, she would be safe. A burn shot through Sasha's shoulder. She cried out from the sharp barbs of pain, and the hands that comforted her drifted away. *Don't forget your skin,* a silky voice echoed inside Sasha's head.

"Wake up, you dumb bitch." A hard slap rocked Sasha's head to the side, and the muffled sounds of laughter filtered in.

The ache of stiff shoulders, the burn of wrists, the sting of icy metal ignited a firestorm of rage inside Sasha's chest. A growl scraped past her lips, but she didn't try to move. She had been tied to a chair. It was a shitty feeling, yet one she'd become quite familiar with over the years.

"Motherfucker," she slurred, battling to open her

eyes.

"You would," a deep voice said right above Sasha. "Fuck my mother. I heard about you."

Sasha sat back against the metal chair she was tied to. Her vision cleared to a wide-open room. She was in a basement, one that had a pool table, couches, and arcade games. It looked like the rec room at the community center. Except this room didn't have children scattered around it. This room had a large group of black men, and they all stood around her to cast icy leers. The man that centered the pack held the hardest glare. It clashed with his little red hat, sitting sideways atop a neat afro, but matched perfectly with the decal of a bloodthirsty dragon on his shirt.

"What's up?" Sasha asked, knowing full-well what the fuck was up. There was blood crusted on her fingertips, the blood of a Black Guerrilla Family member whom she'd murdered for a measly twenty-spot of heroin.

"What's up, she says," the guy in the middle of the pack said through a chuckle. His smile faded quick, and the fiery death-stare returned. "You done fucked yourself, right up your lily-white ass. That's what's up."

Sasha didn't know the man in front of her, never seen his face before, but every shady fucker on the streets knew the logo of the BGF. At least, every shady fucker who visited Harlem.

"Tyrone, right?" she said, staring the tall man in front of her right in his dark eyes.

"I see my reputation precedes me," he said with a little grin. "As does yours, Sasha Lazzari."

"Well then, I guess you know I shouldn't be tied to this chair."

Tyrone knelt down, gaining eye level with Sasha. "Not even a crime boss can get away with slicing up another crew's lieutenant." His hard glare moved from Sasha's face to the fresh needle mark on her arm.

A roiling burn fired up in Sasha's stomach, her foot tapping without consent. This situation was fucked. She'd be able to deal, know exactly what to say, if her head wasn't all twisted. One hit. All she needed was one little hit, half a boot, and the fuzz would clear from her throbbing mind.

"We can work this out," Sasha said, jittering in her seat. The ropes around her wrists pinched her skin, but she couldn't stop squirming. Angry eyes glowered on all sides of her, pierced her nerve, and large hands gripped the handles of Uzis. She was going to fucking die, and the only thing that bothered her about the fact was she couldn't do it wasted.

"I got shit," Sasha said, wriggling as red-hot pinpricks traveled throughout her body. "You want money, guns?"

"You ain't got no shit," Tyrone said, rising to his feet. "Or you wouldn't have been sucking dick in an alley for a hit."

"Fucker." Sasha lunged forward, but the ropes around her wrist kept her bound to the chair. "I didn't suck no dick."

A wicked grin spread across Tyrone's face, and he pulled Roxy's leather pouch from his pocket. "So you don't care about this then, huh?"

"Give it!" A red haze blinded Sasha's vision as she thrashed from side to side. She'd break her fucking arms, rip her hands to shreds to get that pouch. It was all she had left. "I'll tear your fucking throat out."

Laughter echoed around the room, and Tyrone unzipped the pouch. "Look," he said, holding up the needle. "I already reloaded for you."

The brown liquid filling the syringe's tube stopped Sasha's struggle. Her wide-eyes reflected in the needle's shiny metal. Even though the image was slightly distorted, she could see the desperation in her stare. It sickened her, but she couldn't force it away. She couldn't resist the call of that needle's sharp tip.

"You want this?" Tyrone asked, waving the needle in front of Sasha's face. She didn't answer, couldn't with the giant lump rising in her throat.

"I'll untie you," he said, gliding his hand down Sasha's back. "Give you a little taste. Then, maybe we can have a conversation."

"Yeah," Sasha muttered, her gaze stuck on the shimmering tip of the needle.

A man stepped behind Sasha, tugged at the ropes that squeezed her wrists as Tyrone backed away.

"You gonna be a good girl?" Tyrone asked. He pressed the plunger, squirted a healthy dose onto the floor, and Sasha gasped.

"Yes," she practically screamed. She tried to keep still while untied, told her body not to rush Tyrone once freed, but it was useless. The second her sore arms flopped to her sides, she jumped to her feet. Everything spun, faces melded, yet her hand knew exactly where to reach.

Tyrone pulled a gun from his waistband, cocked the hammer, and pointed the barrel in Sasha's face. "Sit the fuck down."

More bullets loaded into chambers. Each click flinched Sasha's already quaking shoulders. She could snatch the gun clunking against her forehead, take out three maybe four of these assholes, but she still wouldn't get that hit. Her legs carried her back to the chair all by themselves, and she dropped onto the hard metal seat.

Tyrone handed his gun to the man beside him and walked in front of Sasha. He stood over her, needle in hand, staring down. "White women are the worst kind of junkies. Y'all are so fucking entitled, you just think everything belongs to you." His smile lingered, but his glare grew fierce. "Ready to behave?"

"Just gimme the needle."

"No." Tyrone unlatched his belt, pulled it from its loops in one swift move. "I'm hooking you up." He bit down on the syringe's glass tube, held it between his teeth, and grabbed Sasha's arm. The thick belt hugged her skin, until Tyrone yanked the strap tight. Then it burned, throbbed, lifted her scorching veins.

A callous grin played on Tyrone's lips as he brought the needle to Sasha's arm, slid its tip into her skin. A drop of her blood swirled inside the tube, then shot back into her veins as Tyrone pressed the plunger. He pulled back too soon. The tube was still half full, and she could barely feel the warmth her body was craving.

Tyrone unraveled his belt from Sasha's arm, and she shook her head. "That's not enough," she said in a rush. "Finish the tube."

"You'll get more when I say." Tyrone pulled a chair in front of Sasha and took a seat. "How long you been doing this shit?"

"I don't know," Sasha said through a snicker. "What month is this?"

Tyrone took Sasha by the hand, looked at the few puncture marks hidden around her scarred flesh. "You only have a few tracks. You been tappin' your toes?"

Sasha lowered her gaze. She shouldn't be ashamed. This was her choice. *She* wanted that drug. It didn't control her.

"Yeah, you have," Tyrone said, his large hand rubbing his smooth chin. He leaned forward and looped the belt back around Sasha's arm. "Does the Don know about your little habit?" He pulled the strap tight, and a shiver ran through Sasha's body. "Tell the truth, and I'll empty this needle into your arm."

The twitch in Sasha's neck went into double-time. It was so close. That glimmering needle was so close to her pulsating vein. "No. Nobody knows." The needle's sharp tip glided into Sasha's arm, and this time a rush flooded her body. She slumped in her chair, which now felt like a fluffy cloud instead of a cold metal slab.

"What are you gonna do with me?" she slurred.

Tyrone refastened his belt, nodded to the man beside him.

"Let's bounce," the guy said, waving his arm.

The wide-open basement cleared out, only Sasha and Tyrone remaining.

He reached for Sasha and she leaned away, wobbling on the edge of her seat.

"Relax," he said, taking a frim hold on Sasha's shoulder. "If I wanted you dead, you'd be in Hell right now."

Sasha tried to shrug away from Tyrone's grasp, but her muscles weren't cooperating. His strong arm circled her waist. Before she could tell him to fuck off, he lifted her to her feet. The fog in her brain made her head so heavy, too heavy to hold, so she rested it against the hard chest beside her.

"For the entire four hours you slept in that chair, I made some calls," Tyrone said, ushering Sasha to the small couch in the far corner of the basement. "A lot of people would like to get their hands on you, and they're all tossing out big numbers." He set Sasha down on the soft couch, his gaze locked on her as he stepped back. "I put you on auction. That was the last big hit you're gonna get. I need you presentable when the buyer comes in."

The bit of information about her ass being sold like chattel should've boiled Sasha's blood. Except she was used to people using her in stupid games. It was the fact she'd be denied her right to get high that set off a raging fury inside her chest.

"Now listen here, motherfucker—"

"Don't worry, girl." Tyrone walked to the wide steel door of the windowless basement, banging twice. "I'll take care of you like the mafia princess you're supposed to be."

Metal hinges squealed as the door swung open.

A woman walked into the room, ran her hand down Tyrone's chest. Her tiny white bra and strip of fabric meant to be underwear gleamed against her sexy dark skin. Her long braids tapped the sides of her arms as she turned to smile at Sasha.

"Keisha here will take good care of you." Tyrone slapped the woman on her firm ass and she yelped, then giggled while trotting toward Sasha. "She's got just enough smack for a quarter-dose, and more than enough titties to keep you busy for the next hour."

"Wait," Sasha called out, but Tyrone didn't look back. The man strolled through the only exit in the concrete room, slammed the door shut behind him.

"What, don't like dark meat?" Keisha asked, propping her hand on her curvy, nearly bare hip. "Didn't think so. You look like a corn-fed farm girl."

Sasha rose from the couch, teetering. The tease of a high she'd been given was starting to wear off. And the woman, no matter how sexy, was bringing her down even quicker with that 'tude. "I've fucked plenty of black women."

"Then what?" A cute little pout struck Keisha's lips as she turned from Sasha. She crossed her arms, which pushed her luscious breasts even higher. "You think I'm ugly or something?"

"Oh, my God." Sasha stood tall in front of the obviously dense woman. "Bitch, I've been abducted. That was right after I woke up to find my girl dead with a needle in her arm." She lifted her finger, wagged it in Keisha's face. "And now, I'm gonna be sold on the Black Market. So, excuse the fuck out of me for being rude."

Keisha shifted in place, hugged herself tighter. "Don't you mean the Black Guerrilla Market?"

A snicker flowed from Keisha's full lips, and the slightest smile cracked Sasha's glower. It was hard not to stare at the long stretch of smooth bare skin, even harder for Sasha not to touch it. She plopped back onto the couch. Her hands couldn't be trusted right now. Hell, her entire decision making process should be brought into question. Shit was going to change if she got out of this unscathed. For starters, she would be taking over the heroin trade in this city and its boroughs. Every shitheel gang slinging smack could squirm under her big ole mafia boot from now on.

"I hope you have more than a quarter-shot on you," Sasha said, glancing at Keisha.

"Sorry." Keisha sat beside Sasha, leaned back against the couch cushions. "Daddy only gave me a tiny ball."

"Tyrone's your father?"

"No," Keisha said, with a bit of a huff. "He's my daddy."

"Right." Sasha held out her hand while scanning the room for Roxy's pouch. "Gimme the ball."

"It's on my body somewhere. You have to find it."

Sasha turned to stare at Keisha. The woman wore the cutest smirk, its wicked sparkle lighting her deep brown eyes. That shine drew Sasha in, let her forget about the light quiver of her fingertips, almost quelled the burn in her stomach. She slouched beside Keisha, sinking into the cushions.

"Just give it to me."

"Come get it. It's not deep." Keisha nodded. She glided her hand down her own stomach, pointed between her legs. "But you can't use your fingers."

The woman was cute as shit, with her button nose and naughty grins. It was a small price to pay in Sasha's eyes. She'd ravage a young, curvy, sex-kitten for much less than a quarter-shot. It was far better than sucking dick.

Sasha dropped to her knees, slid between Keisha's legs. "You ever been fucked stupid by a white woman?" She clutched onto Keisha's hips. A strong yank pulled a gasp from the woman's mouth and brought the silky skin of an inner thigh closer to Sasha's tongue.

"Yeah. I didn't think so," she said, hooking her finger around Keisha's thong and pushing it aside.

***

Vinny

When Vinny opened the door to Fat Tonys, his stomach dropped. The usual flocks of overdressed people didn't swarm the lobby. Voices weren't spilling over from the dining area, and cackles didn't cringe his spine. At midnight on a Friday, that meant trouble. Big fucking trouble.

The hostess podium stood bare, and the two new guys stationed in the corners of the lobby looked clueless, so Vinny headed for the bar. A waitress didn't hurry forward to grope his chest. That was unheard of. Big titty waitresses always served drinks, even in the midst of mob wars.

Vinny rushed past the bar, shivered at the sight of a dark dining area, and dashed up the small steps. Wiseguys didn't fill the table. Just Otis, Kev, and Enzo sat in the dimly lit restaurant, which unsettled Vinny more than if the entire crew had been assembled.

"What happened?" Vinny asked, taking his seat beside Otis.

"I got a call," Enzo said, drawing Vinny's attention across the table. "The Black Guerrilla Family has Sasha."

"What?" Vinny rubbed his head as a stabbing pain infiltrated his temples.

Enzo glanced at Otis, then leaned on the table. "They want a seat at our table in exchange for her."

"They came in our territory, took one of our guys, and expect to live past the night," Vinny said, unable to stop an evil chuckle from slipping out his mouth. "You should call the boys. We'll go into Harlem packing."

"He's right," Enzo said, and Kev squirmed in his chair. "Those fuckers run Harlem because we let them. Now they want more. Fuck that."

Kev huffed, groaned, tapped his foot, but Vinny didn't take his stare off Otis.

"Well," Vinny said, slanting closer to Otis. "You gonna let this shit stand?"

Otis sat back in his chair, narrowed his glare on Vinny. "There's no way she'd be hanging in Harlem, right?"

"No fucking way," Vinny said.

"All right." Otis rose from his chair. A vicious

gaze filled the man's eyes as he looked around the table. "Let's go kill those motherfuckers."

"Wait," Kev yelled, running his fingers through his messy hair. "I did some shit."

Vinny turned to face Kev, resisting the urge to hurl his fist at the first glimpse of Kev's dumb-ass stare. "What the fuck did you do?"

"A few days ago, Sasha wanted me to bring her five-grand. To Harlem," Kev said into his lap. "And earlier, some cops stopped by. Sasha's girly friend Od'd, and Sasha made the pigs take her to Harlem."

"What the…" Vinny slammed his fist against the table, rattling the glasses scattered atop its glossy surface. It was either that, or pound Kev's stupid face. "Why'd you hide this shit from us, asshole?"

"Sasha wanted me to." Kev rocked in his chair, his jaw clenching. "She had that look, like my cousin Jackie."

"Your cousin Jackie is a heroin addict," Vinny shouted, and Kev shrank down. "Fuck!" Vinny could slug Kev, except he wanted to hit himself. He saw the emptiness in Sasha's stare, the jitter of her bones, but he ignored it. He wanted to be close to her, so he ignored her subtle cry for help. Jesus Christ, she'd screamed for help. Sasha and her broken friend were screaming to be saved, and all he did was fuck them.

"I can fix this," Vinny said, looking at Otis.

"No." Otis returned to his seat. His eyes glossed over, but only for a moment before a hard stare gripped his face. "I'm not starting a war, risking this entire organization because Sasha can't hold her own shit."

"Fuck that," Vinny said, straining to keep his voice steady. "Sasha handed you this operation. You fucking owe her."

Otis jumped up, sent his chair toppling to the floor. "I'll take the meeting. But if she's all strung-out, bitch can go to the next bidder in this bullshit auction. I won't have a weak junkie in my family, any part of my family."

The floor rumbled as Otis stomped away. Vinny hopped up from his chair, but Enzo grabbed his arm before he could chase after Otis.

"That won't solve your problem," Enzo whispered, guiding Vinny back to the table. "Sit down, kid. Let's discuss options."

Chapter Eight

Sasha

Women were women. No matter the shade of skin or shape of body, with only two fingers, Sasha could make them shudder. Keisha was no different. The woman squirmed, moaned, gasped for breath beneath Sasha, and all the while Sasha's stare strayed to the small bag of dope beside them.

Sasha ran her tongue up a heaving chest. One hand gripped onto a soft breast, fingers pinching a hard nipple, while the other worked the sweet spot between Keisha's legs. A loud cry of ecstasy filled Sasha's ears, and she glanced at that tiny ball of tar. Five minutes. It would only take her five minutes, tops, to set-up a fix. Then, she could get back to finding out how many times this freaky woman could cum in an hour's time.

"Just go," Keisha said when Sasha moved in for a kiss.

"This'll only take a second." Sasha grabbed the

baggie and jumped to her feet. She snatched Roxy's pouch off the pool table and sat at the foot of the couch to fix up a shot.

"You sure you don't have any more?" Sasha asked, filling her spoon with the water from some random cup nearby.

"Why can't you spoiled bitches ever be happy with what you got?" Keisha asked with more curiosity than spite. It annoyed the shit out of Sasha. The bitch next to her just wasn't getting it. Sasha had been spoiled all right, by death, blood, and disappointment. Drugs were her only solace, only chance to feel something other than coldness.

"You don't understand. I need—"

Sasha choked on her words when spotting the amusement spread across Keisha's face.

"You need more?" Keisha smirked, tossing her long braids over her shoulder. "You're so caught-up on finding the next hit, you can't see what's right in front of you."

Despite the tremble of her hands, Sasha slid the needle into her vein with ease. She pressed the plunger, but only the slightest warmth rushed through her system. It was but a flicker compared to the blaze she had come to love, which made her instantly crave more. She packed Roxy's kit, carefully, then shoved the pouch into her waistband.

"A few hours ago, my cold stiff girlfriend was right in front of me." Sasha picked the longest cigarette butt out of an overflowing ashtray, leaned back against the couch cushions, and lit it up. "Before that, the walls of a tiny torture cell were in front of me."

"What about in between that shit?" Keisha sat up straight, turned to face Sasha. "When you had a table full of strong white men ready to kill for you? Or when you were sitting in a restaurant of rich motherfuckers just throwing money in your face to be in the same room as you? Could you see any of that?"

Sasha glared at Keisha. The scrape of broken glass beneath her skin wouldn't allow her to move, so she didn't backhand the woman. "You don't know a goddamn thing about my life."

"Please." Keisha waved Sasha off. "We all got a sob story. My mama sold me to Tyrone when I was nine for a fifty-spot. You don't see me fiendin' for a hit, do you?"

There was nothing Sasha could say. She'd been given opportunity after opportunity, only to puff them away on clouds of smoke. Keisha had all her opportunities taken from her, maybe at birth. That woman had been abandoned by society, family, justice. Keisha had a real reason to hate, yet she was strong enough to love her own self. Sasha was actually jealous, the same twisted way Keisha must be jealous of her.

The solid metal door creaked open, and a group of all-muscles and no-smiles black men walked into the basement. Sasha wobbled off the couch as Tyrone pushed through the crowd that had begun to surround her.

"It's time," Tyrone said, picking Sasha's flannel off the floor. "Put this on." He tossed the shirt at her chest, then glanced over his shoulder. "The coffee."

A paper cup was thrust into Sasha's hand, a drop

of hot coffee splashing over the brim that stung her skin.

"Drink it," Tyrone said with a bit of a growl. "Keep your marks covered, and try not to act like a crack whore." His glare narrowed, scouring Sasha from head to toe. "I know that's gonna be hard for you to do."

***

Sasha allowed Tyrone to push her up a narrow set of stairs, tolerated the gun he kept jabbing between her shoulder blades, but the quarter-shot business still pissed her the fuck off. It felt like tiny bugs were wriggling beneath her scalp, and it was Tyrone's fault. She scratched her head, neck, arms. It didn't help. The drag of her nails only spread the invisible feelers that wormed under her flesh.

"Who'd you sell me to?" Sasha asked in a bark. If there was a God, it would be Otis who bought her stupid ass. Then, or rather fifteen minutes from this hellish second, Sasha could tear the penthouse apart to find that bag she'd hid somewhere.

"If you say one more word, I'll put a bullet in your junkie brain," Tyrone said, moving the gun's barrel to the back of Sasha's head.

In no attempt to be gentle, Tyrone grabbed Sasha by the arm and pushed her through a doorway at the end of the hall. Her heart leapt into her throat at the sight of Vinny standing in a corner. Then she caught Otis's stare, laced in disgust and aimed at her.

"Deal's off," Otis said, hopping up from the small table that centered the room.

"What?" Tyrone gripped Sasha's arm tighter, pushed her in front of him. "This ain't her?"

Otis cringed, as if a foul odor had just infiltrated his nostrils. "That's the shell of her. I ain't giving you a seat at my table for a half-dead junkie."

"Otis," Sasha called out, but he turned his back. Not even Vinny would look at her, which drove the sharpest of spikes straight into her chest. "These fuckers are gonna kill me."

That stopped Otis in the doorway. He looked over his shoulder, glared at Sasha. His upper lip raised into a snarl, jaw clenching. "You're lucky I don't come over there and put a bullet in your head myself, girl. There's nothing worse than a weak soul."

A roiling blaze scorched the air from Sasha's lungs. She couldn't breathe, speak. Otis, Vinny, and Enzo walked away, out of her life forever, and she couldn't say shit to defend herself. They were right to leave her. She deserved a bullet to the head and was ready to take it.

Tyrone shoved Sasha into the hands of the man next to him. He stomped across the smoky room and slammed the front door shut, closing off the hint of city lights. "Tie her up. She's going to the next bidder."

***

It had to have been an hour, at least. Sasha couldn't see the clock. Hell, this run-down, trash-strewn, graffiti-covered loft probably didn't have a clock. Her hands were tied tight behind her back, but not to the chair she was sitting in. She could easily glance around. Except she didn't need some stupid gadget to tell her what she already knew. It was time.

"I need another shot," she said, unable to control the loud rumble of her voice.

Tyrone rolled a pile of green buds into a blunt wrapper, lit it up, and blew a big puff of smoke in Sasha's face. "Too fucking bad."

"This isn't gonna work." Sasha rocked in her chair, but it didn't slow the whirl in her stomach. "I can't stop shaking."

"These guys don't care about that." Tyrone peeked out the window, grinning. "They just wanna slice you up. I don't think they'll mind if heroin comes out instead of blood."

A loud knock shook the front door, and every one of Sasha's quaking muscles locked stiff. Now that the moment was here, she didn't want to die. Tyler's sad eyes filled her head, clouded her vision of the spray-painted dragon on the wall in front of her. She could've walked willingly to her death, if Tyrone would've just given her a fucking shot.

"Put the hood on her," Tyrone said, looking through the peephole of the front door.

"So much for treating me like a mafia princess," Sasha muttered as a black hood dropped over her head, tossing her into darkness.

"You ain't no mafia princess anymore," Tyrone said, his harsh voice muffled by the hood's thick cloth. "Just another used up meal ticket."

A door's hinges squealed, footsteps rattled the floor, and Sasha curled her bound hands into fists.

There had to be something she could do, a way to save her sorry ass, but all her brain could spit out was a demand to get high.

"This better be her," a man said with a heavy Spanish accent.

"It's her," Tyrone said, and strong hands lifted Sasha from the chair. Her feet barely touched the ground. The tips of her boots dragged as she was carried at a quick pace. Crisp night air cut through her clothes, but she couldn't smell the city's bitter scent beyond her hood.

"*Vámanos*. Get her in the van."

Sasha was tossed against hard metal. The grind of a van's door filled the air before a light sway rocked her body. She rolled to her knees, and the hood was yanked off her head. Her hazy vision cleared, and she glimpsed a warm smirk in the flash of passing streetlights. It was a grin she knew, loved, had been praying to see. It was Vinny's grin.

"Holy shit, dude," she said through a chuckle, falling against his chest. The ropes were cut from her wrists, and she wrapped her arms around Vinny. "I knew you'd come through." He didn't hug back. Not one word flowed from Vinny's mouth, and she pulled away.

The man sitting beside Vinny clutched his Uzi tighter. In the faint light of the cargo van's rear, the ink on the man's brown skin gleamed. "The money," he said, keeping his gun aimed at Sasha. Vinny handed over a briefcase, and the guy set his gun down and opened its lid.

"*¿Nuestra familia?*" Sasha said, eyeing the tattoo of a machete laying across a sombrero on the man's neck.

A low growl rumbled from the man's mouth, and he turned to face the front of the van.

"What's going on?" Sasha asked, scooting along the van's floor to get closer to Vinny.

"Otis wouldn't let me bid on you," Vinny said, his eyes low. "So I had to go through a third-party."

The short tone in Vinny's voice and clenched fists should've warded Sasha away. Vinny was pissed. A whole mess of crazy bullshit must have been whispered in his ear, but she could set him straight. Then maybe, just maybe, she could get a motherfucking hit. "Listen. I don't know what stupid shit you've heard—"

Vinny grabbed Sasha by the wrist, pushed her sleeve up. She tried to pull back, and his tight grip turned crushing. "You got track marks on your arm."

"They did that to me." Sasha yanked her hand away, pulled her shirt sleeve down. "I don't fuck around with that shit. You know me." The shakes had come on so strong she could barely contain them. It wasn't the lies, or Vinny's disgusted glare, that rattled her bones. It was the pouch shoved inside her waistband. The smooth leather pressed against her skin dug into her spine. She could even feel the outline of the needle and spoon through the thick fabric.

Brakes squealed as the van rocked to a stop. Sasha looked out the windshield, grinning at the sparkle of her high-rise building. Somewhere inside her penthouse, which dominated the entire west wing of the top floor, sat a bag of dope. She was sure of it.

Sasha reached for the van's sliding door, and Vinny gripped onto her arm. "Before this starts, I want you to know something." He stared into her eyes with only affection behind his gaze. "I'm doing this because I love you."

Vinny pulled Sasha close, then jabbed a needle into the side of her neck. She hurled her fist, but it missed its mark. A dark haze had taken her down, surrounded her in an endless abyss of black.

***

Vinny

Kev rambled, but the words didn't penetrate the fog that clouded Vinny's mind. He leaned against the doorway of Sasha's bedroom, staring inside. The room had been emptied. Even the toothbrushes in the private bathroom were gone. All cleared out, except for the king-sized bed with Sasha's tranquilized body on it and the mafia doctor who hovered over her. Sasha looked normal while crashed out atop satin blankets. As long as her bloodshot eyes stayed closed, and the twitch of her limbs remained sedated, he could pretend everything was all right.

"You got that, man?" Kev asked. He patted Vinny on the arm, breaking his daydream of a warm beach and a naked, non-strung out Sasha. "That's the most important thing."

Vinny steered his gaze to Kev. He'd never seen such a serious expression on that guy's face before.

Whatever shit Kev just ranted on about must've been pretty fucking major.

"You weren't listening, were you?" Kev asked, his brow crinkling.

"Fuck, man. I'm sorry." Vinny glanced back into the bedroom just as the doctor drew a vial of blood from Sasha's limp arm. "Just tell me that last thing, the important one."

A huff flew from Kev's mouth, and his gaze rolled to the ceiling. "All that shit was important. You seen how my cousin turned out."

"Sasha ain't gonna be giving five-dollar hand jobs in the back of a bar," Vinny damn near yelled in Kev's face before turning toward the bedroom.

Kev latched onto Vinny's arm, held tight. "Just...try to remember, the shit she says, how she acts. It's not her. It's the drugs."

"Yeah." There wasn't a doubt in Vinny's mind he could handle this detox shit, until he stepped inside the empty bedroom. The doctor snapped his black bag shut, walked toward Vinny, and Vinny almost hightailed it out the penthouse.

"She's starting to come around," the doc said. His head shook, gaze falling to the floor. "I'm sorry to see her end up this way. I helped get Sasha back on her feet after the coma. She has the strongest will I've ever seen. If anybody can kick the needle, she can. Just not alone. Nobody can do it alone."

The doc patted Vinny on the arm as he headed for the door.

"Wait," Vinny called out, following the doctor to the bedroom door. "She's all good, right? Her health and shit?"

"My biggest concern is the possible exposure to certain diseases due to intravenous drug use. AIDS has ravaged the drug community. I'll phone you here, at the penthouse, when the blood results come in."

The doctor shook his head and headed down the stairs. Kev blocked the doorway, flashed a pitiful attempt at a confident smile, and then shut the door. Vinny stared at the solid wooden slab, which now had no handle. To be locked in a room with only Sasha and a bed had been a fantasy of his for a long time. Now it was a nightmare.

"Vinny," Sasha slurred, the sheets of the bed rustling. "What the fuck? Did you drug me?"

Vinny forced his sorrow into a hard stare and turned it toward Sasha. "I thought you liked needles."

Sasha rolled off the bed, swaying on her bare, scabbed feet. Her stare shot straight to the spot where the nightstand had been before Kev and Enzo emptied the room out.

"Where is everything?" She opened the closet door, stopped short. Not even one hanger hung on the ghostly rail, every shelf picked clean.

"I had shit in here," she shouted, rushing to the bedroom door. Her palm slid along the metal plate that used to hold a door handle, her fingertips squealing on its glossy surface. "What is this shit?"

"We're gonna hang out for a few days, seven to ten," Vinny said, crossing his arms.

"No, we're not." Sasha banged on the door, shouted at the wood to open up.

"There's nobody out there," Vinny yelled over

Sasha's loud mouth. "Kev won't be back 'til tomorrow." She stopped pounding on the door, but her fists remained clenched as she turned to face Vinny.

"You can't do this to me." She charged Vinny, but he stood tall even when her fists struck his chest. "You know what happened to me. You can't lock me up."

"Sasha!" Vinny clutched onto the sides of her arms, holding tight. "You're not in a dark cell. You're with me, in a safe place. I'm gonna ride this out with you, until the last of that dirty shit leaves your veins."

Sasha shoved Vinny, but ended up staggering herself. "I fucking hate you. You know that, right? I only started hanging out with you because I pitied you. The scrawny punk, alone beneath the monkey bars." She sneered, held a glare of pure hatred. "I should've minded my own business, left you to wallow with your stupid books."

It was probably true. Deep down, Vinny had always suspected it was pity that bound Sasha to him. He never could be man enough to exist in her eyes, not like his brother. It didn't change the fact that he loved her, that he'd sacrifice everything for her.

"You're not getting out of this room."

A roar burst from Sasha's mouth. She glanced around the room, her shaky fingers out at her sides like claws, then stormed into the bathroom.

"You're not gonna find anything in there to throw at me either." Vinny watched Sasha pace around the bathroom, her feet slapping tile. "I cleaned all that—"

Sasha drove her fist into the mirror. Glass shards rained to the floor, and blood squirted from her knuckles. Vinny ran forward as Sasha scooped a large, jagged piece of glass from the floor.

"Let me out, Vinny," she yelled, pointing the shard of glass at his face. Blood ran down her arm, dripped from her palm, yet she squeezed the glass harder. "I'll carve you the fuck up." Her hand trembled, her entire body trembled, but her voice flowed strong.

Vinny stepped closer to Sasha, until the tip of the glass pressed against his neck. "You won't be sticking needles in your arm. Not while I'm alive." He inched even closer. The glass pierced his skin, sent a burn through his body that settled into his pounding heart. "If the drugs are what you really want, you better get to carving."

Sasha's bottom lip quivered, and her eyes filled with tears. She lowered her hand. The piece of glass shattered on the floor, and she fell against his chest.

Chapter Nine

For the first two hours of Vinny's makeshift detox, Sasha flipped out like a rabid dog on cocaine. She tossed hate-filled slurs the way one would throw candy at a parade, mocked the size of his dick, even hurled her tiny fists at his face.

The next two hours were spent watching her writher on the bathroom floor. She clawed at the tile, cried out in pain between dry heaving. Vinny would be in there, holding her quaking body, but she shoved him away every time he tried to touch her. Apparently, his hands felt like acid on her skin. This entire scenario was not playing out as he'd imagined. They were supposed to spend the week in bed, curled in each other's arms, talking about the past and making plans for the future. He was a fucking idiot. Only in his ridiculous fantasy-land could a heroin detox equal a movie-of-the-week romance.

"Vinny," Sasha called out from inside the ball of tremors she had become at the base of the toilet.

He rushed into the bathroom, dropped to the floor at her side. "I'm right here, babe." His hands shook, wanting to reach for her, but his jaw also hurt from the punch he received the last time he tried.

Sasha grabbed onto Vinny's shirt, fast enough to knock a gasp from his chest. "Please," she said, her voice quavering. "Help me."

"I can get you whatever you need," he said, bushing clumps of sweaty, tangled hair from Sasha's frantic eyes.

A small smile lifted Sasha's pale cheeks, and the tremble of her body turned to a full-on quake. "I just need one shot."

Vinny tried to pull away from Sasha, but she clung to him.

"You don't need that shit."

"Please." She let go of Vinny's shirt and slid her hand between his legs. "You help me feel better, and I'll make you feel really good."

"Fuck." Vinny shoved Sasha back. She toppled to her side, her hip smacking against the hard tile floor. "That's what you want to be?" He rose to his feet, stomped to the bed, and pulled a file from beneath the mattress. "Remember Roxy?"

Sasha turned away as Vinny dropped the file on the floor beside her. She kept her gaze on the wall, her shaky hand out to block the folder.

"Look at it!" Vinny grabbed Sasha by the back of the neck, forced her face right in front of the file. He opened the folder's brown cover to a picture of Roxy's first mugshot, and Sasha cried out.

"Possession," he said, flipping to the next

picture. "Prostitution." He kept flipping through mugshots. Each one the woman grew paler, the circles under her eyes deepening. The last photo, of Roxy's stiff blue body sprawled across a dirty mattress pulled sobs from Sasha's chest.

"Is this what you want to be?" Vinny yelled, pushing Sasha closer to the picture. He hated Sasha for making him do this, hated himself even more for actually carrying it out. His mind spun, chest ached. He yanked his hand off Sasha's neck, but she stayed hunched over in front of the picture.

"I could have saved her," Sasha said, running her finger along the glossy photo of Roxy's dead body. "She wanted to be saved."

Tears poured from Sasha's eyes, splashed the scatter of pictures below her, and wails caught in her throat. Vinny wrapped his arms around her shuddering body. "She wanted you to be saved too."

Sasha crashed into Vinny's arms, practically crawled into his lap. Her tears soaked through his shirt, chilled his skin, but that didn't stop him from clutching onto her tightly.

"You need a few joints and a cigarette," he said, rubbing Sasha's back in attempts to quell its shivers.

"You've got weed and cigarettes?" Sasha turned her tear-filled eyes to Vinny, a glimmer of hope shining beneath the watery glaze.

"Of course. I'm not trying to torture you, girl."

Sasha hugged Vinny tight, and he kissed the top of her head even though her hair smelled like vomit.

***

Sasha

Before Sasha fell asleep, Vinny told her three days had passed. She'd hoped two more had slipped by while she slept. Her cheek rubbed against soft pillows, and they scraped like steel wool, but she didn't get out of bed. Seven to ten days. That was the sentence Vinny gave her. She deserved more. A wild animal was more cordial than her behavior as of late.

Seven to ten days. Then, she could leave this too-bright, too-white room. The walls gleamed, shocked her eyes, which was why she stayed in bed. At least that was her story, and she was sticking to it. Embarrassment didn't keep her rooted to the mattress, shame wasn't the reason she pulled the blanket up past her chin, and fear...the anxiety that she'd run straight to Harlem definitely hadn't shackled her body to the scratchy sheet beneath her. That constant dread she'd end up a body in the morgue, on a cold metal slab beside Roxy, couldn't creep from the darkness and drag her down. She wouldn't let it. There was something she had that Roxy didn't, something that always kept her going. People. Sasha had people, good people counting on her to be strong. Whether strength resided inside her or not, she had to display it for them. For Tyler. Her son was out there somewhere, probably waiting for her.

"Vinny." When he didn't answer, she sat up in bed. Her stare went straight to the bedroom door, which was wide open. She tossed the blanket aside, and Kev stepped into the doorway.

"He'll be right back," Kev said, leaning against the threshold. "The doc called with your test results, would only talk to him."

"What was I tested for?"

"I don't know." Kev glanced over his shoulder, twice, jittering in the doorway. "Vinny will be right back, I hope."

A snicker flew from Sasha's mouth, puffing out her tangled hair. "Don't like me no more, huh?"

"No—" Kev shook his head, cringed a bit. "I mean, yeah. I fucking love you. I'm just…the door's open. Man, you're gonna fuck me up and run out of here."

"I'm not gonna fuck you up," she said through a chuckle. "And I'm not running out of here." Her smile faded, sunk into a frown. "I don't know where I'd go, what I'd do if I left this room."

Kev crept inside, slow, with one eye on the door. "You can hang with me. We'll pretend to be tourists, see the sights. I'm getting sick of this mob bullshit anyway."

"That sounds like a solid plan, brother." She scooted to the edge of the bed, patted the mattress beside her. "Sit down. You're making me nervous."

"I guess." Kev looked at the door one more time, then sat next to Sasha.

"When'd you get here?"

"I've been here," Kev said, stealing glances at her bare, scarred legs. "On Otis watch."

Sasha slumped down, trying to follow the drop of her heart. "Otis doesn't know about this?"

"Fuck no. I fucking hope not. He thinks me and Vinny are pissed, taking time off."

A lump rose inside Sasha's throat, but she choked it down. Now would be the perfect opportunity to practice the fake strength she was supposed to be displaying. "I was hoping that was just a scam to keep the BGF from our table."

Kev lowered his gaze, shrugged.

"Nah, it's cool," she said, even though she was weeping on the inside. "Otis has every right to hate me. Do you know where Dez is, Tyler?"

"Back at the holler. I kinda wish—"

A crash erupted from the living room, followed by the thump of heavy boots and the shatter of glass.

"Wait here." Kev jumped to his feet. He pulled a gun from his holster and headed for the open bedroom door. The second he peeked his head into the hallway, the butt of a gun smashed against his face.

Kev dropped to his knees, blood flowing from his nose, and Sasha hopped out of bed. Her shaky legs buckled, and she fell to the floor.

"Sasha Ashby," a silky, Spanish voice said. "I've been looking for you, mama."

Sasha looked at the doorway, finding a familiar smile. "Carmen. The Los Lobos are in New York now?"

"No." Carmen walked into the room, shadowed by large men with large guns. The woman's hips swayed beneath the tight dress that clung to them, her smile growing wider as she stood over Sasha. "I've been calling that bullshit restaurant for a month, trying to get a hold of you. Then my associates with the *Nuestra* told me they bought you on the Black Market, gave me this address."

Carmen's men dragged Vinny into the room, landing punches every time he struggled. They pushed Vinny to his knees in front of Sasha, then shoved Kev down beside him. Vinny looked at Sasha, and a stream of blood trickled down from the cut above his eye.

Carmen pulled a handgun from the holster of the man beside her. She stood behind Vinny, clicked off the safety, and pointed the gun at the back of his head.

"Stop," Sasha yelled. She rose to her knees, and Carmen's men shifted their rifles to her chest.

"These aren't your captors?" Carmen asked, waving her gun between Vinny and Kev.

"No. They're my family." Sasha dropped her gaze to the needle marks on the arm, covered them with her shaky palm. "They've been...helping me."

"You have a lot of family," Carmen said, lowering her gun. "That's why I've been trying to find you." She glanced over her shoulder, sending long waves of brown hair to glide over her tanned skin. "Bring him in."

Sasha looked at the doorway, and growled at the sight of Dante. He was slumped under the grip of Carmen's men, his face beaten to shit.

"Is this guy family too?" Carmen asked, sneering as she pointed at Dante.

A wicked smile crossed Sasha's lips as she stared at Dante's battered face. One word and his brains would be splattered on her way too-white walls. Except there would be no satisfaction, no fun in it for her.

"Yeah," Sasha said, her annoyance dragging the word out. "That asshole's technically my father. What'd he do to you?"

Carmen crashed the butt of her gun against Dante's cheek. "This *puto* tried to take over my operation. Turn my men against me." She struck Dante again, the gun's handle splitting the skin on his cheek.

Dante doubled over, drooled blood onto the clean carpet, and Sasha groaned. Her bio dad was a dumb bastard. There wasn't much she could do for him now, except ask for a quick death.

"He seems to be pretty ambitious," Sasha said, glaring at Dante. "But he doesn't have the brains to back his shit up."

"I'd like to kill him," Carmen said, turning her back to Dante. "String him up in front of my entire crew and gut the fucker." She strolled past Vinny and Kev, as if they weren't held on their knees bleeding, and knelt beside Sasha. "But I'd like your permission. I don't want to burn our bridge, mama." Carmen leaned closer to Sasha, eyed the scabs on both of Sasha's feet and her left arm. "You need a shower, mama. You smell like puke. Do you need *me* to help you get clean?"

Sasha couldn't lift her stare from the floor. She was mortified to be seen like this, in front of an entire pack of Mexican gangsters no less. Never again. She would never tap a vein ever again.

"I am clean," Sasha said, forcing her chin to raise high. "A little soap and water, and I'll be as cherry as pie, doll."

"Good." Carmen rose to her feet, glanced at

Dante. "And him?"

Dante's gaze clung to Sasha, pleading, but she was too numb to care. She'd already taken one hit for him, a three-month long hit in a dark cell. There was nothing left for her to give to Dante, especially not a second thought.

"I'm sorry he caused so much trouble for you." Sasha looked away from Dante's split lips, his swollen eyes. "Do what you have to. You have my permission."

A smile lit Carmen's dark eyes. She waved her hand, and her men carted Dante toward the door. "We should have dinner while I'm in town," she said, oblivious to the struggle between Dante and her men in the doorway. "Catch up."

Sasha squirmed on the soft carpet, more every time Dante called out her name. Her fingers twisted into the ends of her shirt, heart racing. She looked at Vinny, who shrugged under the grip upon him, then at Carmen. "Yeah, I—"

"Your mother's alive," Dante yelled, clinging to the threshold as men tugged his legs. "I can take you to her."

A whirlwind of prickles ignited in Sasha's chest, spread throughout her body. When a blustery fire hit her toes, she jumped to her feet.

"*De alto*," Carmen said, and her men stopped their attempt to drag Dante away.

Sasha walked toward Dante, her fists balling tighter with each step. "You're lying."

"We faked her death," Dante said, without a hint of doubt in his stare. "I told that crazy Mancini bitch, and she did the same thing to you."

Sasha turned her glare to Vinny and Kev, still on their knees. "Y'all saw my mother, right? She was dead." They just stared at her, shock twisting their faces. "Right?"

"I saw her," Vinny said, a slight tremble cracking his voice. "Her body looked just like the one in the alley, the one that was supposed to be you."

The deepest laugh erupted from Sasha's chest, but she wasn't happy. She was furious. Her mother was alive. That dirty cunt left, of her own free will, never once reaching out. Dante knew. The entire time Sasha was locked in a cell, forced to be her dead mother, Dante knew the woman was really alive.

Red. All Sasha saw was red. Without permission, her knuckles slammed against Dante's face.

"Where is she?" Sasha yelled, landing another solid punch before a man ushered her back.

"No way," Dante said, spitting a wad of blood to the floor. "I'm not talking 'til I'm free."

Rage boiled Sasha's blood. The pressure her anger created would blow the skullcap right off the top of her head if not released, and she only knew one way. "I need a knife," she said, holding out her hand.

The men scattered around the room turned to look at Carmen. Carmen nodded, and the handle of a long hunting knife was placed in Sasha's palm.

A wide smile spanned Sasha's lips as she stepped in front of Dante, still caught under the grip of Mexican gangsters.

"Where is she?" Sasha asked, dragging her blade

along Dante's cheek. His skin ripped open in the knife's wake, spilling blood onto Sasha's feet.

Dante shook his head, held his hard glare on Sasha.

"Where!" She sliced his chest, twice, but he didn't make a sound. Now she didn't care what information wormed around inside his head. Now she'd rather walk the Earth, calling out her mother's name, instead of letting Dante breathe for another second.

Sasha drew her arm back, aiming the tip of her blade at Dante's stomach.

"I'll take you to her," Dante yelled in a rush. "I die, and you'll never see your mother again."

Waves of hesitation almost drowned Sasha. She wanted to drive her blade into Dante's smug face, needed to let her fury, sadness, misery out on something. "Fuck!" She turned toward the bed and threw the knife across the room. It sailed over Kev's head, lodging into the wall with a thump.

Of all the things Sasha had been through—losing Candy, a four-year coma, missing her son's childhood—to beg for Dante's life was by far the hardest to swallow. Her snarl wouldn't fade, even though her back was to Dante, even though she was staring at a beautifully lethal woman. "Look, Carmen—"

"I want something." Carmen sat on the edge of the bed as if she owned it and crossed her long legs.

That broke Sasha's scowl. It wasn't the sexy woman on her bed that brought a smile to her lips. It was the confidence that surrounded that sexy woman on her bed. "Sounds like you're already prepared to negotiate."

"Privacy," Carmen said, and her men hurried to collect Vinny and Kev off the floor.

"Sasha," Vinny said as the men shoved him toward the door.

"It's cool." Sasha flashed Vinny an apologetic stare, and he stopped struggling. Even Dante walked out of the room without a fuss, which was goddamn amazing considering the colossal hissy fit he'd just thrown.

"Don't shut that door," Sasha called out as the last man headed for the bedroom door. "It has no handle."

"A room with no handle on the door," Carmen said once they were alone. "And you've been in here for what…three, four days?"

"Yeah," Sasha muttered, crossing her arms to hide both her new scabs and old scars. For the first time, ever, she felt awkward to be in just a tank top and her underwear in front of a woman. It was a shitty feeling. The emptiness left in her body from the poison she'd pumped into her veins was nothing compared to the devastation she felt over losing her swagger.

"Why don't you go shower?" Carmen said, gesturing to the bathroom. "Get dressed, so we can talk."

Chapter Ten

Vinny

It wasn't easy for Vinny to sit on a couch next to Dante. That man ruined Sasha, shot his brother, and constantly escaped death. Vinny could fix the escaping death part. There was a knife clipped to his belt, and men weren't holding him down any longer. In two seconds flat, he could have Dante's throat split wide open. It would fuck Sasha's plans, but screw Ellen. That bitch went through a lot of trouble to leave them behind. As far as he was concerned, that lying, no good woman could stay gone.

"Don't even think about it," Dante said, glancing at Vinny's hand.

Vinny hadn't noticed his fingers drumming the wooden handle of his knife, didn't realize he'd jacked his shirt up for easier access, until now. "I am thinking about it."

"*Silencio*," a man said, clutching his Uzi tighter.

105

Although Vinny didn't know Spanish, the man's voice clearly said shut the fuck up.

"I should be the one slicing you up," Dante whispered, leaning closer to Vinny. "For turning my little girl into a junkie."

"She's like this 'cause you put her in a cell for months," Vinny seethed, hatred locking his jaw into a clamp.

"I almost died getting her out of that cell. My mistake was taking her to you. I should've known a bunch of punk-ass truckers weren't men enough to keep one little girl safe."

Vinny spun on the couch to face Dante, drawing his fist back, and a gun cocked behind him.

"What the fuck is wrong with you *pinche gringos?* You're told to be quiet, and you shout louder. You fuckers want to get shot?"

Kev raised his hand like a goddamn moron. "Will I get shot for rolling a joint?"

This was so typical for Sasha. Vinny got guns shoved in his face while she fucked a hottie. One of these days, the tables were going to turn. Sasha could stare down the barrels of semi-automatic weapons and he'd bang the exotic, big-tittie woman. One of these days.

"It must feel like shit," Dante said, glaring at Vinny. "Knowing the only person in your crew with any balls is a chick."

"You tell me," Vinny snickered. "You've been Ellen's little bitch for how long?"

That wiped the cocky smirk right off Dante's ugly face. For a second, Vinny thought the guy might lunge at him. Dante didn't do shit. Just like a pussy would do, Dante sunk back into the couch cushions.

The men slouched around the penthouse stood up straight, the clink of their guns filling the room. Vinny peeked over his shoulder as Sasha trotted down the stairs, followed by her sexy friend. The color had returned to Sasha's cheeks, a bit pinker than usual actually. To see her fully dressed, head high, walking instead of wobbling brought a smile to Vinny's lips. Then it sparked a scowl. He'd just spent three days trying to bring the old Sasha back, and this bad-ass gangster chick had done it in twenty minutes.

"We're leaving," Carmen said, and her men crowded around her as she headed for the front door. "Grab that *pinche puto*," she said, pointing at Dante.

"Sasha?" Dante yelled as Carmen's men yanked him off the couch.

"I'm working on it, asshole." Sasha kept her gaze off Dante, yet anger still flared in her eyes. It was goddamn beautiful, like she was alive again.

Vinny grinned, waved at Dante as he was roughly dragged out the front door. "Later, fucking pussy."

The hoard of Mexican gangsters filed out of the penthouse, the thump of their boots fading down the hall. Sasha closed the door then walked into the kitchen.

"So?" Vinny asked, leaning on the couch's arm to peer into the kitchen. "What's up?"

Glass clinked, the refrigerator door slammed shut, and Sasha walked back into the living room with two bags of frozen vegetables. She tossed one to Kev then sat next to Vinny, holding the other one against the cut above his eye.

"Sorry about all that."

"Your ex-girlfriend is crazy, in a seriously hot way." Vinny leaned close to Sasha, brought his lips to her ear. "Any chance for a three-way with that one?"

Sasha chuckled. "She's not my ex. Carmen is our old buyer from Little Rock, and I don't think she'd be down for a threesome."

Kev knelt in front of the coffee table, breaking out a joint. "You guys been having threesomes?" He twisted the buds, licked the paper, and popped the doobie in his mouth. "With chicks, I hope?"

Vinny ignored Kev's stupid smile and looked at Sasha. "What does she want, for Dante?"

Sasha snatched the joint from Kev's mouth, took a big hit. "The same thing everybody wants. A seat at Otis's table."

"I got one of those," Kev said, reaching for the joint and getting a palm to the face. "And it ain't done me no good." Instead of attempting to wrangle the doobie from Sasha's grasp, a battle he'd most likely lose, Kev started rolling another joint. "Being a mobster isn't fun at all. Movies are fucking liars."

Kev lit his second joint, and Vinny plucked it from the man's fingers before it could reach his lips.

"You guys suck," Kev yelled, heading back to the table and the dwindling pile of green buds.

"Otis hates me." Sasha sunk down on the couch, curled her legs beneath her. "He'll never take a meeting with me."

"You think Ellen's really alive?" Kev asked through a cloud of smoke, from the only one of three bones he'd twisted.

The look on Sasha's face made Vinny's heart skip a beat. He'd seen hate, lust, love, but this gaze left him breathless. A sliver of the old fire that once lit Sasha's eyes shined through. It was only a shimmer but still strong enough to vibrate the air around her, lift all the tiny hairs on his arms.

"I'll talk to Otis." Vinny reached over the arm of the couch and grabbed the phone. He'd rat himself out, face judgement for going behind the Don's back, if it rekindled the blaze inside Sasha. "But I'm only setting a meeting." He stopped mid-dial, glanced at Sasha. "You're gonna have to tell him about Ellen and all that business with the sexy, crazy, gangster chick."

***

Sasha

Kev practically jumped at Sasha's grub request, so she added beer and cigarettes to the list. He seemed more than happy to go, almost ran out the door. The dude must've been trapped inside this penthouse for as long as her. Judging by the amount of empty Chinese food cartons, overflowing ashtrays, and drained whiskey bottles, she'd guess longer.

Vinny hung up the phone, muttered a jumble of *fucks* and *shits* beneath his breath. Otis must've shot Vinny down. Oh well. Fuck her plans. Fuck Dante.

And fuck Otis. Sasha didn't need the Don of the Lazzari family to find her mother. Honestly, it couldn't take that long to kick open every single door in every country of the world.

"Otis won't talk to me, will he?"

"He's coming here," Vinny said in a grim tone. His shoulders sunk into a slump as he walked back to the couch.

"That's good, right?"

Vinny plopped onto the cushions beside Sasha. "He said he'll be here in an hour. It's a ten-minute drive. That means he's gathering a crew."

"To what, whack us?" Sasha said through a snicker. Vinny didn't laugh. Not even a hint of a smile cracked his straight lips. "Well, damn. I guess power went straight to his head."

"I should've told him about Ellen." Vinny squirmed, holding himself tight. "I just…couldn't."

More than ever, Sasha wanted to dive into Vinny's arms. It was so much more than the crinkle of his brow, or the pout on his lips, that spawned a deep ache for his touch. Vinny had pulled her from darkness. She'd been screaming for rescue, acting out to see if anybody gave a fuck. Of course it was him, and she was a goddamn fool. This time, her need to push boundaries almost cost her everything. It almost cost her herself.

"What?" Vinny asked, leaning back to better glare at Sasha.

"What?" Sasha wiped her face clear, in case a hint of puppy love lingered.

"You're looking at me strange."

Sasha grinned. She'd been busted hurling googly

eyes, and it didn't even bother her one bit. "I just really…" She ran her hand up Vinny's arm, glided her palm along his chest. "I…umm…"

Vinny wrapped his arms around Sasha. His body pressed against her chest, drove her back into the couch cushions. Then, in a rush that sucked the air from her lungs, he kissed her. His tight grip shuddered her bones, and the feeling of his teeth nibbling her bottom lip spread tingles. She didn't think it was possible to feel this good without a spike to the vein. Holy fucking shit was she wrong. Only now, after staggering along the thin line of life and death, did she get what it meant to be truly alive. It was like she'd been living under a sheet of ice, watching the world pass by in a blurry chill, until Vinny's fiery clutch broke her out and warmed her soul.

"I love you too," Vinny said, kissing her cheek, neck, chest.

"Wait." Sasha grabbed Vinny's arm, which stopped his battle with her flannel shirt.

"I'm sorry," Vinny muttered, moving off Sasha. "I thought you wanted to—"

"No." Sasha took Vinny by the hand, pulled him back on top of her. "I do, it's just…Kev said you had me tested. Do I have something?"

"It was the doc's idea. I didn't think you were hooking or anything."

Sasha snickered as images of her, and her switchblade, attempting to hook ran through her mind. In her version, it was more of a robbery than a sex thing. "I don't care about that. I just don't want to give you anything. You're too good to be dirty, like me."

"You're clean," Vinny said, running his thumb along the scars on her cheek. "On the outside." He kissed the tight patch of scars near her chin. "And every part of your insides." His soft lips moved down her neck as he unbuttoned her flannel shirt. He ran his tongue along her breast, grazing her nipple, and a gasp slipped from her mouth. "You're clean, beautiful, and all mine."

Vinny stopped tugging at Sasha's belt and looked up into her eyes. "For the next forty-five minutes at least."

***

A knock rattled the penthouse door just as a surge of ecstasy ran through Sasha. "Coming," she yelled, which wasn't exactly a lie. Vinny thrust deep inside her, setting off an explosion of tingles. His body quaked, a low moan slipped from his lips, and Sasha giggled.

"Get off, bro," she said through a snicker, pushing Vinny off her. "Otis is here." She squirmed out from beneath his solid, sweaty body and grabbed her pants from the floor. There was no time to fuck with her bra and tank top, so she kicked them under the couch and tossed on her flannel. While buttoning her shirt, she headed for the door.

"You good?" she asked in a whisper, glancing back at Vinny. He nodded, hurrying to fasten his belt while jamming his feet into his boots.

Sasha looked at her bare feet, covered in scabs and bruises. Those ugly marks were a part of her now. She wasn't going to hide them, and Otis could go fuck himself if he didn't like it. Her throat sealed shut as she reached for the deadbolt. A hammer pounded her heart when her fingertips grazed metal. She swallowed the bitter taste of fear and opened the door.

Otis narrowed his hard stare at the first sight of Sasha, and she almost hugged the man. Sure, he looked like a phony in a seersucker suit instead of his usual blue jeans and Led Zeppelin shirt, but his glower was the same. It was disappointment, relief, and a fuck-ton of rage. It was the look he reserved for those he loved. He still loved her.

"Thank you for coming," Sasha said, stepping aside to allow Otis inside. A group of armed mobsters didn't follow Otis into the penthouse. Sasha peeked into the hallway, finding only Kev with a grease-soaked paper bag from the burger joint up the block. "You didn't bring a crew?" she asked, turning to face Otis.

"I'm not here to whack you guys," Otis said, shaking his head.

Kev walked inside the penthouse, and Vinny grabbed the bag of food from his hand. "Where the fuck you been?" Vinny peeked inside the bag, cringed, then shoved it back into Kev's hands.

"Hanging in the hallway," Kev muttered, his stare low. "There was...sounds."

Vinny grumbled beneath his breath. He pulled Kev inside the penthouse and slammed the door shut.

Sasha sat at the dining room table, motioned for Otis to join her.

Otis pulled out the chair across from Sasha. A huff flew from his mouth as he dropped into the seat. "If this is about what happened the other night—"

"No." Sasha kept her stare soft and fixed on Otis. "You did the right thing. That was my stupid fucking mess. I'm glad you didn't sacrifice the business for my fuck-up." Her fingers twitched, wanting to reach for Otis, but she held her hands in her lap. "And I'm sorry. My behavior's been...I've been—"

"If this isn't about the other night, then why did you call me here?"

Sasha took a deep breath, but it did nothing to soothe the burn in her chest. Craziness was about to spew from her mouth. This shit was hard to believe, even for her, and she really wanted to believe it. "There's a good possibility my mother is still alive."

Otis sat up straight. He glared at Vinny, groaned, then turned his stare back to Sasha. "I don't know what these two assholes have been telling you to get you sober, but your mother is definitely dead."

"You remember Miguel's crew, from Little Rock?"

"Yeah, Los Lobos," Otis said, nodding. "He ate a bullet last year."

"His daughter, Carmen, is running the show now." Sasha sat back, studying Otis's face. Any second now, his lid would flip, and it'd been a long time since she'd witnessed that hilarious event. "Dante showed up in her hood, stirred up a shit-load of trouble. So Carmen, and a bunch of her men, brought Dante to me, asking for permission to kill him."

"When did this happen?" Otis asked, clenching his fist. The guy looked pissed, and he had a right to be. Not only had some out-of-town crew stomped on his turf, but Dante was a Lazzari. He might have been a Lazzari with a bounty on his head, but that didn't matter in the mobster world.

"A few hours ago," Sasha said.

"I don't see blood painting your walls," Otis said in a sneer. "I can't imagine you'd deny that request."

"I didn't, but the fucking asshole threw a curve ball." Sasha slid her hands under the table. They wouldn't stop shaking. Her body was aching for a hit to ease the tension so she could deal, even though her mind wanted nothing to do with the drug. "Dante said he helped Ellen fake her death, and he told the Mancinis how. Then they did it to me."

The color drained from Otis's face. It looked like the dude might puke, or pass out. "A shotgun blast to the face and two to the chest," he muttered, almost to himself. His gaze veered straight to Vinny. The nod Otis received didn't do the trick, and he shifted his stare to Kev only to get a shrug.

"Where is Dante?" Otis all but growled, squirming in his seat.

"The Los Lobos has him. They're willing to make a trade."

Otis snickered, his head shaking. "There's only ever been Italian families at the table, Sasha. If I bring in Mexican gangsters to run a borough, the other families will butcher me. They'll butcher us all."

Sasha couldn't argue with that. These city men were tolerant, but only when it came to their own kind. "Carmen is sensible. Maybe you can offer her something smaller. There's that money laundering outfit in Chicago. Just give her that."

Otis snorted, stared at Sasha as if she'd just grown two heads. "And what should I do with the Bassini brothers, send 'em pink slips?"

"I don't know." Sasha grabbed a pack of cigarettes off the table, popped one in her mouth. "They're douchebags, take 'em out."

Otis clicked his zippo to life and held out the flame for Sasha. "That kind of shit starts wars." Smoke wafted from the cigarette in Sasha's mouth, and he flipped the lid to his lighter closed. "Arrange a meeting with this Carmen woman. Just her, in my restaurant. Tonight."

Sasha nodded, and Otis rose from his chair. He took a step, paused, and turned to face Sasha. "I'm glad you're back."

Those four little words were equivalent to one giant hug, which wrapped around Sasha tight. The second Otis looked away, she let her smile flow. Then Kev filled her view. The dude looked like a red-headed stepchild who just got included in a family photo for the first time, which wiped the grin right off Sasha's lips.

"What the fuck are you smiling at?" she barked, glaring at Kev as she headed for the phone.

Chapter Eleven

Sasha stood on the sidewalk outside of Fat Tonys. Frosty air cut between the tall buildings, broke through her shirt to nip at her skin. She rocked in place, rubbed her hands together, but couldn't shake the night's wintery breeze from her bones.

"It's motherfucking cold," she said, glancing at Vinny. He lit a cigarette and handed it to her, as if that would somehow keep her warm.

"Thanks," she muttered, taking a long drag. Nicotine shot through her system, actually chasing away a fraction of the chill, and she snickered through her exhale.

The scene outside of Fat Tonys was a goddamn spectacle. It looked like a block party for rednecks in mobster costumes and tatted up Mexican gangsters. Except, instead of shooting the shit with each other, they all continually peeked through the window of the restaurant.

Otis and Carmen seemed quite cozy, chilling in

the heat, chatting over half-eaten plates of pasta while clinking their wine glasses together.

"This looks promising," Kev said, breathing into his hands to keep warm.

"They're probably toasting Dante's death," Sasha grumbled.

Vinny turned his glare off the crowd of gangsters in front of him to leer at Sasha. "You really care if Dante dies?"

"I want to find my mother so I can punch her in the fucking face." Sasha tossed her cigarette to the ground, just as a man in a suit strolled by. The guy clutched his briefcase close, stumbled into the street to avoid the crowd of Mexicans who hadn't even noticed him.

"Keep going," Sasha yelled as the guy tripped on his own feet while gawking at the men on the sidewalk. "You fucking mook."

The men stopped whispering in Spanish. They turned to follow Sasha's glare and the guy yelped like a little bitch, then scurried across the street.

Sasha chuckled. "*Estúpido ciudad maricón*," she said, and Carmen's men snickered.

"What'd you say," Kev asked in a hush.

"She called that guy a faggot," Vinny said, gesturing to the man who ran down the sidewalk on the other side of the street.

Sasha spun to face Vinny. "You learned Spanish?"

"Only the dirty words." He winked. A grin spread across his lips, and Sasha almost kissed him. Jesus fuck! She needed to get as far away from Vinny as possible, before she left his life in tatters.

Like she did to Dez, Tyler, her mother; like she did to every woman who dared to love her.

The door to Fat Tonys opened, Carmen and Otis stepped outside, and every person crowded on the sidewalk turned to stare at them.

"*Obtener el gilipollas*," Carmen said, and her men hurried to the black van parked at the curb. Its sliding door clunked open, and Dante was shoved out of the back of the van.

Sasha couldn't help but smile. To see her dear old dad stumbling on the sidewalk, his hands tied behind his back, a dark hood covering his head, was such a lovely gift. She'd have to find a way to thank Otis. Maybe bake him a cake, after she washed Dante's blood off her hands.

Vinny grabbed Dante by the arm, pulled him toward the double doors of Fat Tonys. "I bet you ain't smiling now, fucker."

"Thank you," Sasha said, holding her hand out to Carmen.

Carmen brushed Sasha's hand aside, slinked so close their chests pressed together. "No. Thank you, mama," she whispered into Sasha's ear.

With a sly smile, Carmen drifted away. Sasha watched the woman stroll to her awaiting van. Whatever the fuck the fabric was called that made-up Carmen's tight pants, Sasha didn't know. Didn't care. To her, it was magic, perfection, goddamn divine. That sparkly, stretchy material showed every curve of Carmen's ass, accentuated her swaying hips, and flaunted the muscles of her long legs. It really wasn't that cold outside anymore. In fact, Sasha was a bit hot.

"You fucked her," Otis said, stepping beside Sasha to join in the ogling.

Carmen climbed into the passenger seat of the van, and both Sasha and Otis held their breath as the magical pants somehow clung to the woman's ass even tighter. The passenger door slammed shut, tires squealed as the van sped off, and the air burst from Sasha's lungs. "Jealous?" She peeked over at Otis, finding a slight grin.

"Shit yeah." Otis patted Sasha on the arm, knocked her to the side a bit. "Come on, let's go carve some answers out of your prick of a father."

"Awesome." Sasha followed Otis down the red plush carpet that led to Fat Tonys, a tiny skip returning to her step.

***

Vinny and Kev had taken Dante to the backroom. Just like in the movies, they sat the man in a wooden chair that centered the wide-open office. All they needed was a harsh light to swing overhead, casting eerie shadows, and they'd be set. Thankfully, the hood still covered Dante's head. Sasha wanted to be the one to yank that cloth from Dante's face so he could see her wicked smile first.

A jitter trembled Sasha's fingers as she stepped closer to the man in the chair. Kev hurried forward, ripped the hood off Dante's head, then grinned at Sasha.

"Dude," she yelled, her glare hardening on Kev.

"What?" Kev shrank down, backed away from Sasha. "I was helping."

Sasha pulled the long knife from the sheath on Kev's belt, then pointed its sharp tip at his face. "Don't help." At least Dante still had a strip of masking tape over his lips she could tear off.

"Listen," Vinny said in a hush, leaning close to Sasha. "If you start with deep cuts, there's really no place to go from there except a sledgehammer to the face."

"Fuck, man." Sasha crossed her arms, the knife's cool blade pressing against her skin. "I know how to torture someone."

Vinny snorted, his face twisting in doubt. "You didn't get anything out of the last guy."

"I got the letter," she said, waving her knife Vinny's way.

"*I* got the letter." Vinny raised his brow, a smug look on his face.

"Oh. Okay." Sasha flipped the knife in her grasp, offered its handle to Vinny. "Would you like to do the honors?"

Dante sat quietly, his stare bouncing between Sasha and Vinny, and Kev inched behind Otis.

"I'll do it," Vinny said, sounding much like a child in a schoolyard dare. "But you're gonna be sorry, 'cause I get answers without cutting."

Sasha twirled the knife, its handle thumping back into her palm. "By all means," she said, backing away from Dante. "Go right ahead."

Vinny wobbled in place, a hint of shock lighting his electric-blue eyes. Otis snickered, and Vinny's stare turned hard. He stomped toward Dante and ripped the tape from the man's mouth.

"No," Dante said, staring up at Vinny. "I'll never

121

tell. And nothing any of you do will be worse than what was done to me in that Mancini house."

A shiver ran though Sasha. *That* she knew was true. She didn't see what was done to Dante while they were being held captive by those insane inbreds, but his body was just as wrecked as hers had been when they escaped together.

"I'll take her there," Dante said, nodding at Sasha. "Only her."

"Fuck that," Otis said. He pushed past Sasha and slammed his fist against Dante's cheek.

Dante toppled over, taking the chair with him. His side crashed to the floor, and a stream of blood flew from his mouth followed by a chuckle.

"Damn, cuz," Dante said, spitting out a wad of blood. "You still got a mean fucking right hook."

Otis grabbed Dante by the shirt, lifted the man to his feet. "And you're still a goddamn liar." Otis bashed his forehead against Dante's nose, which dropped Dante straight to his ass.

"I know that was Ellen's body," Otis shouted, thrusting his finger in Dante's blood-streaked face. "I held her in my arms. I know it was her."

"That bitch was a dead ringer," Dante said between groans as he tugged against the ropes that bound his arms behind his back. "Tits, ass, tight little waist, but the face was like a brick wall. That's why Ellen put buckshot in it."

"No!" Otis drew back his leg. The tip of Otis's boot aimed at Dante's chin, and Sasha pulled him away.

"He's not the one you want to hit," Sasha said, clutching onto Otis tight.

"She wouldn't do that to us." Otis shoved Sasha off of him. "Not with the coma, and Tyler."

"I told Ellen the kid died," Dante said, wiping his already bruised nose on his shoulder. "So she'd stay gone."

"Why?" Vinny asked, stepping between Otis and Dante.

Sadness took Dante's gaze down. Sasha knew that look well. It was the eternal hollowness that consumed one's soul in Ellen's absence.

"He was trying to keep her locked down," Sasha said, which pulled Dante's stare off the floor and to her face. "But she bailed on him anyway."

Vinny shook his head as he glared at Dante. "This fucker doesn't know where Ellen is."

"She's alive," Otis muttered, backing toward the door. "Dirty cunt played me."

Otis yanked the office door open. Its brass knob banged against the wall, cracked the plaster as he stormed out of the room.

"I know how you feel, cousin," Dante called out, smirking.

Sasha brought the edge of her blade to Dante's neck, pressed the knife against his flesh. "Don't move, *daddy*." She dragged the blade, lightly, leaving a thin cut on his tan skin. "Don't even wag that evil tongue of yours."

Dante sunk down, leaned against the wall, and Sasha handed the knife to Vinny on her way out the room. She jogged down the hallway, chasing the sound of Otis's heavy stomps. Just as she ran into the lobby, Otis reached for the front door.

"Dude," she yelled as Otis opened the frosted

glass door.

"I'm out," Otis said without a glance back.

"Otis." The word came out in a weak, pathetic voice Sasha hardly recognized, and Otis stopped mid-step. His body grew stiff, and his hand trembled against the door's handle.

"I can't..." Otis slammed the restaurant's door shut, spun to face Sasha. "I can't believe she left me."

Tears welled in his eyes, and an icy grip clutched Sasha's heart. She pulled Otis into a tight hug. His strong arms wrapped around her body, and she damn near collapsed against his chest. It had been a long time since she'd mopped up her mother's shit, and it felt goddamn amazing.

"She left me too," Sasha said, clinging to Otis as if he were the last joint on Earth. "Bitch pushed me in the cellar, left me to rot in a coma."

"Why?" Otis pulled back from Sasha's grasp, holding onto the sides of her arms. "Why bring her back? She'll just keep hurting us, over and over again."

It was a question Sasha hadn't even considered. Ellen-damage-control was her specialty. If her mother came back, her life could have purpose again.

"She's family," Sasha said, and Otis sagged down. "I miss the shit out of her." If Otis said no one more time, she didn't know how her body would react. She definitely wasn't above stomping her feet and yelling *I want my mommy*!

"Fuck, Sasha." Otis steeped back from Sasha's pleading eyes, then locked the deadbolt on the front door. "You have no idea how much I miss her."

Sasha's smile came too quick for her to stop. "I'm gonna bring her back. She's gonna have a black eye, but I'm gonna bring her back."

***

Vinny

To stand in a room with the Devil incarnate while holding a knife and not spray the walls in red was probably the hardest thing Vinny ever had to do. Hate was strong, enduring, and goddamn exhausting. There weren't many things Vinny hated. In fact, he could only think of one. Dante.

His fingers drummed the handle of the knife in his grasp. Kev kept a lit joint going, passing it quick. The dude was probably hoping Vinny would get too stoned to start slashing. Fat fucking chance. It would take a hell of a lot more than weed to dull his fury.

"How come you ain't cutting me?" Dante asked, glaring up at Vinny from the floor. "I know you want to."

Vinny moved from the open doorway, crept toward Dante, and Kev stood up straight.

"You just let my little girl drag you around by the balls, don't you?" Dante smiled in a come-stab-me-in-the-face way, and Vinny took another step closer.

"Don't worry, motherfucker. There'll be plenty of cutting." Vinny lifted the long, serrated knife while staring down at Dante. "I'm gonna use this

125

here knife to shred Ellen's face, the way she shredded my heart. And I'm gonna make you watch."

A growl erupted from Dante's mouth, which put a grin on Vinny's lips. It wasn't true. Vinny could never take a blade to Ellen's face, but Dante didn't know that.

"All right," Sasha said, walking into the room. When spotting Vinny in the middle of the room, flaunting a knife, and Dante frozen mid-climb off the floor, she crossed her arms. "Am I interrupting?" She took a step back while glaring at them both. "Y'all wanna fight?"

Sasha untied the rope from Dante's wrists then leaned back against the wall, between a rather amused Otis and a jittery Kev. "Go on then, start brawlin'. But I don't think either of you are gonna walk away. It's gonna fuck up my plans, but whatever."

Dante slumped back onto the floor, and Vinny lowered the knife.

"Well damn," Otis said, walking to the small desk tucked into the far corner. "I would've paid good money to see that one." He sat behind the desk, grabbed a rolodex, and slid the phone close. "Where should I book the flight to?" he asked, glancing at Dante.

"I can't do no airplane," Dante said. "Ellen had me put on some watchlist so I couldn't chase her. We'll have to drive, just me and my little girl."

"No fucking way," Vinny damn near growled. Otis might as well take out his checkbook. The fight was back on, because the only way Sasha was leaving with Dante would be over his dead body.

"Fine," Sasha said, and Otis groaned.

"No." Vinny grabbed Sasha by the arm, pulled her into the hall. "He's fucking lying."

"My mom's still alive, I can feel it."

Vinny's grip tightened, though not by choice. His clutch on Sasha's arms was the only thing stopping the shake of his fingers. "I have no doubt Ellen's alive, but that fucker doesn't know where to find her or he'd be with her. It's just a ploy to get you alone so he can take you out."

"He had me alone." Sasha broke from Vinny's clutch. Her hands landed on his chest as she leaned into him. "In that house, he could've pumped me full of bullets. He didn't. He brought me back here, back to you."

Vinny wrapped his arms around Sasha. He didn't want to let go. It was so hard to get her in his grasp, even harder to keep her there. "I'm going with you."

"You can't." Sasha's palms glided up his chest, tickled the sides of his neck, caressed his cheeks. "The people who roll with me always end up dead. I don't give a fuck if Dante dies." Her lips brushed against his mouth, trembling. "But I can't lose you. I love you too much."

Chills ran through Vinny's body, so cold they left a burn. He kissed Sasha, drove her back against the wall. No matter how hard he pressed, he could never get close enough to really feel her body. All the stupid fucking clothes covering them both wasn't helping. Sasha's tongue slipped into his mouth, and he grabbed onto her hips.

A throat cleared beside them, loudly, but Vinny wasn't about to part with Sasha's sweet kiss.

"Y'all are gonna have to take this somewhere else," Otis said.

Sasha pushed Vinny away, looking at Otis. "What? You're not willing to pay big money to see this shit?"

"No," Otis said, cringing. "I'm not."

"The old International is parked in the loading bay," Vinny said, winking at Sasha.

A sinful smirk lit Sasha eyes. It was a look Vinny hadn't seen in years, one he never thought he'd see again, and it drove his mind wild. He almost ripped Sasha's clothes off right there. Otis be damned.

"Fuck yeah." Sasha took Vinny by the hand. She peeked her head into the backroom, glared at Dante. "You got one hour to eat, shit, and wash the stink off your ass before we hit the road."

A smile lit Dante's battered face, and Sasha's stare hardened. Vinny knew that look on Sasha's face too well. It always seemed to appear right before some dumbass who thought they were getting their way marched to their death. The second Sasha had an address, she'd feed Dante a bullet.

"Dumb bastard," she said in a grumble, backing away from the office. Dante's smile faded once a devious grin popped onto Sasha's lips. She turned from the office, tightened her grip on Vinny's hand, and led him down the dark hallway.

Chapter Twelve

Dez

Dez stared at the phone on the kitchen wall. It was strange. Enzo usually called by now, twice, and Otis at least three times. Here it was, ten p.m., and not one call. The conversations had gotten shorter since the incident with Sasha. Otis sounded broken when he talked about how wasted she looked, how he just left her strung-out in a hot house, in Harlem, with dirty street thugs. Sasha was probably dead, that's why they didn't call. They could all be dead.

"Shit." Dez grabbed the phone just as Tyler ran into the room. "What are you doing out of bed?" he asked, returning the receiver to its hook.

"There you are."

Dez jumped at the sound of Jeri's voice. He still wasn't used to having a woman around, but he was starting to love the view. Jeri bent in front of Tyler, a smirk breaking her poor attempt at a tough-guy glower. "You little rascal," she said, tickling Tyler's stomach. Her ass looked great in those tight jeans, and the blonde curls tumbling over her shoulder glistened like sunshine. Yeah, it was nice to have a woman around.

"I don't like you," Tyler yelled, slapping Jeri's hand away. He crossed his arms, tapping his bare foot on the kitchen floor. "I'm ready to go back to New York now."

Dez held in a snicker. It was pretty damn cute to see his son so confident—fucking annoying as hell but still cute. "You can't go to New York. You have school tomorrow."

"My mama's gonna come for me." Tyler thrust his hands to his sides, his little fingers balling into fists. "She's gonna beat up Jeri and take me back to my family."

"Your mama's not coming," Dez said, rubbing his forehead.

"Yes, she is. She's coming, and y'all are gonna be sorry." Tyler ran from the room, his stomps echoing through the house.

Jeri wrapped her arms around herself, which propped up her cleavage so well. "Maybe I should leave."

"No." Dez grabbed onto Jeri's hips. Her tight arms unraveled, and he pulled her close. "Just give me a few minutes to settle him down." He dragged his lips along Jeri's neck, pulling a giggle from her mouth. "Then I'll come back here and get you all worked up."

"You already are, baby." Jeri reached for Dez as he pulled away.

"Five minutes," he said, backing out of the room.

***

Sasha

The strangest mix of belonging and sadness washed over Sasha. Curled under Vinny's arm, in the sleeper cab of her favorite rig, was the best feeling in the world. They didn't even have sex; there was no need. Just the two of them, snuggled in a semi's cab, and a handful of joints generated more heat, more intimacy than pressing their naked bodies together ever could. It had been so long since they sat in silence, enjoying each other's company. For all she knew, it could be the last time. Her mother might finish her off at first sight, and she'd let the woman. It was sad to know this was most likely the last time Vinny's arms would hold her tight.

"Where do you think Ellen's been all this time?" Vinny asked, his breath rustling Sasha's hair.

"Beats me. She had friends everywhere. Fuck, she had a whole family I didn't know about." A shiver cut through Sasha. Now that the heroin haze had faded, the old woman's eyes could haunt her.

The cozy sleeper cab didn't seem so cozy anymore. In fact, the tiny space had become stifling. She had to tell herself, twice, that this wasn't a cell. Her insane grandmother wasn't dosing her on LSD and holding her captive. She could get up and walk away from the truck's tiny cab, which seemed to be closing in around her.

"You're trembling." Vinny lifted his arm off Sasha's shoulder, turned to stare into her eyes. "It's only been two days since the cramps and vomiting stopped. You don't have to do this right away. We can keep Dante on lockdown for a week, or ten."

"No. I have to get this over with so I can head to Kentucky."

Vinny's hands fell from Sasha's body, and he scooted far from grasp. "You're going back to get your husband?" he asked softly, his gaze low.

Every day was just another day Sasha missed Dez. His large hands didn't caress her skin any longer. They flinched from it. Dez was gone to her. He may have never belonged to her in the first place, but Vinny did. Vinny had always been a part of her soul, even before she met him. She knew that the very first time they had sex, in her messy room above a garage as a party raged outside the window. That intense connection scared the shit out of her before, but now she was more afraid to lose it than to become consumed by it.

"I'm going back to get *our* son," she said, drawing Vinny's gaze. "I miss that little bastard, and I got a lot of mom duties to make up for."

A smile lit Vinny's icy blue eyes, which jacked up the pound of Sasha's heart.

"What about Dez?" he asked, inching a bit closer to Sasha.

"I was hoping me and you could...I don't know..." The idiot vibe struck Sasha like a backhand. She had no idea what to say, how to approach a potential dating situation. "...hang out for a while."

"You want to hang out with me?" Vinny glided his hand along Sasha's neck, ran his fingers into her hair. He pulled her close, their chests pressing together. "I'll hang with ya, girl."

Vinny's lips brushed her mouth, and fire spread from her chest to her fingertips. Now, she was ready to tear his clothes off and jump in his lap.

A knock on the window stopped Sasha's hand on her belt. "Come on now," Otis said, his sharp tone muffled by the truck's heavy metal door.

"Fuck." Sasha slouched down on the sleeper cab's thin mattress, hiding from the glower outside the window. "It's been an hour already?"

"Damn, girl." Vinny clutched onto Sasha's hips, maneuvered between her legs. "Be fucking careful out there."

For some dumbass reason, tears welled inside Sasha's eyes. She took a deep breath, forcing them back, and leaned closer to Vinny. "My finger's on the trigger."

His kiss came quick, bringing a shudder to both their bodies. She clung to Vinny's neck, and he nibbled her bottom lip. This moment when the two of them became lost in each other's arms, hidden from the dark world, would carry her through whatever shit she was about to face.

"Come back alive this time," Vinny whispered, his breath running over Sasha's lips.

She snickered, tearing herself from Vinny's grasp. "No promises."

***

The semi's engine whistled to life, and a whirlwind of flaming butterflies spun inside Sasha's stomach. She gripped onto the steel shifter beside her. Its vibration tickled her palm and brought a smile to her lips. That giddy feeling which floated around in her head popped when she looked at the passenger seat and saw Dante's face. Instinct took her hand to the butt of her holstered gun, then her brain kicked on. She couldn't shoot Dante, not until the man gave her directions.

"Sasha, wait," Kev yelled as he ran across the loading bay, toward the idling semi. He climbed up the running board, peeked into her window. "I got something for ya." He shoved a leather jacket through Sasha's open window, dropping it in her lap.

Crinkled leather and the raised decal of a Mack truck bursting through flames stole Sasha's gaze. The weight of her old jacket filled the hole in her chest, which she had feared would only grow wider until now.

She squeezed between the armrest and steering wheel, wiggling into her coat. The jacket's cool collar pressed against the back of her neck, and the scent of weed and whiskey filled her lungs. It ignited a giddy sensation, which triggered a smile.

"Later." Kev jumped from the steel step. His boots squeaked as he jogged to the bay door. A clink of metal erupted and the wide door slid up, exposing the glow of city lights.

Sasha backed the rig out of the garage, slow, so she could keep one eye on Vinny. He stood beside Otis, rocking in place. She could see his frown clearly, even though the overhead lights cast a glare on her windshield.

A lot of things seemed to suck at the moment. Leaving New York and Vinny's side when she felt so weak sucked. But most of all, Dante fucking sucked. The man's wicked smirks, his dark eyes snuffed out the excitement of wielding a big rig once again.

"Been tappin' the vein, huh?" Dante said, as if that were a normal way to start a conversation.

"Don't even talk to me about that shit."

"The needle was forced on me. I didn't touch the stuff after we left that house."

Sasha glanced at the passenger seat. Aside from a scatter of colorful bruises, Dante looked healthy, strong. His bronzed cheeks were no longer sunken, the muscles along his arms had returned to bulging status. Not her. She hunched over the giant wheel of a semi like the ghost of Sasha.

"I'm sorry," Dante said, in an almost genuine tone. "I should've left you my contact info."

"I wouldn't have used it." Even though Dante was the only person who could have understood why she ran to the needle, she probably wouldn't have called him.

Air burst from the brakes as the semi crept to a stop at a red light, and Sasha glanced at Dante. "So, where are we going?"

"West." Dante squirmed in his seat, setting off a squeak of old springs. "South-west."

A mix of a huff and a groan pushed past Sasha's lips. She turned right, merged onto the interstate. "I saved your ass. We're here, in this truck—alone— like you wanted. Why can't you just tell me where the fuck my mother is?"

Dante turned toward his window. The dumb bastard was trying to hide his guilty expression, but his face reflected in the glass clearly thanks to the sparkle of city lights.

"You have no clue where she is, do you?" Sasha asked through gritted teeth, and Dante sank lower in his seat. "Motherfucker!"

She veered across two lanes. Horns honked, cars skidded as Sasha steered to the side of I-95. She parked on the shoulder of the highway, seized Dante by the shirt, and pulled him close.

"You lied to me." Before her brain could protest, she pulled the gun from her holster. Dante flinched as she pressed the barrel under his chin, cringed when she pulled back the hammer. "My mother's been dead this whole time."

"No." Dante lifted his hands, slow. "I swear, Sasha. Ellen's out there, I just don't know where. But you do."

Sasha lowered the gun, released Dante with a shove. The glossy-eyed, far-off stare that accompanied lies was something she learned to spot at age ten. Dante didn't hold that stare. He looked anxious, like a man fiending for his next fix. Except Dante's drug of choice was her mother.

"I have no idea where she is," Sasha said, holstering her gun. "If I did, you wouldn't be in the cab of my truck."

"Ellen always said if you ever woke up, you'd know right where to look for her."

Dante's words knocked a gasp from Sasha's mouth. She slumped behind the wheel of her idling semi. At this moment, she could only imagine her face warped into the signature glossy-eyed, far-off liar's stare.

"Holy fuck," Dante said, in more of a long breath. "You do know where she is."

It wasn't exactly true. She just knew where her mother's secrets were. "Does she know I'm awake, my mother?"

"You were still in a coma when she left me holding my dick in a two-person town in the middle of nowhere Texas. I didn't even know you woke up, until Tony told me." For a second, it looked like Dante might reach for her. Thankfully, for the sake of his own fingers, his hands stayed in his lap. "Your trucker brothers had a lot of specialists brought in. They all said you'd never wake up, ever. Your mother thought she lost you. It hit her hard. She stopped loving life, stopped loving...me."

What felt like a world's worth of tears piled into Sasha's eyes. She rolled her stare up, taking a deep breath. There was no way she'd weep in front of Dante, let that man's safe-looking arms wrap around her, allow him to believe he could comfort her.

Sasha slapped her shaky hand atop the shifter and pushed it into first. "I hope you're good at rolling joints, 'cause we got a ten-hour ride ahead of us."

Dante pulled a pack of Zig-Zags from his pocket and flashed a grin. "Where we headed?"

The diesel engine whistled as Sasha pressed down on the gas pedal, running through gears. "Kentucky." She pulled a sandwich bag of green buds from her jacket pocket then tossed it in

Dante's lap. "To my holler."

***

Sasha stood at the counter of a cramped gift store. The pen in her hand tapped a rack of buttons as she wrote on a postcard. She had to stop every other second to stare out the store's front window. Across the rest stop's near empty parking lot, her rig sat in the spot she had left it with Dante just chilling in the passenger seat. She would've made him join her in this very important pit stop, except she kind of wanted the guy to split on her. It would prove her right about that asshole, and she'd have the extra bonus of Dante being gone. He didn't steal her rig though, despite having plenty of time. At this rate, she'd never be able to shake the guy.

"You can really get this there by tomorrow afternoon?" Sasha asked, handing the postcard and a fifty-dollar bill to the pimply young man behind the counter.

"Yes, ma'am," the kid said, staring at the cash as if it were a brick of weed. "It'll arrive first thing. I'll mail it out express. Promise."

"Thanks." Sasha hurried out of the rest stop, climbed into her truck. Dante looked over at her and smiled like they were best buds, and she snarled. "I'm surprised you didn't take off."

"Nah. I'm looking forward to this."

"Yeah, right," Sasha muttered. "I bet you just can't wait to see my mother again."

"Not that." Dante sat up tall, damn near bouncing in his seat. "This. Getting to know you."

The gleam in Dante's eyes almost looked real, sincere, which pulled a snicker from Sasha's mouth. As if she'd fall for that shit. She could see his angle from a mile off. The guy just wanted to show up with the long lost coma girl and win his woman back. "Bullshit. The only thing you're gonna know about me after this ride is how I like my joints." She pointed at the bag of weed in the center console, then to Dante. "And it's fatter than the ones you've been rolling."

"You don't need to say much for me to see you, little girl." Dante grabbed the bag of weed, started breaking out a joint. "For instance, I now know you hide behind pot when things get uncomfortable, instead of facing your issues head-on."

"Ah, no." Sasha snatched the freshly rolled joint, which still verged on the skinny side. "I'm trying to smoke myself stupid so I can forget you're my father."

A chuckle flowed from Dante's lips. He held out his zippo, lighting it for Sasha, and she pushed his arm away.

"I'm good," she grumbled, whipping out her own lighter.

"You're so much like your mother."

The thought turned Sasha's stomach. She had never met another person as amazing as her mother, but she never wanted to be like that heartless bitch. "I'm the complete opposite of my mother."

"Still hopping between your trucker brothers, huh?" Dante asked, though it was more of a statement than a question.

"No." Sasha hurled Dante a sharp glare.

"You're married to one, and you just fucked the other in the back of this truck."

"You don't even know what you're talking about. You sound like a fucking idiot."

Dante turned in his seat to stare at Sasha. "Your mother bounced between two men, for a long time. Even after one of those men died, she still couldn't choose."

"The man you killed, Charles Ashby—my real father—was the only man my mother ever truly loved. He was the only man she ever trusted. That's why she didn't run off into the sunset with you." Sasha veered her cold stare to Dante. "She might lust after you, but you murdered her one true love. *You* took away her ability to love."

Sorrow claimed Dante's face, twisted it from one of a demon to the fragile old man he actually was. It felt worse than Sasha expected to break him down. She didn't really know Dante, whether he deserved her venomous words. It did seem like he cared for her, those few times he blew through her life and ripped them to shreds.

"You gonna smoke that to your head?" Dante asked, pointing at the joint between Sasha's fingers, which no longer trailed a stream of smoke.

She should make Dante watch her enjoy this doobie solo. If she were a rude motherfucker she could, but she wasn't, so she passed the joint to Dante.

Chapter Thirteen

"I'm hungry," Dante said, shifting loudly in his seat.

Sasha glanced across the semi's wide cab at the man-child practically stomping his feet on the floor mats. This was exactly what she needed, because the morning's vicious rays just weren't enough to fully grate her nerves.

"There's a rest stop a few miles up," Sasha said, trying to rub the exhaustion from her eyes. Either she was getting too old for a ten-hour run, or the massive amounts of drugs she'd pumped into her body the last few months had done some real damage. "You can run in and get a breakfast sandwich." And maybe she'd sneak in a quick power nap.

"No," Dante said in a sarcastic chuckle. "I'm a big man, I need a big breakfast. Take the next exit. There's a diner right off the ramp."

"I'm not pulling off the highway. We're only two hours away."

"Did Dez open a full-service restaurant on your mountain?" Dante glared at Sasha with his stupid man-child expression, and a slew of jumbled obscenities erupted from her mouth.

"I didn't think so," Dante said, pointing at the exit ramp. "Pull off here."

Sasha couldn't put up with this shit for the next two hours, let alone two more minutes. She steered the rig off the highway, fishing out her wallet at the toll booth. "I'm guessing I'll be springing for this entire trip."

A light shrug lifted Dante's wide shoulders, and a grin spread across his lips. "The Mexicans took my wallet."

***

Dez

Just like every morning, Tyler had to run like a chicken with its head cut off to catch the school bus in time. Once the wide yellow backdoor drove from sight, Dez headed back toward the big house. His boy was smart as a whip, yet couldn't figure out time management for shit. Just like Vinny.

A chill nipped at Dez's spine. He shook it off, walking past the ghostly clubhouse and up the hill. The bigger Tyler got, the more he acted like his real father. Soon, his boy would be old enough to realize he wasn't really *his* boy. Tyler belonged to Sasha and Vinny. Dez was just clinging to the two people he loved most through that child, trying to get back what he'd pushed away.

Just as Dez climbed up the porch steps of the big house, the front door flew open. Jeri hurried out of the house, tucking her rumpled top into her crooked skirt.

"I gotta scoot, babe." She dropped her heels onto the wooden planks, slipped her feet inside.

Dez stepped behind Jeri. He pulled her shirt free to slide his hands underneath it. "You still got time."

"I have to run home and change before work." Jeri glanced over her shoulder, which separated Dez's lips from her skin. "I wore this yesterday."

"Call out sick." Dez pinched Jeri's nipple, and her knees quaked. He slipped his hand under the front of her skirt, snuck his fingers between her legs, and a moan flowed from her lips. "You feel hot. There's no way you can work in these conditions." He glided his finger deeper inside the woman who wriggled in his clutch, bringing a quiver to her entire body. Jeri wouldn't be leaving now, not until she came at least five more times.

"Yeah," Jeri said with a bit of a pant. "I got a few sick days."

Dez snickered. He sure did love getting his way. Jeri spun to face him, locked onto his lips. He gripped onto her ass, backed her into the house, and kicked the front door shut.

***

Sasha

Not five feet from Sasha, a waitress dropped her

tray. The woman's skirt rode up her thigh, higher as she reached for the scatter of silverware. It was damn near painful, but Sasha forced her stare dead ahead. Across her sticky table, beyond her untouched stack of hotcakes, Dante stuffed his face. It was totally worth the stop. She'd found Dante's off switch. With a mouthful of omelet, the man couldn't talk to her.

"Not hungry?" Dante said between chops, proving Sasha wrong once again.

Hungry was a thing Sasha doubted she'd ever be again. Her stomach hadn't stopped burning, ripping, churning since…she didn't remember when.

"How long you been clean?" Dante asked in a tone that a gullible asshole would mistake as concern.

Sasha glared over the steaming cup of coffee in her hand, wishing her thoughts were strong enough to maim. "Why?"

"You're pretty pale." Dante pointed the fork in his hand Sasha's way. "And your fingers haven't stopped shaking since we left Fat Tonys."

Not one word passed Sasha's lips. She assumed her death-stares would be enough to say how she felt about this topic.

"I would guess," Dante said, nibbling on toast, "two, three days."

"What the fuck do you care?" Sasha banged her mug of coffee on the table. "Mind your own business."

Dante pushed his plate aside. He leaned back in the booth, lit a cigarette. "Why'd you do it, turn to the needle?"

"Are you serious? You saw where I was, what they did to me."

"I'm sorry your face got marked up," Dante said, a slight tremble cracking his voice. "But my entire body looks like that. The old bat cut me everywhere." His fingers balled into a fist, which shook under its own tight grip. "Everywhere. To me, the poison she put into my veins was worse than all the other shit she shoved inside my body. I enjoy thinking, feeling, even if it's pain."

Sasha wrapped her arms around herself, but she couldn't stop the twitch of her shoulders. She wasn't scared, nervous, ashamed. It was the taste. The sticky, sweet, metallic flavor that hit the back of her throat when she booted up rushed in for the briefest of seconds. What a tease, to have it roll on her tongue only to vanish without a trace. She wanted more. How she hated herself for wanting it more.

"It was the eyes," Sasha said, pulling her leather jacket closed tight. "I couldn't get the old woman's eyes out of my head. She was always staring at me, in my sleep, around every corner on every street. Heroin made it go away. People could touch me, and I wouldn't flinch. I could smile."

Dante slid around the booth, closer to Sasha. The moment his hand landed on her leg, a yelp flew from her mouth. She shoved Dante away and jumped up from the table.

"Breakfast is over," she said through gritted teeth. "Let's go."

***

145

Vinny

Eleven in the morning, and the lobby of Fat Tonys was bustling. It wasn't fancy city folk who rushed around the bar and hovered over tables. It was the staff. They polished, vacuumed, set the restaurant as if it were a stage, and they did all that without bumping into Vinny once.

"Mr. Archer," the hostess called out, hurrying in front of Vinny. "I have the mail, and the menu needs to be approved, but Mr. Lazzari isn't in yet."

"Really?" Vinny moved toward the bar, peeked up the small stairs to find an empty table. "Enzo?"

"Mr. Deluca isn't here either," the woman said, her tone rising to the verge of whiny.

"Here." Vinny grabbed the stack of mail from the woman's hand, allowing her overflowing cleavage to fully shine. "I'll take care of all this shit." He signed the sample menu, handed it back to the woman, then headed for the backroom. What he found inside the private office when opening the door not only shocked him still, but royally pissed him off. Otis, Enzo, and Kev sat around the long glass coffee table, drinking whiskey and snorting lines of cocaine.

"Assholes!" Vinny slammed the door shut behind him and walked toward the desk. "Y'all been up all night doing coke without me?"

"You're no fun," Otis said, sprinkling some powder into a joint. "You would've brought us all down."

Kev snorted a line, then glanced at Vinny. "Sorry, man. I was gonna call you, but Otis pulled a gun on me."

Chuckles rang out, and Vinny dropped the mail onto the desk. A glossy postcard caught his eye, its bright colors gleaming beneath a stack of white envelopes. He pushed the papers aside to see big bubble letters atop a long sandy beach. "Greetings from Maryland," he mumbled to himself, picking up the postcard.

"You're here now," Enzo said, holding out a silver straw. "Come take a hit."

Vinny walked toward the men sitting on the floor, flipping over the postcard. His steps froze at the sight of Sasha's sloppy handwriting, and his heart jumped into his throat.

I hope you like postcards, motherfucker. 'Cause I'm sending them every day to make up for the one I didn't send last year.

A chuckle slipped from Vinny's grasp before his lungs locked up on him. His body ached without Sasha to touch it. All his thoughts spiraled to the worst-case scenario in her absence, but this little square piece of paper helped calm his nerves.

"What did Sasha have to say?" Otis asked, snapping Vinny from a daydream of Sasha's wavy black hair running along his chest.

"What?" Vinny tucked the postcard into his inside pocket, close to his heart.

"That postcard," Otis said, holding out a joint. "It's from Sasha."

"How do you know that?" Vinny took the joint and knelt beside Kev to cut out a line.

"Your face." Otis leaned on the table, practically chewing on a smirk. "You act like a love-sick little bitch when it comes to that girl."

"Fuck you," Vinny said, grabbing the straw from Enzo. For that comment, he was going to keep the cocaine-laced doobie Otis just handed him.

"But seriously," Enzo said, turning to face Vinny. "What did she say? It could be code."

"No. This one was just for me."

"This one?" Otis asked.

"She'll be sending more postcards," Vinny said, leaning down to tackle his thick line.

***

Dez

Sunlight beamed through the bedroom window, warming Dez's bare chest. He rolled onto his side in bed and pulled Jeri close. Her naked body felt like silk against his own. It was a surprise how her soft skin spawned tingles in his fingertips, how perfect her curves fit with his body. He had thought only one woman could affect him that way, but he'd been wrong.

"You should bring some of your shit here," he said, kissing the back of her neck.

Jeri squirmed. The sheet slid down, releasing her beautiful breasts, and Dez couldn't help but wrap his lips around her hard nipple.

"You want me to bring my shit here?" Jeri asked, twisting her fingers into Dez's hair.

Dez ripped the sheet off Jeri, which pulled a soft

giggle from her pouty lips. "Yeah." He maneuvered between Jeri's legs, kissing her stomach. "So you don't have to go all the way home before work when you crash here."

"Really?" Jeri hiked her legs on Dez's shoulders, squeezing his cheeks with her thighs.

The whistle of a diesel engine echoed off the hills outside the bedroom window. Dez sat up straight, and Jeri's legs fell to either side of him. He looked out the window. His heart jumped into his throat at the sight of steel exhaust pipes peeking above the bare trees.

"Fuck." Dez jumped out of bed, grabbed his pants.

"Is it the bus?" Jeri asked, reaching for her top.

Dez glanced at the clock, but only for a split-second. His gaze was fastened on the window, breath choked out by the whoosh of air brakes.

"No," he muttered. "It's still early."

A steel grill glinted in the sunlight as the old black International pulled into the lot. "I think it's my brother," Dez said. It had to be Vinny, which meant Sasha actually was dead. Why else would his brother come home, sporting that ride?

"Your brother?" Jeri hurried to dress, stopped in front of the mirror to smooth down her hair. "I look gross."

"Just give me a minute." Dez shoved his feet into his boots, left Jeri wide-eyed in the middle of the room as he hurried out the bedroom door.

Chapter Fourteen

Sasha

A mini cyclone whirled in Sasha's stomach as she drove past the rusted, weathered sign for Ashby Trucking. The cyclone warped into a twister of razorblades when she parked across from the clubhouse. It had been so long since she pulled a rig onto this lot. She expected it to feel better, like she'd finally found her way home, but only dread stirred in her chest. This place was empty, lonely, rotting away. It was just like her. Only, it didn't feel like the place she was meant to be.

Sasha looked at Dante, who slumped in the passenger seat. His stare lingered on the clubhouse, a half-frown stuck on his lips.

"I should've went along with Ellen's plan," he said, almost to himself. "We'd all be in there right now, chillin'."

"No, we wouldn't," Sasha said with a sneer. Except they probably would be: her mother, Candy, all of them. She wanted to strangle the life from Dante for fucking her world to shit. Instead, she gripped onto her door handle and squeezed.

"Do *not* get out of this truck." Sasha wagged her finger Dante's way then opened her door. His grumbles followed her as she climbed down the running board, only stopping once she slammed the door shut.

She walked to the middle of the lot, which seemed to be as far as her legs were willing to go. She'd been dreaming of a hug from Tyler. Dreams were awesome; they were warm and comforting. Reality fucking sucked. Never had she been so scared. Beatings, callous insults, even bullets she could take, but the fear of being rejected by her son was damn near crippling.

Her gaze veered to the clubhouse. She should just run in there, pillage her mother's desk, and leave. Only, she'd already been spotted. The front door to the big house creaked open, and shivers ran beneath Sasha's skin.

Dez hurried down the porch steps, took one look at Sasha, and stopped short in a skid of dust. His jaw dropped, eyes wide. It looked like the dude just saw a real-life monster, especially with the way he crept toward her. He probably forgot how shredded her face was. The lines of puffy, red skin running along her cheeks sure did surprise the fuck out of her every time she walked past a mirror.

"Hey," she said in a bit of a croak, since her throat decided to close up. "I'm sorry to—"

"I ain't got no money," Dez said, crossing his arms.

By the leer in Dez's eye, Sasha wasn't sure if he'd hug her or hit her. The way his face fought between a smile and a frown, how his entire body quaked except his balled fists sent off some seriously mixed signals.

"Umm, okay." Sasha shrugged, reached for her wallet. "How much you need?"

Dez took a step backward, shook loose his tights fists. "What the fuck do you want?" He peeked around her shoulder, looking into the semi's cab. "Who's in there?"

"Right." Sasha scratched her head, which apparently was full of rocks. She should've prepared for this conversation, maybe wrote a speech. There were a lot of topics to cover, and she had very little time to get through all that shit. Dez would most likely flip out instead of trying to process the fiasco that was her life. She really should've called first.

"Dante's in the—"

Dez shoved Sasha aside, stomping toward the truck. The muscles along his arms flexed beneath his tight t-shirt as he pounded his fist against his palm.

"Stop!" Sasha pulled Dez's arm, pushed his chest, but it was like trying to slow a rock slide.

Dante opened his door, climbed onto the running board. "What's up, *mother* fucker?" A wicked grin spread across Dante's lips as he jumped to the gravel, holding his hands out at his sides.

"Please, Dez." Sasha jumped between the two raging men. Her back pressed against Dante's chest, and she cringed. There was nothing she'd enjoy more than letting Dez loose, but Dante would be completely useless with a shattered face.

"I need him," Sasha said, clinging to Dez's arm. "To find my mother."

That broke Dez's glower, replaced it with shock. He staggered back a step, stared at Sasha as if she were insane. "Your mother's dead."

"Yeah. The same way I was dead."

"Dez?" a woman called out, and the shock in Dez's eyes deepened.

Sasha followed the silky voice to the blonde bombshell on her mother's front porch. She didn't know whether to be jealous or pissed. The bitch was hot. Perfect tits, tight waist, and no scatter of scars on her creamy skin.

"That your woman?" Sasha asked, her gaze still caught on the timid woman who twirled her long, golden hair.

Guilt took Dez's stare down. He rubbed his forehead, muttered some shit about timing.

"That's cool." Somehow, Sasha managed to keep her voice from quaking and her chin high. "I got something going with Vinny anyway."

"Of course you do." Dez stepped so close to Sasha his wide body blocked out the sun, which allowed his electric eyes to shine. "What, you wait fifteen whole minutes after I left to fuck him?"

"She needed a real man," Dante said, and Dez's face turned beet-red.

Dez swung his fist over Sasha's head. She ducked, Dante jumped to the side, and Dez's knuckles slammed against the side of the semi.

"Woo-hoo!" Dante chuckled, slapped his hands

together. "That's why my little girl's fucking your little brother. You're a goddamn animal."

Sasha knew what was coming next. She tried to stop Dez from charging, but he pushed her, hard. Her ass hit gravel just as Dez tackled Dante. She sat on the cold ground, watching the two men roll across the lot while hurling punches at each other. Grunts and the sound of knuckles cracking bones echoed over Dez's new woman's screams.

The dumb broad ran toward Dez, reached for his swinging fist, and Sasha jumped to her feet. She took the woman by the arm, as gentle as possible, and pulled her back.

"You don't wanna get tangled in that mess, doll."

"They're gonna kill each other," the chick screeched as a stream of blood flew into the air from the ball of testosterone on the ground. "Tyler's bus is coming up the hill."

"Fuck." Sasha pulled her gun from its holster, stepped away from the now crying woman, and fired a shot off above her head.

The loud bang stopped both Dez and Dante mid-swing, just in time for the squeal of brakes to ring out from the road.

"Shit." Dez hobbled to his feet, stifling a groan. "It's a fucking half-day." He backed away from Dante, wiped the blood from his cheek and lips.

A bright yellow school bus stopped beside the front gate just as Dante jumped to his feet. The man rocked in place, ready to lunge at Dez, and Sasha aimed her gun right at Dante's face.

"Get the fuck back in the truck." Her stare

must've reflected the murderous thoughts in her mind, because Dante backed away.

Her goddamn devil of a father climbed into the semi, and Sasha holstered her gun before Tyler could hop off the bottom step of the bus.

Dez turned his glare to Sasha, like she was next in line for a beating. "I swear to fucking Christ, if you do anything—"

"I'm not gonna hurt my son," Sasha said, and Dez's woman gasped. Sasha stared at the chick, more like her overflowing cleavage. "That's right, sweetheart. I'm his wife."

"Ex," Dez all but hissed.

"Did you forge my signature on divorce papers and forget to tell me? It would be fitting, since that's how you got me to marry you."

"Mommy," Tyler yelled, running toward Sasha.

Sasha knelt down, and Tyler crashed against her chest. His weight took her back, and her ass hit gravel once again. Except this time, she didn't grumble. She smiled, wider than she thought possible, as she wrapped her boy in a tight hug.

"God, I missed you," she said, soaking in the warmest embrace she'd ever experienced.

"I knew you'd come for me." Tyler wiggled out of Sasha's clutch. He planted his little hands on his hips, and he looked up at Dez's woman. "I'm sorry, Jeri. My mama's here now, so you're gonna have to go."

Sasha had to literally bite her tongue to keep from laughing out loud. Goddamn, she loved that tiny dude.

"Tyler," Dez barked, his sharp tone making

Tyler's body flinch.

"That's not nice, little man." Sasha climbed off the ground, brushing dirt from her pants. "I think your pa really likes…what was it? *Jeri*."

"Apologize," Dez said to Tyler, pointing at the woman who was slowly backing away.

"No," Jeri said, waving her hands. "He doesn't have to—"

"Sorry, Jeri," Tyler said in a long, drawn out tone.

"No worries, buddy." Jeri rubbed the sides of her arms, looking at the sedan parked out front of the big house. "I should go."

"No." Dez took Jeri by the hand, pulled her close to his side. "Stay."

Sasha looked away. She might not want Dez's hands on her body, but she damn sure didn't want to see them comforting some other bitch.

"I'll go," Sasha muttered, keeping her gaze low.

"You just got here," Tyler cried out, tugging on Sasha's arm. "Please, Mommy, take me with you."

"You want to come back to New York with me?"

"Sasha," Dez said with a groan, narrowing his glare.

This wasn't the time for a throw-down. Dez was already riled up, and Sasha had a wild goose-chase to continue. She bent down, looked Tyler in the eyes. "I have to go find my mama. But when I'm done, I'll come back for you."

Tyler pouted, and Dez sneered at Sasha as if *she* were the bad guy.

"But I can come by for dinner tonight," Sasha said, smiling back at Dez. It was rude to invite herself to dinner, but she didn't give a fuck. This was her property, Dez was crashing in her house, and she really missed her kid.

Tyler jumped up and down, clapping, which made landing a kiss on the kid's cheek nearly impossible for Sasha. She latched onto Tyler's shoulders, which slowed his excited hop. "I'm gonna run into town, grab a room, get cleaned up. I'll see you around six."

"Love ya, Mommy." After planting a kiss on Sasha's lips, Tyler took off up the hill toward the house.

"I'll, umm…" Jeri wiggled out from under Dez's arm, walked backward up the hill, "keep an eye on him."

"I hope to see you tonight," Sasha called out as Jeri scurried toward the house.

"Why?" Dez stepped in front of Sasha, cutting off her view of the woman's ass shifting beneath her tight skirt. "You wanna steal my kid and my woman?"

"This bitch is alone with my son. For all I know, she's tying him up and throwing him in a closet right now."

Dez let out a condescending snicker. "She's not from your family. She wouldn't do something like that."

The words hit like a backhand, actually took Sasha into a slump. She had a good comeback, a few in fact, but was far too drained to argue. Dez let out a roar, his fingers clenched.

"Dammit, Sasha. Every time shit gets good for me, you breeze in and blow it all to Hell."

"I know." Sasha lowered her head into her hands, but it did nothing to help the whirl of her mind. She loved Dez, wanted him to be happy. The type of girl he needed to feel whole, she could never be. It wouldn't be fair to keep him on the hook just to appease her own twisted desires.

"I'm sorry." She looked up into Dez's eyes, and his stiff body wilted. "I swear. I won't blow your shit to Hell."

Dez turned his back on Sasha. "You already are." He walked up the hill, blending into the big house's shadow, and Sasha headed for her truck.

***

The front office of the motel had an array of postcards, though none resembled Sasha's holler. She grabbed the only one with tree-lined mountains, dropped a hundred on the counter, and took her key.

Dante was leaning against the semi's grill, tapping his foot as Sasha walked from the office. He smiled at her, splitting his newly busted lip, and she snarled.

"What the fuck is wrong with you?" she yelled, heading for her room. Once inside, she considered slamming the door in Dante's face and locking him out. Except the only thing that douchebag would do while unattended is cause more trouble for her.

"I don't like your old man," Dante said, following Sasha into the small room. He shut the door, plopped onto the only bed, and stretched out. The fucker better enjoy that soft mattress, since this would be the only time he'd spend atop it.

Sasha strained to keep her rage in check. She sat at the small desk, writing to Vinny. It was either now or later from prison, after she got arrested for murdering the fuck out of Dante.

"The guy forced you into marriage," Dante went on, as if anybody was listening. "Turned you into a junkie, stole your property. Now he's got some bimbo playing mom to your kid. I'd kill him if you'd let me."

"What the fuck do you care?" Sasha slammed her pen onto the desk and turned to glare at Dante. "Don't you have your own family to torment? Oh right, you killed them all."

Dante sat up on the bed, stared into Sasha's eyes. "Not all of them."

"I ain't your family, fucking psycho."

"My grandson is goddamn cute as shit." Dante settled back against the pillow, hiking his hands behind his head. "He's got your spunk. Did you ever figure out who the father is?" He paused, waiting for an answer he knew wouldn't come. "No way it's the ape. Tyler is already smarter than that guy."

The sound of Tyler's name slithering from Dante's mouth made Sasha want to vomit. Her fingers wrapped around the butt of her holstered gun. She could kneecap the fucker. In fact, she didn't even really need Dante anymore.

Sasha jumped to her feet, and Dante flinched. Of all the people that man had encountered, she was the only one to strike fear in his gaze. She had to be his kryptonite. No matter what she did to Dante, he couldn't hurt her. Such a weakness must scare the shit out of the man, a thought that brought an overwhelming fluster of joy to Sasha's heart.

A laugh burst from her mouth. She grabbed her postcard and pen then headed for the door.

"Where you going?" Dante asked, moving to the edge of the bed.

"Don't fucking go nowhere." Sasha forced her grin into a glower. "And get the fuck off my bed."

Chapter Fifteen

A light grip clutched onto Sasha, shook her from a deep sleep. She opened her eyes, and there was Dante's face. Her hand flew to the knife on her belt. In seconds flat, she had the blade out and pressed against Dante's neck.

"It's me, little girl," Dante said, raising his hands.

Sasha shoved Dante, scooted away from him. "Why the fuck are you touching me?"

"It's five. You told me to wake you."

The knife stayed in Sasha's hand as she climbed off the bed. "Don't fucking touch me."

"Sorry." Dante lit two cigarettes, held one out for Sasha. "I haven't been able to let anybody touch me either, especially when my eyes are closed."

Sasha took the cigarette from in-between Dante's fingers. Her icy glare melted as shame painted Dante's face.

"Everybody's hands feel like that old bat's hands," he said, staring off into the corner.

161

"Calloused, rough. I think…with Ellen it'll be different. Her hands are a part of me."

Tears welled in Sasha's eyes, mostly because she was disgusted with herself for wanting to hug Dante. She understood the man's pain so well. Vinny was her anchor, the only person whose touch could soothe her soul. She'd do anything to wrap herself in that touch right now. Just as Dante would walk through fire to find Ellen.

"I'm glad you showered," Sasha said, grabbing her backpack. "You're coming to dinner with me."

"Nice. I'm dying to hang with that kid."

"Don't ever fucking talk to my son." Sasha pointed a stern finger before shutting herself inside the bathroom and turning on the shower.

***

Dez

Jeri paced in front of the oven, checking the roast for the ninth time.

"It's fine," Dez said. He walked behind Jeri and wrapped his arms around her. She didn't collapse against his chest like normal. Her shoulders remained stiff, tense.

"Sasha eats with her hands," he whispered into the back of Jeri's neck. "She's not gonna care."

"I care." Jeri turned to face Dez. One glimpse of his half-smirk, and she was putty in his hands. "I shouldn't care," she said after a long exhale. "It's just…Tyler already hates me. I'm screwed no matter what. If I outdo Sasha, I'm evil. If I can't be

162

as cool as her, I'm a loser."

Dez chuckled. He gripped onto Jeri's hips, backed her against the counter. "You can be my sexy, evil loser."

A smile broke Jeri's pout, and she leaned in to kiss Dez. Before he could slip his tongue into her mouth, a diesel engine's rumble rattled every glass in the cupboard.

The stiffness returned to Jeri's shoulders, and she stood up straight. "Oh God. She's here."

"Relax." Dez slapped Jeri on the ass, pulling a yelp then a giggle from her mouth. "This is your shit now."

"Right." Jeri shook her head, her brow scrunched. "My shit?"

***

Sasha

A fiery pound clutched Sasha's heart, harder the closer she walked toward the big house. She climbed the porch steps, glancing at Dante. The guy looked semi-civil. His hair was combed, and his face looked slightly less beaten when cleaned. It wasn't Dez's tantrum that left the shiner, cuts, and bruises on Dante's face. The man spent a month as a punching bag for the Los Lobos. He was damn lucky to still have both eyes. The way Dante stared at her, with such gratitude, told her he knew that fact as well as she did.

"Please," she said, spinning to face Dante. "*Please* don't run your mouth."

Dante lifted his hands, palms out, as if pleading innocence. "I'm on my best behavior."

The front door creaked open, and Dez growled. He stepped onto the porch and crossed his arms, which completely blocked the doorway. "I can't believe you brought him."

"I couldn't leave him at the motel. He'd take off, burn the town to cinders."

"You could've cuffed him to your steering wheel."

Sasha looked at her truck, then back at Dez. "I guess. You got any handcuffs?"

"Mommy!" Tyler pushed past Dez and hugged Sasha. "Who's this?" he asked, pointing at Dante.

"I'm your grandpa," Dante said in a rush, glancing at Sasha.

"You motherfucker," Sasha muttered beneath her breath.

"I have a grandpa," Tyler practically yelled. He took Dante by the hand, and both Sasha and Dez lunged forward.

"No." Sasha jammed her elbow into Dante's side, right in the kidney, as Dez pulled Tyler away. "What the fuck did I tell you about talking to my kid?" she whispered to Dante.

"I forgot," he said, attempting to flash a charming grin.

"He looks like your daddy," Tyler said, staring at Dante.

"He is." Disgust cracked Sasha's voice, and her shoulders fell into a cringe at the omission of her relation to Dante. "But don't touch him, or talk to him. He's a biker. I wouldn't want his douchery rubbing off on you."

"Oh." Tyler took Sasha by the hand, leading her into the house. "Is your mama a biker too?"

"Ew, no." Sasha picked Tyler up, which almost broke her back. She pointed at the picture on the wall of her mother climbing into the old black truck. "That's my mama, right there."

"I thought that was you," Tyler said, looking between Sasha and the photo.

Sasha set Tyler's feet back to the floor, but her muscles continued to burn. "Nah. I was inside her belly in that picture."

Dante ran his finger along the picture, and Dez grabbed his arm.

"Don't touch my shit," Dez said through gritted teeth.

A glare that could shatter bones filled Dante's eyes, but he didn't budge. Except to slowly back away.

"Don't be rude, Daddy. You gotta share." Tyler waved Dante forward. "Come on, mister. I'll show you my guitar."

Dante looked at Sasha, and Sasha looked at Dez.

"Just go get it," Dez said. "Bring it down here."

"Okay," Tyler said, running up the stairs.

Sasha peeked into the living room just as Jeri strolled from the kitchen. The woman stripped off a white apron, smoothed down her sundress, and floated to Dez's side.

The chuckle came too fast for Sasha to stop. This beauty pageant priss standing next to the big-bad trucker was just too comical.

"Is it my hair?" Jeri asked, glancing in the hall

mirror.

Dez narrowed his glare on Sasha. "She's probably just really stoned."

"I am really stoned." Sasha leaned close to Jeri, eyeing the perfect fit of the woman's cutesy dress. "And you look lovely, doll."

"Thanks." Jeri inched closer to Dez, clinging to his arm. The woman did that thing where her stare flashed to Sasha's scars then quickly away. Her mouth opened to pose the dreaded question, then quickly clamped shut. Every person Sasha met did that now. She should just get t-shirts made saying *"They're torture marks"* with an arrow pointing to her face.

"Can I get you a drink?" Jeri asked, finally looking Sasha in the eyes.

"Yes, please," Sasha said. She leaned against the threshold of the living room to watch Jeri's ass sway as she headed back into the kitchen.

"Wine?" Jeri asked over her shoulder.

"Beer, if you have it."

Once Jeri disappeared into the kitchen, Sasha let out a snicker. "Just, wow. *That's* the kind of woman you like?" Sasha chewed back her grin as she stared at Dez. "She's so…Suzie-Q."

Dez grumbled, held his hand out to the living room. "Come inside, insult all my shit."

Sasha walked into the living room and plopped onto the couch. Like a Pitbull, Dante stayed in the doorway, which meant Dez had to keep at the ready in the center of the room.

Glass bottles clinked, high-heels tapped tile, and Jeri pranced back into the living room with three beers. Sasha and Dez got their bottle with a smile, but not Dante. Jeri stood a full arm's length from the man, stretched out to offer the beer.

"I didn't get your name earlier," Jeri said, yanking her hand away once Dante took the bottle. "When you were wrestling around."

Before Dez could cock a fist, Dante sprung forward and took Jeri by the hand. "Dante," he said, his grin coming off naughtier than his flirty tone.

"No touching," Sasha said, downing half her beer. She had to get a nice buzz going before the fighting commenced.

Dante released Jeri, who scurried beside Dez. The way Dez's jaw clenched, the low growl rumbling his throat turned Sasha on so much more than it should. That wasn't her man, not anymore. And besides, if she had her choice she'd rather fuck Jeri.

Tyler bulldozed his way into the room. The neck of the large guitar strapped around his small chest bashed the wall, then teetered a lamp as Tyler hurried in front of Dante. "Here it is, grandpa."

"He's not your grandpa," Dez barked.

Dante knelt down, strummed a few strings on the guitar. "Nice axe, a strat."

"Do you play?" Tyler asked, holding the guitar out for Dante.

"Yeah, man." Dante took the guitar and Tyler ran to flip on a small amp.

Tyler plugged the guitar in, jumping from the loud crackle that erupted from the speaker. "Play me some Slayer."

Dante chuckled as he pulled the pick from

beneath the strings. "How 'bout Hendrix?"

Sasha gawked as Dante played a damn near perfect rendition of Voodoo Child. To see the man create spine-tingling melodies while smiling and singing to Tyler was surreal. In this moment, he didn't look like the man Sasha wanted to carve into pieces. With his hands strumming out beautiful music, and a softness in his dark stare, Dante actually looked…cool.

Shivers ran down Sasha's spine, followed by a wave of revulsion. She finished her beer in one gulp, then hurried into the kitchen for another.

***

Vinny

The door to the backroom opened, and four young women dressed in trench coats walked in.

"All right," Otis said, shoving Kev off the couch. "Now the party can begin." He rubbed his hands together, eyeing up the gorgeous ladies. "Cinnamon, you're with me."

The black girl wiggled out of her jacket, revealing a long stretch of bare skin. Vinny watched her round ass jiggle as she pranced toward Otis, dropping into his lap. Enzo and Kev argued over the sexy brunette, who Vinny knew from personal experience was a cold fish in the sack. In fact, the only one of the First Premier Escorts he hadn't fucked was the blonde, who was staring at him.

"Hey there," the blonde said, strolling in front of Vinny. She opened the flap of her coat, practically shoving her huge, perky, totally suckable tits in his face.

"No thanks, honey." Vinny backed away from the chick.

"What's this now?" Otis asked, looking up from the woman in his lap.

All eyes steered to Vinny, even the naked women who'd draped themselves over his buddies. Each stare held a different level of confusion, from the self-conscious to the clueless variety.

"I…umm." Vinny cringed. There was nothing he could say right now that wouldn't make him sound like a pussy.

"Sasha took your balls with her, huh?" Enzo teased, and Otis busted out laughing.

Vinny held up his middle finger, spanning the room of chuckling fools. "Fuck you all."

The blonde closed her trench coat, leaned close to Vinny. "You got a girlfriend?" she whispered.

As badly as Vinny wanted to shout out *Hell yeah,* the words wouldn't scrape past his throat. He'd never been happier. The girl of his dreams finally wanted him, but the relationship shit was different. He probably should've asked if he could fuck escorts while Sasha was gone, though he probably would've gotten slugged.

"It's cool," the blonde said, with a genuine smile. She sat in the chair beside the desk and grabbed a pack of cards. "We can play rummy."

"Awesome." Vinny scooped up a pile of blow from the coffee table, along with a handful of weed, and settled in behind the desk. "You deal, I'll roll."

***

Sasha

The pot roast was fucking delicious and held the mystical ability to spread a sense of irrelevance throughout Sasha. She'd never used the oven, except to reheat pizza, and it didn't come out looking like the spread on the table in front of her. Hidden behind a large bowl of smashed potatoes, blocked in by a tower of homemade buttermilk biscuits, Sasha watched Dez flirt with a Stepford Wife. It made her feel like a child. The six beers she downed definitely wasn't helping that matter.

"So, school," Sasha said, looking at Tyler. "How you liking that?"

"I don't know." Tyler pushed the meat around on his plate. "Uncle Otis got me into a special school, back in the city. I was gonna have music studies after math, but now I'm here."

"Your uncle Otis is a cool guy," Dante said, helping himself to a second plate.

Tyler dropped his fork, sat up straight. "You know my uncle?"

"Yeah. We call ourselves cousins, 'cause we're so close in age, but Otis is actually my—"

Sasha waved her steak knife Dante's way. "The lip," she grumbled.

"I miss my uncles," Tyler said, so softly it barely made a peep. "My home."

Dez reached over Jeri, taking Tyler's hand. "This is your home." He tried to sound comforting, but the statement came out fake as hell. The image, though, of a legitimate mom and dad seemed right for Tyler. It was a far better picture than the scuzzy thug section at her end of the table.

"I'm gonna grab another beer," Sasha said, rising from her chair.

Jeri jumped to her feet. "I'll get that for you."

"It's cool. I know where it is." The words sounded cocky. It wasn't what Sasha intended, but she really didn't give a shit.

Once inside the kitchen, Sasha didn't stop at the fridge. She walked into the corner, opened the thin pantry door, and slipped inside. This little cubby had always been her hideaway. Amongst the jar-lined shelves, words couldn't sting and nobody would see her cry. How she loathed her stupid eyes for shedding tears right now. Her brain didn't care that she'd lost Dez. At least that's what she'd commanded it to think.

The overhead light clicked on, and Sasha yelped. She looked at the door, finding Dez's wide body filling the skinny frame.

"This isn't where we keep the beer," he said softly.

"I know." Sasha took a quick swipe at her eyes, then grabbed a jar of peaches. "I need these, for the road." Dez reached for her arm, and she pushed her way past him.

After grabbing a beer from the fridge, she peeked into the dining room. Jeri gathered up the abandoned plates as Dante stared at the woman's cleavage.

"Where's Tyler?" Sasha asked. She shoved the peaches in her jacket pocket and twisted off the cap to her beer.

"He has to finish his homework to get dessert. It's sort of like...a rewards thing."

Sasha nodded while taking a swig off her bottle. "That's smart."

"It was Jeri's idea," Dez said, lowering his gaze.

Of course it was that woman's idea. Jeri was goddamn perfect, in every goddamn way possible.

"I gotta get some shit out of my mother's desk, in the clubhouse," Sasha said, backing toward the doorway.

"I took all your mother's shit out of her desk."

Sasha snickered as she placed her near empty beer on the counter. "All the shit *you* knew about." She walked into the dining room, forcing a smile for Jeri as she leaned beside Dante. "Thank the nice lady for dinner. You're leaving," she whispered.

Questions filled Dante's stare, and Sasha sharpened her glower.

"Thank you, Jeri," Dante said, rising from his seat. "Dinner was awesome."

"You're leaving?"

Dante shifted his gaze to Sasha, who nodded, then looked back at Jeri. "I guess I am. It was nice meeting ya, sweetie."

"I'll be right back," Sasha said, ushering Dante toward the foyer. "Gonna walk him out."

Sasha pushed Dante out the front door and down the porch steps.

"What's up, little girl?" Dante asked, shrugging out of Sasha's grasp.

"You're done in there. I just gotta grab some shit, kiss my boy goodbye, and we're hitting the road." She stopped beside the semi, pointing at the passenger door. "You can wait in the cab."

"But—"

Her arm stretched farther, finger growing stiffer. Dante slumped, trudging toward the truck, and Sasha headed for the clubhouse.

Chapter Sixteen

The secret compartment in the top drawer looked exactly the same to Sasha. Her mother's little black book, filled with the old pickup and drop-off locations in code, sat in the exact same spot. Pictures, notes, pills and dried up weed. It wasn't any different than the other millions of times she'd snooped in her mother's hiding spot over the years. Which meant she didn't know how to find her mother. She had nothing to go on. This entire time, she honestly thought she'd find a letter in the secret spot she shared with her mother. At the very least she expected a post-it, or a motherfucking clue.

A rolling fit of rage spread out to claw every muscle in Sasha's body. She couldn't take the emptiness, not from this drawer or her weak chest. A cry burst from her lips. She ripped the drawer from the desk and flung it against the wall.

Boots thumped outside the doorway of the backroom, right before Dez walked through the threshold. He looked at the desk drawer in pieces on the floor, then at Sasha fighting to control the quake of her limbs.

"Are you clean?" he asked, narrowing his gaze.

"Of heroin, or disease?"

Dez shrank down. His nose scrunched, as if the foulest odor just wafted up his nostrils.

"Yes, Dez. I'm clean." She stepped out from behind the desk, shaking off her jitters. "How do you even know about that?"

"Enzo and Otis used to call every day, but a few days ago the calls stopped."

Sasha all but melted at the softness in Dez's gaze. His frosty blue eyes, strong arms drew her closer. "This shit with my mom has everyone fucked up."

"I bet." Dez moved toward Sasha, falling into the shadows of the dark room. "It must be crazy for you. I'm sorry I haven't been..." He slid his fingers along Sasha's hand, up her arm, to her neck.

Air rushed from Sasha's lungs, replaced by a fiery burn. Before she could think, their mouths were gliding atop one another. His kiss felt wrong, but she still ran her hands up his chest.

Dez backed Sasha against the desk, clutched onto her hips. A stabbing ache pierced her heart. Vinny's face flashed through her mind. It was him she thought about, his hands she wanted on her body. She pushed Dez away, shook her head.

"Don't," she said, to both herself and Dez.

"What?"

"If I fuck you in the backroom of our clubhouse, we'll spiral back into each other. But we want different things. We don't fit right. You'll end up miserable, and I'll end up…" Sasha couldn't say it. She didn't want to be a junkie, couldn't stomach people thinking of her in that way.

Dez grinned, caressed Sasha's cheek as if the scars weren't thumping beneath his fingertips. "You'd end up running off with a stripper."

A giggle slipped from Sasha's lips. It wasn't funny, but it was either laugh or cry, and Dez had already caught her with tears. Her time with Dez really was over. It was a bittersweet sorrow, to let each other go after all the years of clinging. They could finally have a chance at happiness; it was just sad they couldn't find it together.

"Dez?" Sasha looked up into his eyes. The man's defenses were down, which was a rare occasion. If ever there were a time to get her son back, it was now. "I wish you'd consider moving back to New York. You and Tyler can have the penthouse. You can bring Jeri if you want."

"I don't—"

"If you don't like that place, I'll buy y'all another pad. In any borough." She latched onto Dez's hand. "He needs to be with family. You both do."

"I don't know." Dez stared off into the corner, then stood up straight. "What's that?"

"Don't change the subject."

"No. For real."

Sasha followed Dez's pointed finger to the now broken drawer. Taped to the underside of the cracked wood was a folded piece of paper with Sasha's name on it.

"I knew it." Sasha dropped to her knees and tore

the letter from the drawer. A giddy sensation struck her in the chest at the sight of her mother's sharp handwriting.

"What does it say?" Dez asked, kneeling in front of Sasha.

It didn't say anything, but it meant everything. "It's coordinates," she said. "Somewhere in Mexico."

"Tyler." Jeri's panicky voice called out from afar.

By the time Sasha could jump to her feet, Dez was halfway across the clubhouse. She ran outside, sprinting after Dez up the hill.

"He's not in his room," Jeri said, meeting Dez in the middle of the lot. "And he didn't answer when I called for him."

"Dante," Sasha said, running to her truck. She looked inside, mocked by an empty cab. "Son of a bitch!"

"No," Dez muttered, running his hands through his long hair. "Tyler," he shouted into the night sky.

"I'm up here."

They all looked up at the big house to see Tyler's little head in the attic window. The kid smiled, then waved, and Sasha wanted to wring his neck.

"What are you doing up there?" Dez yelled, his voice trembling.

"Helping grandpa find my missing grandma's ring," Tyler said, as if that should be common knowledge to every person on planet Earth.

"Get downstairs, now," Dez damn near growled, and Tyler's wide eyes backed into the shadows of the window.

"I'm sorry," Jeri said, hurrying after Dez as he stormed toward the house. "I didn't know Dante came back into the house."

"It's not your fault," Sasha said, surprising Dez so much he almost tripped up the porch steps. "Dante's a sneaky fucker."

Tyler ran out the front door, and Dez scooped him up.

"Dante," Dez growled as the man walked out of the house.

"I'm going." Dante hurried past Sasha without a glance and climbed into the semi.

"Sorry," Tyler said, kicking his feet until Dez put him down. "He said it was important."

Sasha stepped onto the porch, stood in front of Tyler. "Don't punish him. It was Dante's fault."

"You gonna punish Dante?" Dez asked with that cute, devious gleam in his eyes.

"Fuck yeah. Have been this whole time."

"Good."

Sasha almost reached for Dez but forced her hands to remain at her sides. "Think about what I said, about New York."

"Call me when you get done with this crazy shit." Dez flashed a smile, which jacked up the beat of Sasha's broken heart pieces.

"You're leaving?" Tyler asked. His little voice, crammed with sorrow, shattered Sasha's broken heart pieces to dust.

"Yeah." Sasha knelt down, rubbing the sides of Tyler's arms. "I'm really gonna miss you, little man."

"You'll come back, take me to New York,

right?"

"I'm working on it." Sasha pulled Tyler close, hugging him tight. "Your mama gets shit done," she whispered, kissing her boy on the cheek.

Tyler's bright smile etched into Sasha's mind, carved away all the painful memories that lingered within. She hugged him one more time, landing another kiss. Her stomach dropped as she rose to her feet. She'd insert herself right in the middle of this happy family, bring Vinny along for the ride instead of Dante, if she didn't have a mother to punch in the face and drag home.

Jeri sprung forward, and Sasha flinched when the woman hugged her. "It was nice to meet you, Sasha."

Sasha wrapped her arms around Jeri, slid her hand to the arch of the woman's back. She pulled Jeri closer until their chests pressed together. "It was nice meeting you too, doll."

A deep shade of pink rushed in to claim Jeri's cheeks, and Sasha grinned as she backed away. She dipped her head to Dez, blew a kiss to Tyler, and headed for her truck.

***

After stopping to mail a postcard sealed inside an envelope to accommodate the polaroid of her and Tyler, Sasha was back on the highway. She glanced at the passenger seat, catching a stray grin in the passing streetlights. The smile on Dante's lips seemed unnatural, like blue bread. She preferred a frown on that asshole's face.

"I can't take you anywhere," she said, glaring at Dante.

"I could've laid the ape out on three separate occasions. My conduct was quite impressive. I'm proud of myself."

To keep from snickering at the serious tone in Dante's voice, Sasha glowered. "You got the kid in trouble."

"Fuck. Really?"

Now Dante frowned, which brought a warmth to Sasha's chest. The man should be miserable. Dante and his stupid sperm was the catalyst that kick-started the nightmarish reality called Sasha's life.

"Yeah, really. You made him sneak off, got everybody worked up, and now he's punished. You fucking suck."

Dante shifted in his seat, jaw clenching. "Dez fucking sucks. That animal has no business rearing a child."

The tremble of Dante's voice took Sasha by surprise. If she didn't know any better, she'd have sworn the guy actually gave a fuck.

"What'd you really do?" Sasha asked, glancing at Dante. "In the attic?"

Dante's leather jacket crinkled as he pulled a small felt box from his inside pocket. "It's Ellen's wedding rings." He flipped the top open. A huge diamond shimmered in the dashboard lights, resting above a white gold band with black tribal marks etched into its surface. "Our wedding." Dante tugged at the chain around his neck, pulled out a matching band.

That psycho of a man *did* have a heart. The

thought was downright terrifying, and a bit nauseating. A man with no soul was predictable, craved only death and destruction. It was the assholes that were chock-full of emotions who were really dangerous. Those guys broke every rule, burned every bridge to chase their depraved desires.

Sasha shrank down in her seat, leaned away from Dante. That motherfucker was going to get her killed. She could feel it in her bones.

"Did you find what you were looking for?" Dante asked, staring at Sasha like a junkie waiting for a fix.

"Yeah." For a split-second, Sasha considered shooting Dante in the head and kicking his corpse onto the side of the highway. Instead, she handed him the piece of paper her mother left for her. Riding with Satan was better than riding solo. Somebody had to roll the joints.

"You're slacking," Sasha said, tossing a bag of weed into Dante's lap.

Dante went straight to work, battling to break up the tight buds in the bouncy truck. The entire time he twisted the bone, his eyes stayed on the scribbles of her mother's handwriting. "It's coordinates. Where we headed?"

The *we* part of Dante's statement made Sasha cringe. "Mexico," she grumbled, glaring at the asshole who was getting harder to hate in the passenger seat.

"Why don't you let me drive for a bit?"

"Ha!" Sasha clutched onto the steering wheel, almost hugged it. This was her father's truck, her real father, and she wasn't going to let her wannabe dad drive it off a bridge. "Wield my rig," she muttered beneath her breath. "Do you even have a license?"

"No," Dante said, sneering, as if he'd been asked to solve a simple math equation. "Do you?"

Sasha sat up straight. She did have a driver's license, when she was Sasha Ashby. Sasha Lazzari never had a chance to get one before she died. And now that she was nobody, government issued IDs didn't much matter.

"Well, no," Sasha said, holding her chin high. "I don't need a license. I'm dead."

Dante handed Sasha a lit joint, clutching onto the paper with only one line of numbers on it.

"I'm gonna need that back," Sasha said, struck by the possessive glare in Dante's eyes. "Eventually."

"I can't believe she took off on me."

"What'd you do?"

"What makes you think I did anything?"

Sasha narrowed her stare, veering it to Dante.

"Ellen caught me fucking a redhead, in our bed."

A snicker pushed its way to near escape, but Sasha held it back. It must be true what they say about apples not falling far from trees. "Redheads are hard to resist."

"Right," Dante said, turning to face Sasha. "Ellen always has to have a shit-load of hot chicks around, but God forbid if you touch any of 'em."

Dante had no idea. He'd just described Sasha's entire childhood. "Did my mother ever—" She stopped herself. A stupid question, one she really didn't want to know the answer to, almost tumbled from her dumb mouth. If lady luck loved her, her words would be lost under the thump of tires on pavement.

"You want to know if your mom likes the ladies?" Dante looked at Sasha with only sincerity, and her throat loosened enough to allow for a gulp. "Not the way you do, little girl. That doesn't make you different. Some people just like both."

"I don't like both." A knot, one Sasha hadn't even known was tied, unraveled in her chest. She'd never been honest before, with anybody. The sense of freedom, of knowing her own self was better than any drug she could slam into her veins. "I'm only attracted to women."

"What about your trucker brothers?"

The tone in Dante's voice reflected only curiosity. There would be no judgement in the cab of this truck. Sasha could speak her mind, process her thoughts out loud, maybe gain a grasp on who she really was, and something told her Dante would understand.

"It's different with them. I've been with Vinny for...ever. Being with him is like being with myself, safe, fun. And Dez..." Sasha hit the roach in her tight clutch, its red-hot tip burning her fingers. "Dez is the perfect man. He's so rough but still sensitive. He has morals and actually stands by them. I never really wanted to be with him." She squirmed in her seat, in her own skin. "I wanted to *be* him."

"You shouldn't want to be other people." Dante leaned on his armrest, moving close enough for Sasha to feel his electric vibe. "You're fucking awesome just the way you are."

The nicest thing anyone had ever said to Sasha had come from the person she despised most. It kind of drained the joy from the experience.

"Coming from you," Sasha said, glancing at Dante. "That might be an insult." She pointed at the center console, and the bag of weed she knew was lost somewhere within it. "I think we need to have a serious conversation on joint etiquettes."

Chapter Seventeen

Vinny

Twenty-four hours had passed since Vinny walked through the front door of Fat Tonys. The girls were long gone, his buddies had crashed out around the spacious office, but a restless jitter ran through Vinny, keeping him wide-awake.

As quiet as a coked-out person could be, he opened the door of the backroom and slipped into the hallway. The staff buzzed around like busy bees. It was strange, like deja vu. The same people scurried across the same freshly vacuumed carpet, setting the same tables. It was almost as though an entire day hadn't been lost to a snow-blinded haze.

"Mr. Archer," the hostess said, slinking out from behind her podium.

Vinny had never noticed before, but that woman had a smoking hot figure. His fingers twitched, wanting to clutch onto the chick's hips.

"What's up, darlin'?" he asked, gripping onto his

185

belt to keep from seizing the woman who would gladly duck into a closet with him.

"This came." The hostess held out a postcard, her gaze low. "I'm pretty sure it's for you."

The postcard's glossy front gleamed in the restaurant's harsh lights, driving Vinny's pulse to race. More strange, as guilt rushed in. This postcard just had to arrive at the same time as his thoughts to bend the woman in front of him over her podium.

Vinny stood up straight, cleared the dirty thoughts from his mind, and took the postcard. "Thanks, Donna." She flashed a sweet smile before hurrying off to bark orders at the busboy.

"Kentucky," he muttered, running his finger along the picture of green mountains. He flipped the postcard over, grinning at the first sentence.

Cocksucker Dante is a motherfucking liar. You were right. He doesn't know where my mom is, but I think I can find her. Just gotta get Dez to let me in the clubhouse. I got to see the munchkin. Fuck, he got big.

A long sigh sunk Vinny's chest. He drew the postcard close, but it didn't soothe the ache that scorched within. Sasha was back at the holler, alone, with Dez. His brother would throw Sasha against a wall, and it'd be so long Vinny.

He'd see. If another postcard came, and it wasn't a Dear John letter or full of barbed insults to cover guilt, then his girl really would be his girl. Tomorrow afternoon seemed like an eternity away. Thankfully he was coming down from an extended cocaine bender, hard, and would most likely sleep through the entire wait.

Vinny pulled his shades from his inside pocket, slid them up his nose, and strolled into blinding rays of daylight.

***

Sasha

Sasha walked from the rest stop, jogging across the parking lot to her idling semi. Vinny was going to end up getting two postcards a day at this rate, but fuck him if he didn't like it. Sending those stupid little cards with their shitty pictures was the only way she could be close to him. Sure she could call him, but this was way more fun.

Dante stared Sasha down as she climbed into the cab, a stupid smirk on his face.

"What the fuck are you looking at?" Sasha asked, hardening her glare. "'Cause I can tell you what I'm looking at. Not a joint."

"You smoke too much," Dante said, even though he grabbed the bag of weed and magazine he'd been using as a tray.

"I don't know who the fuck you think *you* are." Sasha pulled back onto the highway and opened up the motor. "Telling me I smoke too much."

"*I* think I'm your father."

Before the last word could babble out of Dante's mouth, Sasha had her knife out of its sheath. She swung her arm toward the passenger seat, without looking, stopping the blade only inches from

Dante's neck.

"Now," Sasha said through clenched teeth. "Why'd you have to go and say a thing like that?"

With two fingers, Dante pushed Sasha's hand away. "All right, little girl." Once Sasha sheathed her blade, Dante continued his rambling. "I have a theory about why you're so cold to me."

"I don't want to hear it."

"I think you're so excited to be my daughter you don't know how to show it. So you act out."

"Ha." Sasha leaned close to Dante, stretched to reach his face. "Ha!" She settled back into her seat, chuckling. "You're hilarious, man. You do know I don't really need you anymore, right?"

"Please." Dante lit the freshly-rolled joint then passed it to Sasha. "Who would roll all these joints?"

A snicker erupted from Sasha's mouth. "I can roll and drive." Hell, she could roll in a pitch-black room with one hand tied behind her back. There really was no reason for Dante to be riding shotgun in her truck. The fact the man sat comfy in his seat should be an extra incentive to toss his ass out of her cab. But he was still hanging around. She was still letting him hang around. It made perfect sense, in her warped mind. She'd always been drawn to toxic elements, felt a need to be punished. Dante was for sure the ultimate punishment, in anybody's life.

"You were here to be my human shield, but now I'm thinking...my mom probably won't start shooting unless she sees you."

"Oh yeah," Dante said, staring out his window as

they drove down an off ramp. His wide shoulders sagged, lower the farther they sped into the swamps of Mississippi. "Where we going?"

Sasha glanced at Dante, finding a deep-seated fear brewing within his stare. The guy must really believe she'd kill him. She'd never taken a life in cold-blood before. A fucker had to seriously piss her off for things to turn bloody. Dante had given her plenty of reasons to justify unloading a clip in his face, but that was in the past. To kill him now seemed petty. He'd have to screw-up in her presence. Then she'd have no problem stopping the fucker's black heart from beating.

"We're going to Mexico," Sasha said, turning onto a dirt road. She tried not to sound sinister. Or maybe she was trying extra hard to sound sinister. Either way, her words came out with a very sinister edge.

"Look, Sasha—"

"What were you gonna do, that night?" Sasha had Dante on the ropes. If the dumb bastard thought these were his final moments, he'd probably tell the truth. "When we were by the cellar, and you lifted that gun, you were gonna shoot me. That's why my mom jumped in front of me, isn't it?"

"No. Your mother jumped in front of you because she never learned to trust anybody. After visiting her childhood home, I understand why." Dante rocked in his seat, like a lion ready to pounce. "I was gonna shoot Ellen in the leg, and knock you out with the butt of my gun. Then we could've finished staging the body, and you would've been fine. But everything got fucked."

189

Dante snatched Sasha's hand, squeezed tight. "I blame myself for your coma, every day. Hurting you was never my intention. I can't stand that I took so much from you."

Sasha yanked her hand from Dante's grasp. His touch was too safe, comforting, and she couldn't stomach it. Only Dante could fuck up a person's ability to hate.

"We're here." She parked beside her old pickup dock, staring out at the sun's low rays as they glistened across the gentle gulf. The dock's tall lamp was broken in half, its top end tilted and blowing in the breeze. This place looked like *it* had fallen into a coma as well. Another beautiful spot ruined by her absence, by the people who stole her from this world.

"Get out of the truck," she grumbled, her glare fixed on the decrepit dock.

"Sasha, you don't have to do this."

A huff soared past Sasha's lips. To pull out her gun and keep up this charade would be cruel, and that was something she'd never been. Sasha turned to face Dante, softening her stare. "We're going to Mexico." She pointed out the windshield, to the glimmer of light bobbing in the distance. "That's our boat. Get out of the truck."

"Shit," Dante said through a long exhale. "I thought you were gonna off me, little girl."

"I'm not like you. I can't just end people."

Anger didn't puff Dante's cheeks. His lips weren't pressed tight in offense. He just gazed at Sasha with a hint of a smile. She opened her door. The interior of her semi had become hot, confined, suffocating. An epitome of Hell. The affection that spewed off Dante turned the air to acid, darkened what little light remained of the day. She had to get away from his warmth, ignore it, and never, ever admit to liking it.

***

Two minutes of peace were bestowed upon Sasha while Dante took a leak. It was the best two minutes of her life. She could breathe, smile at the prospect of seeing her mother again, even giggle a bit. Then Dante stepped beside her, and her cheerful vibe burst.

"Who exactly are we meeting?" he asked, lighting a cigarette.

"Why? You been fucking people over internationally?"

Dante shrugged, snickered a bit. "Maybe."

A boat's motor revved, waves rushed onto shore, and the now faded letters of *Gulf Runner Tours* glinted in the low light.

"It's my uncle Felix," Sasha said as the boat moored beside the dock. "And he don't fuck around, so you better show respect."

"Uncle?"

"Yeah." Sasha turned to face Dante, holding a smug grin. "From my real father's side."

Dante's jaw clenched, his dark gaze narrowing.

"Don't say it," Sasha said, her grin widening. Any mention of Charles Ashby twisted Dante's knickers into a bunch, which was always entertaining to watch. If the guy didn't like the fact that another man had raised her, then he shouldn't have left her ass. "I don't even like you thinking about him."

"I know the feeling," Dante muttered, though not low enough.

The clink of bullets loading into chambers rang out. Men with rifles hurried off the boat, and Sasha stood tall as gun barrels pressed against her chest. None of the men surrounding her looked familiar. Beyond their angry eyes and snarled lips, she didn't see the wide brim of Felix's hat.

"Oh, hell no!" A young woman pushed her way through the crowd of armed men, backhanding the tallest one. "We talked about this on the boat, *el estúpido*."

Sasha stared at the girl who couldn't have been more than eighteen as she scared off a pack of hardened, rifle-wielding, tattooed cartel members. It was so hard not to get turned on. Sasha told herself, repeatedly, she was looking at a child and standing beside her father while on a mission to find her mother, but the chick's curves were amazing. Her hips were just the right size for clutching onto. She had thighs that could crush like a vice, and breasts one could bury themselves deep into.

"Sasha. My favorite cousin."

"Cousin?" Sasha's lust turned to shock, more so when the chick wrapped her in a tight hug. "Angelina? That can't be you."

"You don't recognize me?"

The chick stepped back, opened her jacket. The long stretch of brown skin, between her tight tank top and even tighter jeans, caught Sasha's stare.

"Good lord, you got big," Sasha said, forcing her gaze to lift from Angelina's chest.

"I can't believe your stoned, coma-mind forgot me," Angelina teased. She zipped her suede jacket, eyeing Sasha over. "My father would've flipped to see you awake."

"Where is Felix?" Sasha glanced at the boat, expecting to see the gleam of a white hat, but only glimpsed a group of young men leaning on their rifles.

"My father passed, almost a year ago. Cancer, a messy fucker."

"I'm sorry...I didn't know." A wave of sadness washed over Sasha. There were very few people who'd supported her throughout her life without strings attached, and now there were even fewer.

"Of course you didn't. You've been busy." Angelina ran her fingers along Sasha's scarred cheek, a mix of anguish and venom filling her stare. "*Pinche maricones.*"

Sasha chuckled. The girl was so much like her father. How Sasha hoped nobody ever thought that about her and Dante.

"Who's running the family now, with Felix gone?"

Angelina turned her stare to Dante for the briefest of seconds. "Who's your friend?"

That would be one hell of a story to tell. No way Sasha was opening the sperm-donor daddy can of worms.

"That's my prisoner," Sasha said, and both Angelina and Dante raised a brow. "Well..." Sasha crossed her arms, glaring at Dante. "He's more of a hostage."

A mischievous giggle slipped from Angelina's mouth. She took Sasha by the arm and headed for the dock. "You'll fit in just fine in my *barrio*." With a wave of her hand, the men hurried forward.

"Tie up that stupid *pendejo*," Angelina said, gesturing to Dante.

"Sasha," Dante called out as men stomped toward him.

Their eyes connected, just as two dudes clutched onto Dante and forced his arms behind his back. Dante's stare screamed for mercy, and Sasha shrugged.

"So," Sasha said, pulling Angelina closer. "Please tell me you have some killer buds on that boat."

"You fucking know it." Angelina hopped onto the boat, flashing a devious smile. "Let's sneak down to the cuddy cabin, like the old days."

Chapter Eighteen

The hours-long ride to Mexico had been the most relaxing moments Sasha had experienced in…what might've been ages. Sasha couldn't remember the last time she'd kicked back and chilled. Angelina had confided in her the hardships of running the cartel, and Sasha actually had solid advice to offer. Plus, the joints never stopped flowing. That young woman, with her nineteen-year-old lungs, could give Sasha a run for her drug money.

By the time Sasha stepped foot off the boat, onto the dusty soil of Mexico, her head felt like a warm, fuzzy, happy balloon. It was perfect. The buzz in her brain masked the onslaught of vendors, who rushed her in a sprint to be the first to sell some poorly weaved straw hats or sloppily painted maracas.

Angelina and her men strolled down the wide, wooden dock. Dante lingered behind them, though not far due to the rope around his neck and hood over his face. The villagers took one look at

195

Angelina, surrounded by rifle-bearing men, and scurried back to their clay houses. The empty sandy roads, with their now pitch-black homes, seemed eerie under the silvery glow of moonlight.

"The people love me here," Angelina said, rolling her eyes. She stood beside Sasha, watching a woman in a tattered dress drag her teenage son into a small hovel. "I could help them all, and I would, if the fuckers bothered to talk to me."

A pout took hold of Angelina's lips, but only for a second and barely big enough for Sasha to see.

"It's better they fear you." Sasha looked at Angelina, nodding. "It's the ones who love you that end up hurting you the most."

"Like your *madre*?"

"*Si*," Sasha said with wide eyes. "Like my *madre*."

A slight rumble vibrated the ground. Sasha turned to stare down the only road that led away from the village, squinting from the beams of headlights cutting through a cloud of dust.

"Right on time," Angelina said. A wave of her hand sent a line of men in front of them, creating a wall of fully-loaded guns.

Angelina grabbed a rifle from the man beside her, then pulled Sasha into a crouch. "You never know, *amor*. Everything's a trap in the Yucatan."

Sasha glanced over her shoulder, straining to find Dante beyond the men who'd walled her in.

"Don't worry," Angelina said, loading a bullet into the chamber of her rifle. "Your boyfriend will be fine."

"Ew." Sasha darted her stare dead-ahead,

cringing. "He's sort of…family."

"Oh." A sly grin spread across Angelina's face, lighting her deep brown eyes. "The *pendejo* belongs to your *madre*, *si*?"

"*Si*," Sasha grumbled, taking another glance behind her.

Angelina nudged Sasha on the arm, winking. "I see. You need the man to shoot in the head in front of your mother, so she'll stop running and playing silly games."

"That's my back-up plan," Sasha said, her words lost under the rumble of engines. A fleet of black SUVs skidded to a stop, kicking up a puff of sand. Sasha couldn't see shit. The people around her, however, didn't hack up a lung or rub their eyes like she did. Everyone around her stood firm, aimed their guns into a haze of dirt and darkness.

The word *clear* rang out in Spanish from the men in front of Sasha, and Angelina rose to her feet.

"It's all good, *amor*. Let's head to my villa, figure out your coordinates."

"Is there a place I can get a postcard?" Sasha looked beyond the settling sands at the rustic village.

"*¿Qué?*"

"*Turistas letras.*"

"No," Angelina said. Her nose scrunched as she gestured to the ghostly, shabby town. "I'll get you some, later. Come."

A grunt pulled Sasha's stare. Two men struggled to handle Dante, barely able to contain the man despite his bound hands and veiled sight. She reached out, patted Dante's shoulder as he was shoved past her. Dante must've known it was her touch, because his tight muscles loosened and his legs shuffled onward a bit easier.

Sasha backed toward the awaiting convoy of SUVs while staring at the moonlight shimmering off the gulf. She should've called Vinny. It would've ruined the whole sentimental postcard bullshit she was trying to pull off, but that didn't seem so important anymore. Vinny's rough, strong voice rang in her head. But it was only memories of soft words spoken long ago. She could've had the real deal, heard a true I love you before her plans went to shit, like usual.

***

Felix had liked to call his house a villa, but Sasha knew a goddamn mansion when she saw one. Tall double doors opened to the shine of marble floors, priceless statues, and golden trimmed walls. Every fucking thing glimmered, and it only gleamed brighter beyond the foyer.

Although Sasha had never been in one, she imagined this was what a museum would look like. Vases on pedestals, stone busts of men with funny mustaches, shimmering suits of armor were still scattered around the large study. The collection of cute little eggs and fancy lamps in the sitting room had grown since she'd been there over five years ago. All that shit had always made Sasha nervous, except for the paintings that lined the walls in every room. She could stare at the deep colors, follow the hints of brush strokes for hours.

"Do you remember the layout?" Angelina asked from the curved staircase that centered the wide open main room.

"For the most part." Sasha lingered in front of her favorite painting. The picture of a lone castle twisting toward a starry night sky should send eerie vibes, but the dark tone and warped background only soothed her mind.

"You're in the spare room, across from mine," Angelina said, making her way upstairs. "I had your bags put up there. I have some business. I'll see you at dinner."

Sasha hurried toward the stairs, the thump of her boots echoing throughout the airy house. "Angel. Where's my...hostage?"

A snicker flowed from Angelina's mouth as she stared down over the banister. She could tell Sasha was hiding something, and probably knew what. Every crime family in the world must know her life's story by now, since those fuckers did nothing but gossip.

"Jose," Angelina called out, and one of the men stationed by the front door hurried forward, clutching his rifle tighter. "Take my cousin to the *pendejo.*"

Sasha had to force her stare from the locks of Angelina's black curls, the sway of her luscious hips as she strutted away. Angelina was her cousin, for Christ's sake. They had no blood ties, but Sasha could still see the child in the young, teenage girl. It was gross. Sasha was fucking gross, because that young, semi-related, teenage girl sparked her pulse to race.

"*De esta manera*, Ms. Ashby," the man said, heading for the wide hallway behind the staircase.

She followed the man through the kitchen, which must have undergone a renovation recently. The wood-burning stoves and ice chests that surrounded the room the last time Sasha had visited were replaced with modern, stainless steel appliances. Beyond the kitchen, the hallway got tighter. Sasha had never been in this part of the house, where the walls and floors were made of faded wood and sand littered every corner.

Sasha's elbow bumped the wall and she jumped to the side, crashing against the opposite wall. Fire seared her chest, burning away any trace of oxygen. She couldn't do this. It was too much like the corridor she had escaped in the Mancini's basement. Only now, she was walking toward her cell instead of running away from it.

"I don't—"

"It's okay," the man said. His rushed steps stopped in front of a thick wooden door, a puff of dust kicking up in the narrow hall. He slung his rifle over his shoulder so it rested against his back and unlocked the door. Hinges squealed and echoed down a long set of rickety stairs as the door was pushed open, and Sasha's knees almost gave out.

"He's down there." The man pointed into the dark doorway. "Locked up good."

The wooden walls around Sasha seemed to stretch out, grow tighter. She closed her eyes. The guy's footsteps thumped away, but she couldn't move, couldn't do anything except suck down gulps of stale air. She was alone, in this cramped hallway of her nightmares. At least now, nobody could see her curl into a ball on the dirty floor and weep like a baby, which was about to happen any minute.

"Little girl?"

Dante's voice flowed up the crooked steps, and Sasha ran toward it.

"Dante!" Her boots hit the dirt floor at the bottom of the steps, slipping. She teetered, bumped against a stone wall. Her mind whirled as Dante glared at her from behind rusted iron bars. There was no great bond between Sasha and Dante, yet panic ran through her. After what happened to her, she couldn't bear to see another person trapped in a tiny cell.

"That's fucked up," Dante practically growled, reaching through the bars to point a stern finger at Sasha.

"I'm sorry." Sasha rushed toward Dante's cell, grabbed onto the cold bars. "I had no idea she'd take it this far. I thought they'd lock you in a fancy suite, with whores and a fruit tray or some shit. I didn't even know they had a dungeon here."

"So you're just gonna play along, punish me because you can't stand the fact I'm your real father?"

"No." Sasha squeezed the iron bars, strained to keep from clutching onto Dante in search of comfort. He had saved her from a cell much like this one once. Although she was free to walk around as she pleased, it still felt like she was trapped inside that cell. That is, until Dante breezed back into her life.

"I'll get you out of this shit. Here." Sasha tore

through her pockets, collecting handfuls of weed, papers, and cigarette packs. "Take this, to hold you over." She shoved her stash onto Dante's hands, the quake of her fingers slowing at the feel of his skin. "This type of shit usually takes lengthy negotiations."

Dante tucked the weed into his pocket and lit a cigarette. "You're bullshitting me. You probably set this up so you can run off with Ellen."

"I swear." Sasha pushed her shaky hands into the cell, latched onto Dante's arm. She kept her stare low, away from the metal cot in the corner. "I don't want you in here. I'm gonna get you out."

"Go," Dante said, wiggling out of Sasha's grip.

"What?"

"I'm good." Dante reached through the bars, took ahold of Sasha's trembling hand, and squeezed lightly. "You shouldn't be in a place like this. Go on, little girl. Get the fuck out of here."

The words were like a sledgehammer, breaking free an invisible shackle. Sasha sprinted up the stairs. She wanted to look back, flash a comforting smile Dante's way, but fear wouldn't allow for it.

"I'll get you out," she yelled over her shoulder before bursting through the doorway at the top of the stairs. The walls swayed, her lungs clenched shut. She had to keep going, escape this corridor where sun didn't shine, breathe in air that flowed on a warm breeze.

Sasha pushed her wobbly legs, forced them to move faster. Sweat poured from her brow, doing nothing to cool the heated waves rolling beneath her skin. She glimpsed a hint of light beaming through a door's seams. The tiny shimmer strengthened her will, cleared her blurry vision. Her hand steadied, enough to grip the handle, and she yanked the door open.

The gleam of metal appliances greeted her and a brightly lit, empty kitchen welcomed her to stay. She slammed the door shut behind her, gasping to catch her fleeting breath. The momentary lapse of courage, which had carried her punk-ass this far, fled her body. She slid down the wall, pulled her knees to her chest. Tears streamed from her eyes, thumped along the scars on her cheeks, and she wiped them away. This couldn't happen. She couldn't lose her shit here, alone in Mexico, so close to her mother's touch.

Within her mind, Sasha screamed at her muscles to quit their quivering. Much to her surprise, her body actually listened this time. She rose from the floor, lifted her chin high, and left the kitchen.

***

Sasha stepped out of the shower, careful to avoid the mirror. She snatched a towel off the silver rack and wrapped it tight around her mangled body. The icy water had done wonders at chilling out her fiery soul. If only she had a joint.

Water dripped, splashing the marble floor as Sasha opened the bathroom door. She stopped short once she caught sight of Angelina sprawled out on her bed puffing on a freshly lit doobie.

"Hey," Sasha said, hurrying to dress.

Angelina rolled onto her side, held the joint out

to Sasha. "Who is that man to you?"

"What's this now?" Sasha took the joint, turning her back to Angelina. The seconds of distraction that puffing and brushing her hair provided was enough time for her to come up with a ton of bullshit, but she was so sick of lying.

"I had cameras installed last year, everywhere. The kitchen, every bedroom." Angelina pointed up, at the oversized smoke detector on the ceiling. "Even in the old parts of the house and basement."

Sasha sat on the edge of the bed, keeping her back to Angelina. The girl behind her had only seen the hard Sasha, and the pout stuck on her lips clashed with that façade.

"I think you know who he is."

"I do," Angelina said, scooting closer to Sasha. "And I know what happened to you, and that the people who hurt you disappeared when you rose from the dead."

Sasha could feel the warm body behind her damn near vibrating. If she tilted back, just a tad, she'd fall against a soft chest. There was a good chance delicate hands would hold her, but she didn't budge. Her entire life, she'd used people to fulfill her needs. She wouldn't do it again, not to the daughter of a man she considered family.

Angelina crawled to the edge of the bed, stared at the side of Sasha's face. Sasha glanced Angelina's way for only a split-second, which lured Angelina even closer to her.

"Why won't you look at me, Sasha?"

Angelina's hand landed on Sasha's shoulder. The grip, although light and tender, seemed to have enough power to crush the frosty layer that clutched her bones.

"Did you know," Angelina said, caressing Sasha's arm. "I had a huge crush on you when I was fourteen? You blew into town, took out all those men, and the people whispered your name for years. After that, I was never able to let a man touch me again."

That drew Sasha's gaze, her wide eyes veering to Angelina. "You were having sex at fourteen?"

"Weren't you?"

Sasha shrugged. She shouldn't be used as an example, for anything. "I'm sorry I ruined sex for you."

"Oh no." Angelina planted her hand on the mattress, leaned against Sasha's chest. "I have a wonderful sex life, now that I know what I want."

A sexy, young woman pinned Sasha to the bed. It was strange. Sasha was the one who made women's bodies quiver, who warped their rational thoughts to wild, lusty desires. She played the man. Yet here she was, on her back, a prisoner to her trembling muscles and Angelina's sensuous leer.

Angelina's lips brushed Sasha's neck. When hard nipples rubbed against Sasha's chest, she gripped onto Angelina's hips. The idea was to push Angelina away. Sasha was a fucking idiot. She should've known once her hands clutched onto luscious curves, they wouldn't be letting go.

"This isn't right," Sasha managed to mutter. It was amazing her brain allowed for speech at a time like this. Strands of silky hair caressed her skin. The scent of roses and vanilla filled her head. Just the fact she could produce a single word was a goddamn miracle.

Angelina glided her hands along Sasha's arms, across her palms, locking their fingers together. "I've fucked every *juera* who stumbled into my country, but none of them were you. You're even more fierce and beautiful than the first time I saw you."

A passionate kiss landed on Sasha's lips, shocking her. It took a few seconds and the sliding of Angelina's tongue into her mouth before Sasha pulled away.

"I can't."

"You can't?" Angelina said, climbing atop Sasha's lap. "Or you won't."

It was a tough question, one Sasha had a bit of trouble answering. Won't was such a harsh word. It ruled out so many possibilities.

Sasha looked up at Angelina, finding a naughty stare. One glimpse of that girl's crooked smirk, and Sasha's already low morals blew to dust. "I can't," she mumbled, chewing back a smile.

"Okay." Angelina leaned down, kissed Sasha on the neck. "You don't have to do anything, *amor*." The soft lips tickling Sasha's ear came with tingles of mind-numbing proportions. "Just lay back, let me take care of you."

Any attempt to resist would be useless at this point. Sasha's tank top had already been hiked up, and Angelina's tongue was on its way down her neck. Angelina was so powerful, so strong. Sasha had never been handled this way by a woman before. It excited the fuck out of her. If this was how all those girls she fucked felt while trapped in her clutches, she was owed a whole mess of thank you letters.

Chapter Nineteen

Somewhere between the three orgasms Sasha had, and the five she gave, sunlight faded to night. She should enjoy this. A tranquil buzz radiated throughout her body, which was currently snuggled against a naked woman, but she couldn't relax. Every second she wasted was another second her mother had to sneak off, disappear into the millions of other faces in the world. Plus, her level of scumbag was verging epic. Not only was she rolling in a soft bed with a gorgeous young woman while Dante withered away in a dark cell, but she'd cheated on Vinny. Already.

"Angel?" Sasha sat up, which pulled Angelina's lips off her shoulder.

"He's down the hall," Angelina said, hopping off the bed.

"What?" Sasha grabbed the joint from the ashtray, watching Angelina wiggle back into her tight jeans.

"Dante." Angelina pulled on her halter top then

plucked the joint from Sasha's lips. "Your *real father*. I had him confined to the suite at the end of the hall. Gave him a few whores and a fruit plate."

A smile lifted Sasha's cheeks as she leaned closer to Angelina. "Seriously?"

"Of course." Angelina planted a quick kiss on Sasha's lips before shoving the joint back between them. "You're family. I'll do anything for you."

Sasha climbed off the bed, collecting her clothes. "We can't be family anymore. You just fucked the shit out of me, and family don't do that."

Angelina leaned against the closed bedroom door, her gaze narrowed on Sasha. "We can do anything in my world. You should stay here, with me."

It was a gracious offer, delivered in a chilling tone. Something told Sasha it wouldn't matter how she answered. If a spoiled teenager with an army of seasoned killers wanted something, that spoiled teenager would get it. Fucking the sexy, young chick didn't seem like such a great idea now.

"I have a son, with a man I really care about back in the states."

That would've ended the conversation, in a perfect world. Unfortunately, Sasha had created a world of shit for herself to live in.

"You can bring them here," Angelina said, her face completely blank and unreadable. "I don't mind sharing. We'll talk more, at dinner. Finish getting dressed. I'll get Dante."

"What? Now wait a minute." Sasha hurried across the room, but Angelina slipped out the door and slammed it in Sasha's face.

"Oh…" Sasha raised her hand, palm out. "…no she didn't." Sasha might have to bitchslap that little brat. Or better yet, she'd wait and let her mother do it.

***

Sasha hurried down the wide staircase. Her boots squeaked against marble tile when she hit the bottom and cut to the left. Candlelight gleamed from the dining room's doorway. Sasha practically barged inside the room, stopping short. Dante sat alone at a long table, eclipsed by the shimmer of china plates and real silver silverware, and Sasha almost hugged him. The way Dante jumped up from his chair, rocking in place…it looked like the man wanted to hug her too. The whole situation was a bit unsettling, and extremely awkward.

"Hey," Sasha said as she dropped onto the chair across from Dante.

"You came through, little girl." Dante smiled—a true, warm smile—and Sasha actually felt like a little girl staring up at her daddy. "But I knew you would." He sat back in his seat, glancing at the fancy spread of gold-rimmed plates and wine glasses around the table. "I like your girlfriend's style."

"She's not my girlfriend," Sasha said, a little too fast. She forced her tight shoulders to loosen. "Angelina is an old family friend."

"Right." Dante leaned onto the table, staring into Sasha's eyes. "Are we prisoners again? Because it's hard to tell with all the women, liquor, and great food."

"We're not gonna be prisoners."

"Aw, shit." Dante pulled a pack of smokes from his pocket and lit one up. "We're fucked."

In a thump of combat boots, Angelina and her entourage of gun-toting men strolled into the room. "I have good news," Angelina said, plopping into her chair. "My man has an address to go with your coordinates. It's only ten miles from here."

Sasha sat up straight. It took everything she had to keep from running out the house and into the desert to scream her mother's name.

"I'll assemble a team," Angelina said. She gestured to the wait-staff across the room, which sent them into a fluster. "After dinner. Maybe we'll go in right before dawn, *si*."

Dante coughed, shifted in his seat, cleared his throat, but Sasha refused to look his way. It was best for everybody that she stared at her wine glass. To see annoyance on Dante's face, the asshole who started this jumble-fuck, would only flare her temper. And Angelina. Her dear friend, her hottest lay, the girl who'd given her the best night she'd had in years sounded so excited. She'd never wanted Angelina to be one of the many people crushed beneath her train-wreck of a life, but it was too late. She'd fucked the girl. Now she had to hurt the girl. It wasn't what she liked, just what she did.

A plate of crazy looking food that was either cut to resemble a bouquet or was actual flowers landed in front of Sasha and she leaned back. "Angel—"

"Leave us," Angelina said. Before her arm could wave, the room cleared, leaving Sasha to stare into

Dante's nervous eyes and Angelina's pissed off glare.

"You're not going to stay with me, are you?" Angelina asked through clenched teeth.

Sasha stared down the table at Angelina, holding a hard edge to her gaze. "No, I'm not. But if you need anything, I'm always a phone call away."

Angelina drummed her fingers on the table. Not one hint of emotion crossed her face. Sasha had expected shouting, foot-stomping, maybe a gun to the head, but silence was far worse. A bullet could be seconds from Sasha's brain, and she wouldn't know what the fuck had happened until her ass was roasting in Hell.

"I see," Angelina said, settling back in her chair. "You're a hard one to get, Sasha Ashby. But you will be mine." The words were spoken in such a flirty tone, they could never be mistaken for a threat. "I can wait, *amor*. Family life isn't for you. You belong here, with me, where the action is. You'll see."

It could be true, probably wasn't, but damn well could be. Sasha snickered, until Dante chuckled. Then she grumbled.

"And you," Angelina said, turning her stare to Dante. "Is there something wrong with the girls I sent you?"

Dante stopped picking at his food and set down his fork. "The girls were hot as hell, *muy bien*," he said in a choppy, thick-tongued attempt at Spanish.

"Then why you no fuck them?" Angelina asked with a mouthful of what turned out to be tamales wrapped in cornhusks.

"She has cameras," Sasha said, pointing at the ceiling. "In every room." The fluster that lit Dante's eyes warmed Sasha's soul. It was worth keeping the guy around, permanently, if only to watch him squirm.

"I have a woman," Dante said, into his lap. Must be a pep talk he had with his cock on a daily basis, because it sounded rehearsed. "I cheated on her once. I'll never do it again."

"Aw," Angelina said, pushing her plate aside to lean on the table and swoon over Dante. "It's so *romántico*, no?"

"No," Sasha sneered, narrowing her gaze on Dante. "It's bullshit. He knew your girls would tell you, and you'd tell me. The fucker's just slinging angles, trying to get back in my mother's good graces, and he thinks I can do that for him."

Angelina stared at Dante, a slow nod rocking her head. "*Serpiente*," she said, before turning to face Sasha. "You see. That's why I need you by my side. You can teach me how to spot *puto* liars."

"That, my dear, is a talent you can only acquire through experience," Sasha said, tearing into her food.

"You sound just like my father."

That was one pretty amazing compliment, and a man Sasha was proud to be compared to. She grabbed her wine glass, lifted it high. "To Felix."

After glasses clinked and smiles faded, Dante cleared his throat. "In all honesty, Sasha is right. The man she knows would've ran that very con, but I'm not that man anymore." He pulled the little black ring box from his pocket, running his thumb

213

along its felt top.

"I think he's serious," Angelina said, gesturing to Dante. "The man has *la mirada de amor*."

"We'll see," Sasha muttered. There was no way she could eat now, after Dante murdered her appetite. If he was for real, the man had far more willpower than she could ever hope to possess. If it was lies, she was slipping. Either way, her affection for Dante was starting to outweigh the hatred she harbored toward him, and it fucking sucked. Hating was easier than forgiving, than love.

"So." Angelina rang a crystal bell, which triggered a rush of men in butler suits to file into the room. Plates were cleared, and ashtrays full of cigarettes and joints were set in the center of the table. "What shall we do while we wait for dawn? I just opened a donkey show in town, brings in lots of *turistas*."

"A donkey show?" Sasha asked, reaching for a joint.

"*Si*. It's when the *chica* and the donkey fuck," Angelina said, nonchalant, as if they were discussing a new strand of weed. "The men love to see it, and some women."

Dante took a long hit on his own joint, which transformed his wide-eyed stare to a scrunched, confused leer. "The girls want to do this?"

"*Si*. It's *voluntario*. So, should we go?"

That was a question Sasha never expected to ponder. Did she want to see a chick fuck a donkey? It would definitely be a once in a lifetime experience. Dante looked pretty intrigued and completely disgusted, which blended to form a fucking hilarious expression.

"You know what?" Sasha said, and Dante held his breath. "Maybe next time."

"Yeah," Dante said through an exhale. "This is kind of a serious trip."

Sasha nodded, ignoring Angelina's snickers. "Right. We'll come back for a party trip, do that…then."

Angelina sat back in her chair, straining to wear a disappointed glare. "I guess we'll just have to do lines and watch children's movies, since neither of you have any *cojones*."

***

Sasha didn't do any lines. She didn't trust herself to stay on the rails, even with something as harmless as cocaine. The inability to trust her own self, know her limits, hurt worse than the pain she felt when coming down from heroin. She did, however, put some powder in the joints. Smoking coke didn't count as doing drugs, at least according to Vinny. He'd made sure to give her a whole list of do's and dont's right before she left. Too bad he didn't include fucking a sexy Spanish cartel princess on either of those lists, then she'd know whether she was supposed to feel like shit right now.

Three in the morning rolled around quickly, and Sasha found herself alongside Dante, following Angelina toward the wide front door of the villa. "Were you ever able to get me a postcard?"

Two men opened the double doors, letting in the

sounds of waves rushing onto a shore, and Angelina turned to face Sasha. "No. Sorry. Do you need to send a letter?"

"No. I'll do it when I get back. Listen." Sasha took Angelina by the hand, pulled her away from the armed men assembling right outside the open front door. "I'd like it if Dante and I went alone."

"Really?" Angelina crossed her arms, eyeing over Dante. "You trust him?"

"Fuck no. But I know my mom. If she sees an army of Mexicans pull up, she'll take off and I'll never find her."

Angelina rocked in place, her stare bouncing between Dante and Sasha. "If that's what you want, *amor*, I'll make it happen. But…" She gripped onto the sides of Sasha's arms, brought her lips to Sasha's cheek. "Be careful, my love. The Yucatan is a dangerous place."

"Don't I know it." Sasha flashed a smile, walking away from the luscious lips she longed to kiss. "If I'm not back in twenty-four hours, send in the army."

"Oh, I will."

Sasha tapped Dante on the arm and headed for the door. Men stepped aside as they walked toward the first SUV parked in the cobblestone driveway. Dante hurried to jump in the passenger seat, but Sasha's steps slowed. There was an electric vibe coasting on the air. It only drifted in during the wee hours before dawn. Here, in a place where a salty breeze grazed her skin, and the rush of waves always thundered, the crackle in the air seemed to double. She wanted to enjoy that, real quick, before sucking the ghost of her past back into her life.

After one last look at the stone fountain, sparkling in the moonlight, Sasha climbed into the SUV. The key was dangling from the ignition, and fully-loaded rifles decorated the backseat. It would be perfect, if not for Dante's shit-eating grin.

"You fucked your cousin," Dante said with a mocking chuckle.

Sasha started the car. Its engine rumbled, covering her mix of cusses and grumbles. "She's not my cousin."

"*Now* she's not your cousin. But, Saint Ashby—"

"Shut the fuck up." Sasha drove off the compound, flooring the gas once hitting open road. Ten miles of desert rested between her and her mother. The one thing she never thought possible was about to happen, and she could barely wait another second. She was about to feel the only hands that ever truly completed her soul on her body once again, hear the only voice that could fully calm her mind. Her chest wouldn't be empty anymore, and the world could be bright again.

Sasha pushed down harder on the gas pedal. The motor revved, the backend skidding on sand. Only eight more miles.

"Don't you want to slow down?" Dante said, fastening his seatbelt. "There could be cops or some shit."

"There ain't no police out here. And if I wanted to slow down..." Sasha pulled a small lever beside the shifter. The transmission locked into four-wheel drive, the SUV bucked as the front tires gripped pavement, and she floored the gas harder. "...I'd fucking do it."

"I snagged you some joints."

"I don't want no joints," Sasha said in a bark, keeping her eyes on the pitch-black road ahead.

"Say what?" A zippo clicked from the passenger seat, and the sizzle of paper burning filled the cab. "Sure you do, little girl."

"You don't know me," Sasha yelled, thrusting her finger in Dante's face. Tires squealed as the speeding SUV swerved, rattling everything in the cab as the car bounced on and off the road. Sasha shifted her attention back to the windshield, finding cacti instead of faded lines. She tapped the brakes and cut the steering wheel.

The SUV fishtailed back onto pavement. Once all four wheels gripped road, Sasha barreled down on the gas again.

"No." Dante turned off the ignition, pulled the key from the column. "You *are* gonna slow the fuck down."

"What the fuck?" Gravel crunched as the car slowed to a stop, and Sasha spun in her seat to glare at Dante. She didn't get to hurl her death glower. One look at Dante's hard stare, and she shrank down in her seat.

"I know you, little girl. You're a self-sabotager. You don't have happiness because every time it gets near you, you fuck it in the ass. I ain't gonna let you fuck this up for me." Dante jammed the key back in the ignition, cranking the engine to life. "Now, you're gonna sit back, smoke a joint, and drive this car like a normal fucking person."

Sasha opened her mouth to lay into Dante, and he shoved a joint between her lips. She sat there, stunned, smoke rising into her eyes. This motherfucker had a lot of nerve. She'd let him have it, as soon as she thought up a legitimate rebuttal. A dark cloud of devastation did follow her around, but she didn't create it. Or did she? Every decision she'd ever made had been rooted in fear, fear strong enough to form such a destructive cloud. She fucked Dez right after Vinny, because in that one night she fell for Vinny so hard it scared the shit out of her. The sergeant at arms position would've been hers, but she ran from the dreaded burden of responsibility. Everything! She *did* sabotage everything. Candy, Tyler, her mother…

Dante placed his hand on Sasha's knee, squeezed lightly. "You got that shitty habit from me. But our two wrongs can make a right, as long as we stick together."

Sasha reached for Dante, and he latched onto her hand. Waves of affection stemmed from his grip, strength flowing from his fingertips. She'd never touched Dante before, not like this. His skin pressing against her own generated a spark, one she'd only felt in her mother's presence. She nodded, almost telling herself it was okay to release the hatred she held toward the man. It was okay for her to like her shady asshole of a father.

"I'll keep it under fifty."

***

Two joints, and a semi-slow ride down a

deserted road later, Sasha parked in front of a skinny dirt path. She cut off the engine and reached into the backseat for a rifle.

"What's up?" Dante asked, checking the side mirror.

"We're here." Sasha gestured to the sandy hill outside Dante's window, then loaded a round into the rifle's chamber.

A pink flush rushed in to claim Dante's tanned cheeks. The big, strong man looked like a kid about to embark on his first date, especially with the way he bobbed to see through the gray haze of dusk. "There's nothing out there."

"A villa should be on the other side of that hill. If we drive up the path, she'll hear us coming and split."

Dante grabbed a gun from the backseat and hopped out his door. Before the guy could run off and blow their only chance, Sasha hurried after him. Dude was quick, halfway up the hill before Sasha reached his side.

"Damn, man." Sasha latched onto the back of Dante's jacket, pulled him to a stop. "Now who's sabotaging shit?"

A gleam of light peeked beyond the sandy hill. Sasha inched forward, glimpsing the corner of a brown stucco villa. Her heart leapt into her throat. It was a good thing, because she was just about to yell out for her mother.

"What's the plan?" Dante asked, crouching lower as he crept up the hill. "You take the front, I'll cover the back?"

Normally that'd be the plan, but Sasha wasn't

about to do this alone, or let Dante out of her sight. "No. We'll sneak onto the porch, kick open the front door, and storm the house. Together."

"All right, little girl." Dante flashed a smile, clutching his rifle to his chest. "Let's do it."

Sasha followed Dante into the shadows. Every step forward made her throat clench tighter, drove her heart to pound faster. This was really happening. She was about to see her mother. After all the horrors, blood, tears, she was about to see her mother, feel that magnetic vibe, and the world would be right again.

Sand crunched beneath Sasha's boots as she jogged to keep with Dante's pace. The guy was like a fucking ninja. Dante slid from one dark corner to the other with barely a sound, like a shadow himself. He must be a professional stalker by now, after all the years he'd spent sneaking on and off her compound.

They stopped beside the wide trunk of a palm tree. Sasha peeked out, staring into the front window only feet away. A figure moved beyond the glass, and she flinched. She pressed her back against Dante's side. Instead of revulsion, comfort ran through her. She looked up at Dante, finding a confident stare shining down at her.

"It's now or never," he whispered, straining to hold back a grin.

Sasha pushed off the tree and hurried toward the porch. Before she reached the top step, Dante was at her side. Without a second of hesitation, he lifted his leg and kicked the front door open. Sasha stormed inside the brightly lit house, her rifle aimed out.

A crowd of men turned to face the now shattered door, which stopped Sasha and Dante in their tracks. Rifles veered to Sasha's chest, and harsh words were shouted in Spanish.

"Drop the gun," she said to Dante, tossing her rifle to the floor. "*Estamos aquí para ver a Ellen.*"

Bullets loaded into their chambers, and snarls decorated the men's faces.

"That's funny," said a man with a thick Spanish accent from somewhere within the horde of angry Mexicans. The crowd parted, and a tall man stepped forward to stand in front of Sasha. "We're here to see Ellen too."

Winter in Mexico sucked. With everybody wearing long sleeves, covering their tattoos, there was no way for Sasha to know if she was cool for kicking in a door, or totally fucked. One wrong word and bullets would fly her way.

"Well then." Sasha lifted her hands, slow, and inched backward toward the kicked-open door. "Y'all were here first, so we'll just go. Let you guys have at it."

Boots thumped on the porch behind Sasha. The air grew thick as another group of men rushed through the doorway to shove the barrels of their guns into her back.

"Your mother," the tall guy said, narrowing his psycho-killer eyes. "She took many things from me. That *punta* owes me."

Sasha shook her head, keeping her hands high. "Nah. You got me mixed me up with someone else. I'm not Ellen's kid."

"This not you?" The man held his hand out, and a short dude placed a thick book in it before scurrying back into the crowd. He opened the cover, flipping through pages of pictures.

"This is you," he said, showing Sasha a picture of herself and her mother by the pool table in the clubhouse. "And here." He turned the page, pointed at a shot of them in the cab of a semi. "Here." Every page had another picture, going back to when Sasha was a child.

The man flipped to the last page, holding up a black and white photo of Ellen and Dante at their wedding. "I have Ellen's husband, and daughter." He smirked, which warped his dark stare into a menacing leer. "It's a good down payment. *Tomarlos*."

Dante lifted his arm, fist cocked, but before he could hurl a punch the butt of a rifle crashed against his temple. He dropped like a sack of bricks, landing at Sasha's feet.

"Wait," she called out as men closed in on all sides of her. "I have money, *mucho dinero*."

A grin lifted the tall man's brown cheeks. He leaned close to Sasha, his long black hair gliding over his wide shoulder. "*Chica*, you are money."

The worn butt of a handgun filled Sasha's view. A loud crack echoed in her head, before the sting of the hit splintered out. She dropped to her knees and face-planted the floor. Somewhere above the buzz in her ears, and the throb in her brain, she heard laughter, then...nothing.

Chapter Twenty

Vinny

A knock rattled the front door of the penthouse and Vinny sat up on the couch, blinking back the haze of sleep. He never made it past the living room. There was no point in going upstairs anyway. His room was crammed with Sasha's shit, and her room...only a bed remained in her room, and the lingering memories of her agonizing detox. He never wanted to go in that room again, except to light it on fire.

The door shook under another barrage of knocks, followed by the chime of the doorbell.

"All right," Vinny yelled. His stiff muscles burned as he rose from the couch, bones cracking. "I'm coming." He grabbed his glock off the coffee table, dragged his ass across the room, and opened the door.

Marco crossed his arms, leaning against the threshold. The man's long coat brushed the wall, and he dipped his head so his narrowed eyes showed just below the brim of his hat. It was some real deal mobster shit.

"You boys must've had one hell of a night," Marco said, forcing his grin into a scowl.

"The boss started it," Vinny said, heading for the first glass of water he saw. "Why didn't you use your key?"

Marco walked inside the penthouse, closed the door behind him. "Kev took it from me last week. Some bullshit about broken locks."

"Right." Vinny set down his gun on the kitchen counter and grabbed a spare key from the hook on the wall. Marco was one of the originals, from when Tony ran the family. Sasha had trusted the man with her life, which was why Vinny made the guy his right hand and gave him free reign over Manhattan. A borough was one thing, but he wasn't trusting city folk with Sasha's secrets. His girl's little mishap with heroin was nobody's business, unless Sasha decided it would be.

"The locks are fixed," Vinny said, tossing the key to Marco. "So, what's up?" He sat on the couch, pulling a semi-crushed pack of smokes from his pants pocket. "Otis finally crawl out from beneath his pile of cocaine and whores?"

"Ain't seen the boss yet," Marco said, sitting on the loveseat. His foot tapped the floor, gaze darting away every time it landed on Vinny.

"Fuck." Vinny lit his cigarette, throwing the lighter onto the coffee table. "You got that look. Did Manhattan burn to the ground?"

"Nah, boss."

Vinny cringed, as he always did when Marco called him boss. The title never sunk in. He was the VP of Ashby Trucking, not the boss in an Italian mob family.

"Business is good," Marco said, with a sour look that stated otherwise.

"Then what?"

Marco reached into the inside pocket of his coat. "You got some mail."

The scrunch of Marco's nose, refusal to maintain eye contact hit Vinny in the gut like a sucker punch. Sasha broke it off with him, on a postcard no less, and everybody must've read it.

Vinny crushed out his cigarette in the ashtray, snatching up a joint as Marco pulled an envelope from his pocket.

"A letter?" Vinny dropped the joint and grabbed the envelope. Scrawled on the front, in bright blue ink was Sasha's chicken-scratch excuse for handwriting. This couldn't be good. Nothing good ever came inside envelopes. Eviction notices, past-due bills, letters from over-priced specialists saying the love of your life would never wake up was what came in envelopes.

Marco fished the joint off the floor, sparking it up as Vinny tore open the envelope. Vinny took a deep breath, and looked inside. A smile popped onto his lips at the sight of a postcard and a polaroid. The picture brought a wall of tears to his eyes. Outside his clubhouse, Sasha knelt beside Tyler. Her arm was wrapped around the boy's little shoulder, holding snug as she planted a kiss on his laughing face. It was the greatest picture Vinny had ever seen throughout his entire life.

"What is that?" Marco asked, gesturing to the photo in Vinny's now shaky hand.

Vinny took the joint from Marco and with great reluctance handed him the picture. A laugh, warm and genuine, flowed from Marco's mouth.

"Look at this," Marco said through a wide grin. "We should have this blown up, hang it at Tonys."

"Yeah," Vinny muttered, reading the postcard. "Maybe."

"What'd Sasha say?" Regret crossed Marco's face the second the question left his lips. "Unless it's personal."

"No. She's going to Mexico. Sent me the coordinates for where she thinks her mother is."

"You want me to have it translated to an address?"

"Fuck yeah." Vinny gave Marco the postcard, then snatched back the picture. They could make a million copies of that photo, hang them wherever the fuck they pleased, later. He needed this little piece of home close to him right now.

"Jesus." Vinny settled back, finally relaxed enough to smoke his joint. "You scared me, man. Looked like you had bad news."

"There is something else." Marco shifted in his seat. Guilt rushed in to paint his face in a pinkish tinge. "After I got the letter, another postcard came into Tonys. Special delivery."

Vinny narrowed his stare. "And you read it?"

"It's a postcard. How am I not supposed to read it?"

The hand gestures of the overdramatic Italian

next to Vinny started, and he grumbled. "Fork it over."

Marco placed a postcard on the cushion beside Vinny, a picture of swamplands gleaming on its glossy surface.

"Mississippi?" Vinny said. He grabbed the postcard, flipped it over.

I'm a few miles from our old dock. I don't know what's gonna happen over there. Mexico's a fucked up place, and I left a lot of loose ends when I went into that stupid coma. If you don't get any more postcards, if you never hear from me again, I need you to know I didn't run. I'm done running, except back to you. I love you, Vinny. I've always loved you and always will.

"That—"

A lump formed in Vinny's throat, choking out his words. He coughed, took a few hits of his dwindling joint, but it wasn't budging.

"That sounded like a…"

Marco nodded. Leather crinkled as the man sunk down in his seat. "It sounds like one of those letters a soldier sends before going into battle."

"Fuck!" Vinny jumped to his feet, headed for the stairs.

"What?" Marco rose from his seat as Vinny stormed up the staircase. "Where you going?"

"Hop a flight to Mexico." Vinny pushed open his bedroom door, only to have it fly back in his face. Every piece of furniture from Sasha's bedroom was stuffed in there alongside his own shit. Did he even need spare clothes to rescue his woman? He had credit cards and a driver's license. That should be all he needed to book a flight to Mexico.

Vinny turned away from his bedroom door and ran back down the stairs. Fuck his clothes. There was no time for stupid shit. Sasha was in trouble. He could practically hear her calling out for him at this very moment.

"Don't you want to wait?" Marco hurried across the room, blocked the front door. "See if another postcard comes?"

"There ain't gonna be any more postcards." Vinny grabbed onto Marco's arm but he didn't push, not yet. He'd give the man one chance to move, before the guy got shoved.

"You can't take guns on an airplane," Marco said, standing tall in front of Vinny. "When you land, you'll have no weapon, no connections. Do you even speak the language, know anybody in that wretched country?"

"I know an important name, Felix Vega. And I have coordinates." Vinny snatched the postcard from Marco's hand, then pushed the guy from his way.

"Don't tell Otis," Vinny said on his way out the front door. "He'll just come after me, then everything'll get fucked up." He slammed the door to his penthouse shut, leaving Marco inside, and hurried down the hallway.

The elevator neared, and he picked up his pace. No time to push buttons and wait. He'd take the stairs. Marco could burst out of his penthouse at any moment, try to stop him. He couldn't afford bullshit delays, not when his girl needed him.

***

Sasha

A light slap tapped Sasha on the cheek, pulled her from a spiral of colors and shapes. She tried to lift her arm, but her entire body felt so heavy. The tap on her cheek grew stronger, each hit spreading sharp pangs throughout her already throbbing brain. She wished her hand worked properly right now so she could punch whoever was fucking with her face.

"Sasha."

Dante's muffled voice trickled into Sasha's ears, and she forced her eyes to open. The blur that clutched her vision cleared, letting Dante's panicked stare filter in.

"Jesus Christ," Dante said, pushing some scrap of wet fabric against her head. "I thought they cracked your cantaloupe."

"I'm good," Sasha said, in a bit of a slur. Her hand finally decided to work, flying to the pulsating ache on her forehead. A long gash ripped beneath her fingertips, filling her palm with blood. A burn radiated from the cut on her head and she groaned, her arm flopping back to her side. "Head wounds bleed a lot."

Dante took Sasha's hand. He leaned close to her face, cradled her arm to his chest. "Don't freak out now."

"What?" Sasha pushed against Dante, tried to

pull her hand from his grasp, but his wide body kept her pinned to the cold floor beneath her back.

"We're in a cell."

"What?" Sasha yanked her arm free from Dante's grasp and sat up, wobbling. Her side slammed against a stone wall, jagged rock digging into her skin. She'd scream but feared only vomit would spew out if she opened her mouth.

"It's all right, little girl."

"No!" Sasha pulled at her shirt, at her skin. It was too tight, everything was closing in on her. She couldn't look up from the sand covered floor, see the sparky walls, glimpse the words painted in blood.

I am Ellen.

"No, I'm not," she muttered between hectic gasps for air, which never came. This cell—her cell—had no air. It never had any fresh air.

"Listen to me." Dante clutched onto the sides of Sasha's arms. He knelt down, until her eyes connected with his gaze. "You're not alone in that cell. We're not in a basement. There's a window." He pointed, but Sasha didn't dare look. She couldn't see where she was, what Hell she'd been dumped into.

"You're not alone," Dante said, staring into Sasha's eyes. "I'm here. I'll die before I let anybody hurt my little girl."

Dante glided his thumb along Sasha's cheek. His gentle touch soothed her raw soul but couldn't stop the tremble of her body. He pulled her close, wrapped his strong arms around her, and she buried her face in his chest.

Now, she got it. She finally understood why her mother had chased this man for so long. While tucked within Dante's arms, Sasha felt untouchable. Nothing the world dished out could harm her, not while this barrier of strength shielded her.

"I'm sorry," Dante said, resting his cheek atop Sasha's head. "All my choices fucked your life. It kills me I've hurt you. I've never loved anybody as much as I love you, my little girl."

"Don't say that." Sasha pushed off Dante's chest, glaring at him. "People only say that kind of mushy shit when they think they're gonna die."

"I've been waiting a long time to say that kind of mushy shit to you." Dante drew Sasha back into his embrace, dropped a light kiss on the top of her head. "And I'm gonna tell you I love you more often. Every fucking day."

A snicker flowed from Sasha's mouth, slowing the quake of her limbs. "That's gonna get old."

Dante held tighter, and the spikes of terror that pierced Sasha's mind faded to dull blades of anxiety. She peeked over his arm, taking in the cramped space around her. It was definitely an upgrade from her last cell. Same ridged stone walls, filthy concrete floor, except the cot shoved against this cell's corner had a shit-stained mattress. And the window! Stars gleamed against a black sky outside the thin opening in the wall high above. She couldn't fit through that window yet, but after ripping out the center bars she'd squeeze her ass out even if it ripped her skin.

"All right." Sasha pulled away from Dante's clutch and patted down her pockets. She had no cigarettes or weed. The fuckers even took her zippo, and she'd had that one forever.

"Motherfuckers took all my shit." She jumped to her feet. Oh, how she loved anger. It had the ability to sweep in, overshadow any trace of fear invading her mind, and send a surge of fire through her blood. She glanced down at Dante, looking quite snug on the dirty floor. "Did they leave you any weed? I need to think."

"You don't need weed to think."

Sasha glared, a low growl rumbling her throat. Don't need weed to think? This guy was living in an ass-backward crazyland. "Maybe *you* don't need weed, but—"

"Will you just stop focusing on weed and think up a way to get us out of here."

"Me?" Sasha paced within her limited space, kicking up a cloud of dirt. "Why does it always gotta be me?"

Dante coughed, swatting at the puffs of sand wafting up from beneath Sasha's shuffling boots. "You know people here, speak the language. Just start dropping some names."

Sasha stopped circling her cell like a caged animal. That was actually a great idea. She did know people, really important people, who didn't take kindly to second-rate wannabe gangsters.

"Fuck yeah," Sasha said, eyeing the solid wooden door that kept her confined in this small stone cell. "We'll be out of here before…" She turned toward the window, rose to the tips of her toes. The thin opening was far too high to glimpse anything other than dark sky. It was night, which meant an entire day had passed since she stepped foot into the villa that was supposed to harbor her mother. The woman was gone. She'd probably left before Sasha even arrived in Mexico. Her mother was gone.

A clink rang out from the cell door. Dante jumped to his feet, stepped beside Sasha as the door flew open. Four men rushed inside the cell, hovering beside the door with their rifles at the ready, as a white man in a lab coat stepped inside.

"Take the girl first," said the doctor-looking guy, pointing at Sasha.

Two men inched toward Sasha. In the low light, she glimpsed the fringe of a tattoo on one of the guy's neck. The symbols were ones she recognized, ones that brought hope. "I'm a friend of the *Llamada de la Muerte.*"

The men stopped short, glanced at the white guy that crowded the doorway.

A cruel grin swept the man's face as he leered at Sasha. "Tito was already here, gave the okay."

"The okay for what?" Sasha yelled, backing away from the two men who crept toward her.

Dante decked the guy in front of him, then charged the men who reached for Sasha. A gunshot thundered the air before its white flash could stun Sasha's eyes. Dante flew backward, trailing a stream of blood from the bullet hole in his stomach. His side hit the stone wall, and a spray of red burst from his mouth.

"No," Sasha cried out as Dante dropped to his

knees, holding his gut. Dark red streaks of blood flowed between Dante's fingers, his eyes wide. Just as Sasha ran for Dante, a strong hand gripped onto her arm. She was yanked back, and a needle was jammed into her neck.

"Great, you damn near gutted him," said the doctor guy, staring down at Dante groaning on the floor. "I guess he's first."

Sasha slumped to the ground. She couldn't move. Her arms, legs, every muscle was locked stiff. Not even one toe would wiggle on her foot. She tried to call out to Dante, but her jaw wouldn't even open.

"Little girl," Dante shouted above the sounds of a struggle. "Sasha!"

The slap of fists and shuffle of boots ended with a grunt. Dante fell to his side on the ground in front of Sasha, his body just as stiff and frozen as her own.

"Can't...move," she muttered, in somewhat of a slur since her jaw refused to unclench.

Dante's frantic gaze was dragged from sight, leaving Sasha to stare at the sparkle of stone walls.

"Hit her with a light sedative, and put her on a slab. I gotta get to the other guy before he bleeds out."

The ends of a white lab coat fluttered above Sasha, cloaked her in shadows, then glided away. A man placed his rifle on the ground, only inches from her face. In her mind, she grabbed that gun and blasted everybody's ass to shreds. Reality was a cold, hard bitch. In the real world, she lay paralyzed, helpless, transferred from a cell of dirt and stone to one within her mind.

A needle slid into Sasha's arm, but she didn't feel shit. It was like her entire body had floated away, leaving only her useless thoughts. The back of her shirt was hiked up, and the ground started to move beneath her. She was being dragged out of her cell and into a narrow hallway. Tinges of red stained the sand, and streaks of blood painted the brick walls, blurring as they passed by her still legs. A thick haze clouded her vision in gray, and that familiar metallic taste hit the back of her throat. There was no fighting it. She was going under, fast, and at this point her best hope would be to never wake back up again.

Chapter Twenty-One

Vinny

Vinny stepped out of the airport, onto the sidewalk of Merida, Yucatan and took a deep breath. Thick air filled his mouth, crammed into his throat. He coughed, covered his nose in a hopeless attempt to block the rancid stench from his nostrils. Mexico held the distinct odor of sweaty balls. He thought New York City was bad. At least he couldn't taste the air there.

Men and women hustled along the sidewalk, lugging suitcases around Vinny. He strolled past a line of taxis, avoiding eye contact with the men rushing forward to spout out some shit in Spanish. A ride wasn't what he needed. He needed a fucking clue. The entire plane ride to Mexico, he'd tried to form a plan. It wasn't until his ass was fifty-thousand feet off the ground that he realized how stupid he was. There was no plan to form. Mexico wasn't a town; it was a goddamn country, full of strange people speaking weird gibberish.

He couldn't just go to the nearest bar and flash Sasha's picture, mostly because he didn't see any bars. The scenery wasn't at all what he'd expected. Beyond a dark patch of sand dunes and palm trees, he glimpsed the glimmer of a distant city's light cutting into the night sky. That was it. Old women in shawls weren't trying to sell him a bunch of crap they'd made. Cowboys didn't ride horses along dirt roads. Everything he'd ever seen in every movie was complete bullshit.

A tall man with dark skin, covered in tattoos, grabbed onto Vinny's arm. "Come with us," he said as another, even bigger guy seized Vinny's other arm.

"What the fuck?" Vinny hurled his elbows, and the men tightened their grip. Not one person broke their stride on the sidewalk. Heads didn't even turn when Vinny slammed his forehead against the asshole's nose on his right. Blood flowed down the man's chin, splashed the sidewalk, and not one woman shrieked.

The men pushed Vinny toward a black van, and he struggled harder against their grip. This was un-fucking-believable. Not five minutes in Mexico, and he was being taken off the street like a little bitch. The van's side door slid open, and the butt of a gun filled Vinny's view. He tried to duck, but solid metal smashed against his face and knocked the world from sight.

***

Sasha

A fuzzy blur was all Sasha could see, but her ears worked just fine. Low gargles echoed over loud rips and sharp clinks. The mumbles, which resembled her name spoken with a mouthful of water, guided her back from a gray fog. She forced her hazy eyes to focus, and Dante's pale face blurred into view. Terror clouded the man's stare, his mouth caught open in a silent scream.

Her hand flinched, slapping icy metal. She was on a steel table. They were both lying on steel tables, except Dante's body rocked in violent tugging motions.

Sasha strained to lift her head, and a wave of terror nearly pushed her back down. Dante's chest had been cut down the center, his skin peeled back to show bloodstained ribs. The man in the doctor's coat stood over Dante, blood up to his elbows, surrounded by bowls of fleshy gore on ice.

"What…what are…?" Sasha muttered, falling back against the table.

"Shit," said the guy carving up Dante. "The chick's coming 'round. Hit her with more paralytics."

"Stop," Sasha slurred. Another garble erupted from Dante's mouth, his arm flailing Sasha's way. She tried to jump up, run to him, but her body was too heavy to budge. "Stop!"

"Sorry," the man said, pulling a large piece out of Dante's chest and placing it in a bowl. "You two are young, strong, and American." The guy pointed his scalpel at Sasha, a thick bead of blood dripping off its tip. "I'll clear a mil with you guys' organs, finally get out of this filthy country."

The man went back to work at ripping and pulling Dante's insides, and Sasha thrashed her weak arms. She'd kill this motherfucker. One hand, that's all she needed to pull her limp ass across the floor and stick a scalpel in that douchebag's eye. Except not even one finger would obey her mind's commands.

"Sasha," Dante said in a low sputter.

All on its own, her arm reached for Dante. Their fingertips grazed and Dante gripped onto her hand. She could feel his fear, his agony in the tight clutch. Then, his hand slipped away.

"Love..." he choked out, "love...you."

"Daddy," Sasha cried out. That man *was* her father, her daddy, and he was dying right in front of her. She screamed at her own body, demanded it to rise off the table. Her head lifted half an inch, and Dante's stiff shoulders fell limp. His bluish lips no longer trembled, but his eyes, now blank and empty, stayed wide open.

It couldn't be real. This had to be a fucked-up nightmare. The strongest, most fearsome man she'd ever met couldn't have been stripped to pieces before her eyes. Her father couldn't really be a bunch of weird-shaped parts in bowls of ice.

A young man stepped beside Sasha's table. The kid couldn't have been more than fourteen, yet his eyes held the stare of an old man who'd seen horrible things. He shoved Sasha back onto the table, jabbed a needle into her neck.

"That's the heart," said the bloody doctor, in a

chirpy tone. He strolled around the puddles of red, leaving Dante's torn open body to stand over Sasha. "You're next."

Sasha rolled her head to the side, which was the only movement her body would allow. Dante stared at her with dead eyes. He looked so scared, so alone on that shiny table with his chest split open. That would be her fate soon. A light tug rocked Sasha to the side, and the sound of a rip filled her ears. That would be her fate now.

Tears rolled down Sasha's cheek, warming her frosty skin. "Daddy," she muttered as a wall of waterworks blurred Dante from sight.

"Don't worry, dear. It'll all be over soon."

The man above Sasha tugged and pulled at her gut. She could feel pressure but no pain, not where he was cutting. All her pain circled inside her heart. Dante was dead. She'd never see Tyler's smile, never feel Vinny's rough hands on her skin, never hear her mother's voice ever again.

A loud crash filled the room, and the man digging into Sasha's stomach jumped back. His hands rose, higher the farther he backed from the table. A series of pops rang out. The man staggered, and the scalpel tumbled from his hand as bullets pelted his chest and face.

Sasha tried to roll her head to the other side, take a peek at who was shooting up the room, but only got halfway before her cheek flopped back to the cold table.

"Sasha!" A shadow fell over Sasha. She peered up, squinting to make out the figure hovering at her side. "Sasha, can you hear me?"

"Mama," Sasha slurred at the first glimpse of red nails.

"No, *amor*. It's me, Angelina. But—"

"What the fuck?" a woman shouted from the corner. "We're too late."

Sasha knew that voice, sharp, silky, but she couldn't place it.

"Sasha's still alive," Angelina said, moving from Sasha's view. "All her parts are here, somewhere."

"You killed the fucking doctor."

"Shit. I can…"

The jumble of voices faded, so low Sasha could no longer hear them. She felt so light, so empty. Warmth waited for her. It was just within reach. Something told her if she closed her eyes right now, it'd all be over. The ache of her shattered heart, the girl with all her missing pieces would be over in the span of a blink. So she closed her eyes and slipped into the black.

***

In a field of sunflowers, on a gentle hillside, Sasha lay on her back. It was warm here, but she knew it would be. Anyplace was better than where she'd just come from.

"You still owe me," a squeaky voice whispered. Soft lips brushed Sasha's cheek, and a lock of scarlet hair fell over her face. She inhaled deeply, breathing in the scent of lavender.

"Candy." Sasha rolled onto her side, staring into the greenest eyes she'd ever had the pleasure to glimpse. "Fucking shit, girl. I've missed you."

Candy propped onto her elbow in the tall grass, gazing at Sasha. Her eyes narrowed, and she leaned close. "You still owe me," she repeated, nodding as she backed away.

"I know." Sasha couldn't help but smile. She still remembered that conversation clearly, as though it didn't happen six years, a coma, and two stone cells ago. "But I can't keep my—"

An electric jolt ran through Sasha. She sat up straight, looking at Candy. The girl had the cutest crooked grin as she nodded slowly.

Candy wrapped her arms around Sasha, kissed her hard. Their lips glided, skated, caressed one another. Then, as quick as she drifted in, Candy drew back.

"Don't forget your skin." Candy winked, hopped to her feet, and hurried up the hill.

Sasha watched Candy run into bright beams of sunshine. Her wavy hair flowed behind her, the ends of her sundress fluttering to flaunt long legs as she ran away.

Once the sun's rays swallowed Candy up, Sasha rose to her feet. She stared down the hill, at a steep descent into darkness.

"I can't keep my mother waiting," she said, stepping into the shadows.

Chapter Twenty-Two

Fingertips slid down Sasha's arm. Someone clutched onto her hand and squeezed. She could actually feel the gentle touch, along with a red-hot prickle in her own fingers and a searing burn in her gut. A cry scraped past her throat, erupting as a whimper.

"That's it, sweet girl," said a soft voice. This time, Sasha knew exactly who that voice belonged to. How she could've ever forgotten that wonderful sound, she'd never understand.

"Come back to me, Sasha."

"Mama." Sasha blinked back a haze, and there she was. Ellen Ashby, the unstoppable, and apparently unkillable, president of Ashby Trucking. She'd found her mother, and it stung. Dante was supposed to be at her side for this moment. He was supposed to see this.

A flood of grief rushed over Sasha, mixing with the joy that already filled her chest. She was so angry, happy, full of pain.

The surge of emotions warped into strength, and Sasha used it to draw back her fist. With all her weight, she lunged forward and clocked her mother square in the eye.

"What the fuck?" Ellen yelled, stumbling back as she cradled her face.

Sasha's swing took her down, off the edge of a couch. Her hands flew out, stopping her just in time to keep her face from kissing a tile floor.

"Bitch," Ellen said. She grabbed Sasha beneath the arms and shoved her back onto the couch.

Splinters of sharp prickles spread out from Sasha's stomach, rippled beneath her flesh, but she ignored that shit. The fire in her chest, whirlwind inside her mind had to be dealt with immediately.

"You left me," Sasha yelled, cringing at the childish tone that infected her words. "You faked your death and left me, forever."

Ellen knelt down beside the couch, took Sasha's hand. "The doctors said you'd never wake up. *You* left me."

"No." Sasha yanked her hand away. "I caught you faking your death. You were gonna leave me anyway."

"Do you even remember the last conversation we had?"

Sasha sat up, despite the grate of her insides. "Of course I do. It haunts me. I thought you died thinking I didn't love you. That I didn't care."

"So did I." Ellen squeezed onto the couch, held Sasha in her arms. "So did I."

Sasha fought to keep from bursting into an insane-like happy chuckle. Her imagination couldn't hold a candle to the true sensation of being wrapped in her mother's arms. Every piece of herself she'd lost, soul and flesh, was worth just one minute of this woman's embrace.

"What happened to you?" Ellen asked, pulling back to stare Sasha over. "There's scars all over your body, they look old. Except for the track marks on your feet and arms." Ellen lifted her hand to whack Sasha upside the head. Her jaw clenched, and she lowered her arm to her side.

"What the fuck, Sasha?"

"I met your mother," Sasha said, and Ellen rose to her feet. "She put me in your old room."

"No." Ellen staggered back a few steps. A glaze coated her eyes, her bottom lip trembling. "I'll skin that bitch."

"You'll have to go to Hell to do that. That's where I sent her, and all your brothers." Sasha lowered her stare. She'd murdered her mother's entire family. A bit of the asshole vibe wormed its way in to pluck at her conscience. It didn't bother her one bit the Mancinis were dead. Those fuckers deserved it. The absence of guilt is what got her. She should feel bad. Her mother had to have been close to those freaks at one point.

"I'm sorry for your loss," Sasha muttered into her chest.

"They're not who I'm grieving for."

"Dante." Sasha sank into the couch cushions, holding herself tight. That one word had brought an ocean's worth of tears to her eyes, but she couldn't let them out. If she broke down here, so far from Vinny, there'd be nobody to put her back together.

"He was coming to win you back," she said, keeping her gaze low. "Snuck into the attic at the big house to get your old ring. Even turned down two fine Mexican whores."

A low, sorrow-filled laugh pulled Sasha's stare to the center of the room. Her mother stood hunched over, head buried in her hands, shoulders trembling. That's when Sasha realized her mother wasn't snickering. The woman was sobbing.

Sasha pushed her weak body off the couch, forced her wobbly legs to stand. She limped toward her mother, ignoring the ripping sensation in her side. The strongest woman in the world just lost her source of power. Sasha was all too familiar with that feeling. Except her reason to fight had just returned from the dead. Dante wouldn't be coming back.

The pain in Sasha's body dwindled under her mother's agony. She held her mother tight, caressed the woman's shuddering back, kissed the top of her head. It would work. It was the same exact way Dante had comforted her only hours ago when they were locked in a cell, so she knew it was a surefire method. "I hated Dante but I really, really liked him."

"Tell me about it." Ellen pulled back from Sasha's embrace, wiping away smears of black eyeliner. "What are you doing up? Back to the sickbed with you."

Gently, Ellen wrapped her arm around Sasha and guided her back toward the couch.

"No." Sasha squirmed out of her mother's clutch, teetering from the world's sudden sway.

"I'm good." She lifted the end of her t-shirt. A long line of black stitches cut across her stomach, which had been the only unscarred part of her body. "What'd they take from me?"

"A kidney," Ellen said, hovering at Sasha's side like a gnat. In seconds flat, the woman applied a thick glob of ointment and wrapped a layer of gauze around Sasha's waist, all with a cigarette dangling from her lips.

"That's it?" Sasha shrugged, waved her mother off. "Nah, I'm fine." She glanced around. The dark paintings on the wall, marble floor, and tall posts surrounding a big bed of satin sheets brought a smile to her lips. "We're back at Angelina's villa."

"Yeah. I ran to her for help when I saw Tito's men hauling you away."

Sasha headed for the jean backpack on the corner of the bed, slow, since the ache in her side decided to flare-up into a fiery scorch. She tore through the bag, pulling out her spare cargo pants.

"What are you doing?" Ellen asked, picking the rejected clothes that Sasha tossed off the floor.

"I gotta find a postcard, for Vinny, and maybe a phone. He's probably freaking out right now."

Ellen pulled a picture from her pocket, staring down at it with a hint of sorrow in her eyes. "Whose child is this?" She held up the polaroid that Sasha had mailed to Vinny days ago, pointed at Tyler.

"Where did you get that?" Sasha snatched the picture from her mother's hand. Instead of answers, she received a hard glare. It was true Ellen form, which brought a smile to Sasha's lips.

"This is my son, Tyler."

"When did you wake up?" Ellen asked, staring at the picture in Sasha's hand.

"A year ago, maybe two."

"But—"

"Dante lied to you." Sasha slumped onto the bed, holding the picture close to her chest. She'd always resented Tyler for having the stare of a man she loathed. But now, after everything, she was glad the kid had inherited Dante's haunting eyes. "I didn't lose my baby. I just missed his childhood."

Ellen stood, stunned, her eyes wide. "The baby lived?"

"He's Vinny's," Sasha muttered, running her finger over the picture. The picture that shouldn't be in Mexico. She turned to face her mother, resisting the urge to latch onto the woman and shake. "Where did you get this?"

"Sasha, I—"

A loud crash erupted from outside the bedroom door. Sasha pulled on her pants, tucked the picture into her backpack, and grabbed a handgun. "What the fuck is going on out there?"

"Yeah," Ellen said, scratching her head. "Don't get mad."

Sasha rolled her eyes. Of all the openers, that was probably the worst. She could sit around, try to decipher her mother's bullshit in search of explanations, or she could just walk her ass into the hallway and find out what was up.

Gun in hand, Sasha limped across the room. She opened her door, just as a roar flowed from the end of the hall.

"Fuck," she said, cringing at the series of bangs

coming from the padlocked door at the far end of the hallway.

Ellen stepped beside Sasha, holding out a key. Sasha stared at the door, which rattled on its hinges under a barrage of pounds. The grunts, yells, and bangs grew louder. It sounded like a pack of wild baboons had gotten loose inside that room, and they were properly wrecking shit.

Sasha took the key from her mother's grasp and headed down the hall. "Are you torturing somebody in there?" She leaned close to the door, jumping back when a thud cracked it up the center.

"Sort of," Ellen said, flashing a wicked grin that could give the Devil a run for his pitchfork.

"Listen," Sasha yelled through the door. "I'm coming in." The ruckus stopped, and she popped open the lock. "If you don't want to eat a bullet, you better simmer down." She lifted her gun then shoved open the splintered door.

What Sasha found amid the room of broken furniture, shattered glass, and ripped linens was the last thing on Earth she expected to see. The gun slipped from her hand, and a giggle burst from her mouth.

"Vinny," she said through a giant smile.

A long exhale sunk Vinny's chest, his tight shoulders sagging. "Jesus fucking shit, girl." He rushed toward Sasha, wrapped his arms around her and squeezed tight.

The cry that belted out of Sasha's mouth couldn't be stopped. Sharp barbs of pain shot from her gut, ricocheted throughout her body. The scrape of red-hot razorblades on her insides, and the tingles spawning from Vinny's touch on the outside were too much to handle. Her knees gave out. She dropped to the floor, taking Vinny with her.

"Have you been shot?" Vinny practically yelled in her face, since he was still cradling her in his arms. He pulled up Sasha's shirt, gasping at the wide stitches peeking out from beneath a blood-soaked bandage.

"I'm okay." She didn't give a shit about her ripped-up flesh, stolen organs. Her fingertips were gliding on the stubble of Vinny's chin, the frosty gleam of Vinny's eyes were shining down on her, and those lips…if only she had the strength to lift herself up and kiss them.

"Did you get my postcards?"

Time seemed to stop as Vinny smiled. He leaned down. Prickles of electricity nipped Sasha's lips, right before his kiss rushed in to silence them. His embrace was hard, forceful, yet it was the most passionate hold she'd ever experienced. She'd always felt this undying hunger from his touch. The sensation had been so strong she'd mistaken it for lust, but she was wrong. She didn't know what true love was, not until this very moment.

"Careful with my girl," Ellen said from the doorway. "She got carved up like a Thanksgiving Day turkey."

"No fucking way," Vinny whispered. He shifted his gaze from Sasha to the doorway, and a laugh flew from his mouth. "Ellen, you're a goddamn asshole. I should've know it was you who grabbed me." He helped Sasha off the floor. Once she was steady on her feet, he let go to better hurl a glare

251

Ellen's way. "I hope you're happy. I trashed all your fancy shit."

"It wasn't my shit, kid."

Vinny scooped Ellen into a bearhug, lifting her feet off the ground. "Otis is pissed at you."

"I bet." Ellen boosted a pack of cigarettes from Vinny's pocket, then took his lighter. "It ain't easy running the club, is it?"

"Ha!" Vinny snatched the freshly lit cigarette from Ellen's mouth. He took a drag before passing it to Sasha. "She doesn't know, huh?" he said to Sasha, even though his taunting grin stayed on Ellen.

"Know what?" Ellen asked, knocking another cigarette loose from Vinny's pack.

"We need to have a talk," Sasha said, holding her side to combat its ache. "Where's Angelina? She has all the weed."

Sasha pushed past her mother and staggered toward the stairs at the other end of the hallway.

***

A cool breeze rode on the waves of the gulf, adding a chill to the humid air. Sasha never found Angelina. She did find a pile of joints in an ashtray, which she immediately took onto the veranda to enjoy while watching gentle waves crash onto white sands.

Her mother and Vinny had found her before she finished the first joint. By the third, she had thoroughly blown her mother's mind. It wasn't the info about Dez's new woman shacked up at the big

252

house, playing mommy to Sasha's kid that stunned the woman silent. The little tidbit about Otis playing Don to the Lazzari family was what did the trick. Too bad Sasha didn't know CPR, because the next thing she was about to tell her mother might give the bitch a heart attack.

"Tyler's in trouble," Sasha said. Vinny tensed up, shifting the wicker loveseat they were cuddled on, but Sasha kept her stare on her mother. "Only you can help him."

Concern washed over Ellen's face, shining bright in the remnants of day. "Who do I have to kill?"

Sasha almost burst into tears. It was goddamn amazing to have her mother back, and downright terrifying. If she said the wrong thing, hurled the wrong glower, the woman could run off. She didn't know if she'd survive losing her mother again, but she was one-hundred-percent certain she'd never live through the loss of her son.

"Right now, Tyler is the heir to the Lazzari empire. He can't live that kind of life. The boy sings, writes poetry, plays guitar. He has a future, bigger than blood and guns."

"I don't understand how I can help," Ellen said, grabbing another joint from the ashtray.

Sasha waited until the doobie was placed in her hand. She needed a hit of smoky courage to bark this order out.

"The plan," she said through a billow of smoke, "was for you and Dante to take over my position. But now…" Sasha took two more hits then passed the doobie back to her mother. The woman was going to need that joint in a second. "You have to marry Otis, give him a son. So they don't take mine."

"Excuse me!" Ellen hopped to her feet, walking to the edge of the stone patio. The way her mother rocked in place, staring out at the long stretch of sand meant trouble. The bitch was about to split, and this time Sasha was too sore to give chase.

"I just saw the man I loved split open." Ellen charged toward Sasha, hands on hips, glaring down. "I literally held his heart in my hands. And now you want me to marry Dante's cousin, spit out babies. Girl, do you know how old I am?"

"Come on," Sasha said, her stare bouncing between Vinny's and her mother's wide eyes. "Just brush the dust off your twat. You gotta have a few eggs left in there."

"That's fucking selfish, Sasha." Ellen crossed her arms, shook her head. "Your kid's too good for that life, but I can sacrifice mine?"

The statement was so ridiculous Sasha couldn't even laugh at it. "Oh please. All you've ever wanted is one of your children at the head of the Lazzari table, right? Well, it ain't gonna be me, and it *ain't* gonna be my son. So if you don't do this, you ain't getting your way."

"No." Ellen took a step back from Sasha, her glare hard. "I'm not going back to the states."

Sasha rose to her feet. Every movement ignited a sharp ache, but she stood tall in front of her mother. "I'm the underboss of the Lazzari family. The Don told me to bring you back, so I will be bringing you back. When you get to New York, you can do whatever the fuck you want."

"Ellen," Vinny said, leaning forward in his seat. "I've never asked you for anything, but Dez has been raising the kid. Tyler's not conditioned for this life, for these people."

"Holy fucking shit," Ellen said to the sky. Her stare lowered from the puffy clouds and narrowed on Sasha. "You let Dez rear the kid?"

"I was in a coma. And you ran off, so you don't get a say."

The steam ran out of Sasha's sails, and she staggered on her feet. Her legs wobbled, the world taking a quick spin. She slumped back into her seat, groaning as a ripple of red-hot pinpricks ravaged her midsection.

"Are you gonna do it?" Vinny asked, looking up at Ellen with a giant puppy-dog stare.

"Of course I'm gonna do it." Ellen dropped back into her chair with a huff. "It's the motherfucking Lazzari family." She grabbed a banana from the bowl of fruit on the table, tossed it at Sasha. "Eat this, you look like shit."

Boots thumped from within the house. Sasha looked over her shoulder as Angelina walked onto the veranda.

"There you are," Angelina said, standing in front of Sasha.

Sasha sat up straight, taking in the amazing sight of Angelina's curvy hips confined by tight leather pants. "Goddamn, girl." The sting in her side faded as a much hotter burn flared in the deepest parts of her soul. It had to be that skimpy halter top. The stretchy black fabric, flaunting cool bronze skin, crumbled her sorry-ass excuse for willpower and allowed a surge of desire to rush in.

"Where you been?" Sasha asked, forcing her hands to keep at her sides. "You look...fucking incredible."

Sasha glanced at Vinny, finding a somewhat curious expression. The shrug of her shoulders and scrunch of her brow had to announce her guilt, yet Vinny smiled and nodded. Hell, it looked like he might pat her on the back.

"I have a gift for you." Angelina waved her arm, and a butler-looking dude scuttled forward with a silver platter. He lifted the shiny lid, displaying a severed head.

Vinny jumped back, shaking the seat, and Sasha leaned forward. Her first instinct was to touch it. The face, frozen in a silent cry of terror, looked so fake. The blood seemed too bright, its skin far too droopy.

"It's Tito," Angelina said. She grabbed the head by its blood-clumped hair. A squish erupted as she lifted it slightly off the tray. "He's very sorry for all the trouble he's caused."

"That's umm..." Sasha stared at the frayed ends of puffy skin, which dripped blood onto the silver platter. "Am I supposed to keep it?"

"Do you want to keep it?" Angelina asked, lifting Tito's head higher.

"No."

The head slopped back onto the tray, and Angelina wiped her hands on her butler man's coat. "Feed it to the dogs," she said, shooing the man away. She sat in the chair across from Sasha, without a glance at Ellen or Vinny. "The *Llamada de la Muerte* is no more. It seems I have a lot of new territory to cover, almost more than I alone can handle."

Of all the offers Sasha had received in her life, this was the most tempting. Only a fool would pass on an opportunity to live in a tropical paradise, with a smoking-hot woman, in a land where laws didn't exist. In which case, Sasha was a goddamn idiot. New York City was her home now, and she couldn't wait to get back into that concrete jungle.

"I don't think you'll have any problems handling your shit," Sasha said, eyeing the row of blood-tipped knives strapped to Angelina's leather pants.

"Your man," Angelina nodded at Vinny but kept her gaze on Sasha, "is stupid, using his real name to fly into *my* airport."

A coldness filled Angelina's eyes, almost masking the tiny sliver of compassion that hid within. Almost.

"Thank you," Sasha said, and Angelina smiled. Confusion gripped both Vinny and Ellen, but Sasha knew how close Vinny had come to eating a bullet. If Vinny had disappeared in this brutal country, on some bullshit mission to save her dumbass, she'd be devastated. Living in the places where Vinny had lived wouldn't have been possible. She would've ran into Angelina's arms, jumped headfirst into the girl's gangster-life fantasy. Angelina was smart for picking up on that minor weakness. The girl was even smarter for not enacting the plan, because now Sasha craved that bitch more than she ever had before.

"*Las cosas cambian,*" Sasha said with a slight

smirk. "You never know, doll."

"*Si*." Angelina rose to her feet, heading for the house. "Will you be staying, so you can find ways to repay me for my heroic rescue? Or should I have the boat prepared?"

Vinny ripped his gaze from Angelina to stare at Sasha with pleading eyes. She chuckled, until the burn on her side turned her laugh into a groan.

"I have to get back," Sasha said, staring out at the stretch of water that stood between her and her home.

"That's what I thought," Angelina said from the back door. "I already had the boat gassed up. It's ready when you are, *amor*."

The wicker bench shifted as Vinny leaned close to Sasha. His arms circled her chest, warm breath flowing over her ear. "Can't we stay for a little bit. I wanna roll in that white sand with you, when you're all better."

To lay in Vinny's arms atop soft sands, with warm water rushing up to kiss her feet, sounded like pure bliss. Anything could happen between this moment and the one where they walk into Fat Tonys. She may never have another chance to fuck her man on a beach in Mexico.

"Guess we can stay for a few days," she said, running her fingers into Vinny's tangled hair.

The End

Epilogue

One year later

Sasha stood in Central Park, feeling like a complete dumbass. Couples sat on checkered blankets, giggling at each other's bullshit, and she was about to be one of those assholes.

"Why are we doing this?" Sasha asked as Vinny spread an ugly plaid blanket out on the grassy hill. She hugged a small basket to her chest, as if that would somehow shield her from what was to come.

"Don't be weird," Vinny said, stretching out on the blanket.

Sasha dropped the basket, plopped down beside Vinny. "You're being weird, wanting to have picnics in the park. It's strange."

As usual, Vinny ignored her rantings and groped her body. "So, what'd ya bring?"

A wide smile spanned Sasha's lips. She flipped open the lid to the basket, sinking her fingers into the pile of joints within. A nice big fatty fell into her grasp, its smooth paper tickling her skin. She lifted the doobie from the basket, held it up in front of Vinny's eyes.

"You just brought weed?"

"No, stupid." Sasha reached into the basket and pulled out two frosty bottles. "I got beer too."

A devious grin lit Vinny's eyes in blue flames. He pulled Sasha close, taking a beer from her hand. "Spark it up," he said, snapping his zippo to life.

Sasha leaned back against Vinny's chest. A cool spring breeze flowed over her skin as they puffed and passed. A picnic in the park was actually a great idea, though she'd never admit it out loud. With Dez and Jeri in the penthouse next to their own, and Tyler running back and forth every minute, it seemed like ages since they'd sat in silence just enjoying some kind bud.

"How about that one?" Vinny asked, pointing at a tall blonde chick walking her dog on the trail. "The way she struts...she'd be a wild one in the sack."

"Too skinny," Sasha said, taking a sip of her beer. "I like curves on my women."

A chuckle shook the chest behind Sasha's back, and Vinny dropped a kiss on the top of her head.

"I know what you like," he whispered, his breath spreading tingles in every spot it grazed along the side of her neck. His hands slid under her shirt, and he caressed the long scar on her stomach. She was running out of unmarred skin. Her entire body looked like a fucking patch quilt, but Vinny didn't seem to notice. He pawed at her just as much as ever, maybe more, and it didn't bother her one bit.

"You like that one," Vinny said, gesturing to a

young Latino woman sitting alone on a bench. The way the chick clung to her ratty backpack, flinching at every laugh, struck a nerve with Sasha. If she didn't have Vinny at her side, she could be just another lost, lonely girl on a park bench.

"She looks hungry," Sasha said, staring up into Vinny's eyes. "I bet she'd be mighty grateful to get a hot meal and a warm bed for the night."

Vinny glided his thumb along Sasha's cheek. "Why don't you go over there and fetch her?"

"I got the last one. It's your turn."

"No." Vinny guided Sasha's back onto the blanket, eased between her legs. "I brought that coat-check girl to you last week."

Sasha grinded against Vinny, dragging her lips along his mouth. "And *I* seduced her right out of her tight dress for you."

"Mommy," a high-pitched, very Tyler-sounding voice called out.

"Tyler?" Sasha pushed Vinny off of her as Tyler ran beside their blanket. "What are you doing here, little man?"

"Daddy brought me." Tyler pointed across the grassy hill, at Dez standing beside a black sedan. "Grandma broke her water."

"So," Sasha said, sitting up. "She can go get another one."

"But Uncle Otis said you have to come. Now."

Sasha stared at Tyler, fidgeting like a frog on a hotplate. "Wait. You mean Grandma's water broke?"

"Duh," Tyler said, glaring as if Sasha were dense.

"Shit!" Sasha jumped to her feet, tugging at Vinny's arm. "My mama's having the baby. We gotta go."

Vinny hopped to his feet, started jogging up the hill, then doubled back for the blanket. Sasha and Tyler stood next to each other, heads cocked to one side, watching Vinny bumble around like a chicken without a head. There were only two things in front of him; and still, he couldn't figure out whether to grab the blanket or the basket first.

"I got this," Tyler said. He snatched the blanket off the grass, wrapping it around his neck like a cape. With a smile and a wink, he took off in a sprint up the hill. "Come on, y'all," he hollered over the flutter of the blanket, which glided on the air behind his scrawny legs.

Sasha picked the basket off the ground and took Vinny by the arm. "Let's go meet the new prince of the Lazzari family."

"After Ellen pops out that baby," Vinny said, pulling Sasha close. "We should grab *our* kid and head to Mexico."

"That's an idea," Sasha said, chewing back a smirk. "But, we might need to bring a sitter. I promised Angelina I'd check out this donkey thing."

Vinny hurled a leery stare, and Sasha pulled a joint from behind her ear. She sparked it up, snugging Vinny's arm as they followed Tyler up the hill.

Acknowledgements

This book, and the entire Ashby Holler series, wouldn't have been possible if not for so many amazing people.

First and foremost, I need to acknowledge how awesome my readers are. It's the comments and reviews from you guys that keep me trucking down this bumpy road called publishing.

I'd really like to thank everybody at Limitless Publishing. The marketing team, my incredible editor Tiffany Cole, Lori, the cover designers, and everyone else has made me feel valued and like a part of their family.

Speaking of family, mine are real troopers. There are a lot of ups and downs in publishing, and my family has been there to support me through good times and bad.

My critique partner, Kaelan Rhywiol, is not only a ridiculously talented author, but my rock in rough seas. She always believes in me, even when I don't, and never fails to deliver a swift kick in the ass when I get too mopey.

The support in the online writing community is so vast, there are just too many people to thank. So I'm sending out big hugs to all my #amwriting #amediting #writerslife friends.

While this is the final book in the Ashby Holler series, it's not the last you'll be seeing from me.

-xoxo

About the Author

Jamie Zakian lives in South Jersey with a rowdy bunch of dudes, also known as family. A YA/NA writer, her head is often in the clouds while her ears are covered in headphones. On the rare occasions when not writing, she enjoys blazing new trails on her 4wd quad or honing her archery skills. She's a card carrying member of the Word Nerd Association, which means she's probably stalking every Twitter writing competition and offering query critiques so keep an eye out.

Twitter:
https://twitter.com/demoness333

Website:
http://www.jamiezakian.com/